Tom McCulloch has published poetry and short stories in various journals including Other Poetry, Northwords, Northwords Now, Eildon Tree, Markings, Buzzwords, and Wilderness magazine (New Zealand). He was long-listed for the Herald/Imagining Scotland short story competition 2011. The Stillman is his first novel.

THE STILLMAN

Tom McCulloch

SANDSTONEPRESS
HIGHLAND | SCOTLAND

First published in Great Britain by
Sandstone Press Ltd
Dochcarty Road
Dingwall
Ross-shire
IV15 9UG
Scotland.

www.sandstonepress.com

Editor: Moira Forsyth

The publisher acknowledges subsidy from Creative Scotland
towards publication of this volume.

ISBN: 978-1-908737-67-0
ISBNe: 978-1-908737-68-7

Cover design by Mark Blackadder, Edinburgh
Typeset by Iolaire Typesetting, Newtonmore
Printed and bound by Totem, Poland

For my family.
And Bev, for lighting the way.

One

It all begins with death, it all ends with death. The crow lies on the low concrete wall outside warehouse 21. The beak is slightly open and bright blood spatters the snow, guts grey and spilling. Siberia's gale has momentarily dropped to a stabbing breeze. The oily feathers barely move. In an hour or two they'll be frozen. I bend closer, studying the scene, like a TV detective. There's no surrounding tracks or marks. Did the crow just fall out of the sky? It must've been some height to splatter viscera like that.

I look up. Sky the colour of wet pebbles. The first bird I've seen for days and it's dead. What would it be like to never see any other kind of life-form again? Nothing but people.

The crow's feathers give an indignant ruffle. No wonder, imagine being gawped at after your suicide leap. Savage, dying insults, that's what I'd scream at the gathering crowd and their repulsed but fascinated stares. I give the crow its decency and look away. Des is leaning against the big red warehouse door, wearing that greasy fur hat he says he got in the navy.

'When's the delivery due?'

'96 barrels coming in.'

'I know that, but when?'

Des stares at the snow, as if he's wondering how long it's been falling. I can't remember either, it buries memory as it smothers the landscape. I've never known a man to stare like Des. Sometimes he still seems to be up on deck, lost in the ocean, pondering whatever he ponders.

I follow him inside. The high racks of barrels stretch three hundred feet into the darkness. The smell of whisky is strong. Des opens the tea-hut door. We call it the tea-hut but it's just a small room for taking a break. And I've never seen anyone drinking tea. Mostly we sit and mostly in a loaded silence. The barred window is frosted up, accentuating the nearness to each other. I sit on the bench, chin down into my jacket. I move my feet on the gritty floor. The raspy noise cuts into the silence and Malky sniffs. I stop moving my feet.

'If you farted in here it would freeze in the air. If you were first in the next day you'd walk into a wee smelly cloud. You'd know it was a fart but you'd know it couldn't have been you, so how did it get there?'

Nobody bothers to reply to Camp Gary. He probably doesn't want a response anyway. But I know we're all now thinking about it. Five grown men wondering if it's possible for a fart to freeze. Times like these I'm glad when I hear the lorry rumbling closer. Then the driver's face is at the door and he's calling us a bunch of lazy bastards and he wants the barrels off pronto. I've seen this driver before, the one with the wraparound shades, who sits in his cab dreaming he's an Apache helicopter pilot, swooping low over the Tora Bora.

The light. I can't get enough of it. The way it pours through the open warehouse doors as I wait a hundred feet away in whisky dark for the next barrel to come rolling out of the gloom. There's no place for colour here, never has been, a monochrome edgeland, ever cold. How could it be otherwise? Given time most things eventually come to chill us, become grey.

Our three evenly spaced heads bob in silhouette, passing the barrels along. The heavy trundles echo and undulate, separate and combined, like intertwining sine waves; now louder, now quieter, the barrels slowing down, speeding up. I glimpse ghost-stencilled letters, numbers, feel the breath I can't see. My hands are warm for the first time today. It's too noisy to be certain but I know Camp Gary is whistling that same tune I've never placed and never asked him about. I'm glad I can't hear him. I don't want to admit that at this particular moment I'm oddly content as well, bent like a blind cripple in winter's bleakest prison.

Not that I belong here. The distillery, sure, but not these forlorn warehouses. I'm a Stillman. I take care of the nine copper-pot stills where the whisky's born. It's me who selects the middle-cut, the heart of the spirit, swinging the collecting pipe in the spirit safe at that moment of utmost *gravity*. But we aren't producing anything at the moment. Winter closedown; mid-December to mid-January. I've been exiled to the warehouses. I don't like this time of year. I find it unnerving when I open the door and there's no smell of pot ale, no Christmas-lit Stillhouse floating on the night. The distillery exists to pulse, to breathe.

I turned 50 yesterday. So many years in the one place. The celebrations were the very definition of muted. My wife bought me Homer Simpson socks, a frying pan, and a posh bottle of red, Burgundy I think. If there's a message in this I don't feel much like looking for it. Recently she's been *getting into wine*. Always been aspirational, not that it's stopped her battering the cheap voddie. She was pissed off when I started drinking the birthday bottle before it had properly breeeathed. But nothing was said. It was my birthday. It was my day.

'I told you take it out to defrost,' she says, soon as I'm in the door.

'I thought I had.'

'You know what thought did?'

Thought could have done a lot of things so nothing really leaps out.

'No. I guess you don't.'

She clatters in the cupboards. My cup of tea's getting cold and it's a provocation to sit here supping away when she's rushing around getting dinner ready. I should help but don't. There's a fizzing sound coming from the living room, see, I'm trying to work out what it is. Could be a sitcom's canned laughter, crowd noise on the Boy's football manager Xbox game.

'You going to drink that?'

I shrug. She's forgotten to put the sugar in. I know I shouldn't say it. 'You forgot the sugar.'

She freezes at the cooker, slowly places the tin of beans on the counter. 'You know how busy I was today?'

I rub at a black mark on my boiler suit. Nothing I say can be right, not now. I listen to her go on and on and don't touch a drop of the tea. I say something in apology. It isn't meant and she knows it. Our fragmented ghosts in the dark window, what a true reflection they are.

At some point my son appears in the doorway, watching us with that smirk I can't fathom. It's starting to spook me but then he is fifteen; essentially unknowable. It's why I've started calling him 'the Boy'. The pathetic explanation that mum and dad are just *talking* will never work on that smirk. He'll leave on his own terms and I won't realise when he finally does. At least I understand where he gets it from. I've always known when to make the timely exit. I stand, taking care not to scrape the chair. *So that'll be that then, eh?* my wife says, *end of discussion. Jim Drever has decided enough is enough, he's made his point.*

'There's logs that need chopping, need a good fire the night.' The cold catches my throat as soon as I open the back door. The security lamp clicks on; white dazzle in already white dark.

'As you wish, Jim.'

It could be a sigh of resignation. More likely relief that I am finally going, exiting the frame.

'I'll give you a shout for dinner, shouldn't be too long. Lucky we didn't finish the rest of that stew. You want chips or tatties?'

'Whatever you like.' Not because I have no preference, I do, I want chips. More because I want to give the impression that I hold to higher ground, unconcerned with such trivialities. Victory! She'll be glaring out the window as I cross to the shed. But when I look back she's at the cooker laughing, mobile phone clamped to her ear. I think about the dead crow, *viscera*.

That reassuring mustiness, smell of fathers, grandfathers. I leave the shed light off and feel my way to the old easy chair leaning against the back wall. I know the outline of every jar of assorted nails, each plant-pot and tool. Nothing moves unless I move it. That's why I come here. I pick up the axe, running a finger along the iron head and settling it across my lap. The night's made for a George Romero movie, doesn't even need a full moon.

5

I'll do some major axe damage when the zombies come staggering round the side of the house.

I'm sweating after six swings. The logs split easily. They're well-seasoned and I wonder where Malky got them. He'd come round last week, big smiles, asking if I wanted to buy 200 kilos of larch. The man's an entrepreneur, wasted in this place. I soon build up a pile that'll last a few days. And we'll need it, been eight or nine below for over a week, like a fuckin walk-in freezer. I stop for a rest, wiping the shavings from the head as I stare at the distillery.

All these years since childhood but it could be anytime. As if I haven't moved. The cold tang of ten thousand nights and the same sad bleating sheep somewhere on the juniper moors. The access road winds in front of our terrace, over the weighbridge and up to the main site. The back-shift's up there, the Filling Store glow seeping out from behind the Dark Grains Plant. 120 casks we collected from the bonded warehouses this afternoon, they'll be emptying them into the collecting vat for hours yet. Fogged breath. Cold-finger cigarettes. The cooper's adze echoes, slicing the bung flush, the white of fresh oak like a new layer of skin.

And the Stillhouse, forever drawing my eye. A dark silhouette that shouldn't be silent. Two more weeks of closedown. Two more weeks in the warehouses. These days they call it a secondment. I'm counting the minutes. Nineteen years I've worked in the Stillhouse. That ever-present thruuum. I pad across the scuffed yellow floor, checking hydrometers, temperatures. Distillation is in itself a distillation, of process, chemical and electrical determinism, the regulation of time. Narrow parameters always reassure me. I'm comfortable within set limits, I guess, where the hazards are long neutralised, problems foreseeable.

There's four places set, three taken. Me, my wife and the Boy. My wife's evangelical when it comes to eating together. She'll quote you some expert, *the setting aside of family time is essential to harmonious functioning.* I'm unconvinced. Mostly we just sit in silence and surely conversation is essential to harmonious functioning. Not that the silence is total. If I close my eyes I can tell who's responsible for each sloppy sound we make when eating. It's all to do with the extent the lips are left open, the slight differences in the air inhaled with each mouthful.

The Boy has his iPod in. Anonymous thrash metal leaches out of the headphones. When his mother tells him to remove them he ignores her. I nudge his arm and he ignores me too. Then my wife is shouting and the Boy eventually deigns to comply. I'm impressed again at the effortless way he can draw his mother's fury to a savage peak and then calmly capitulate. Artfully done, giving the sense that it's his mother who's actually the defeated one.

'Is she coming?'

My wife finishes texting before answering. 'She's late.'

I glance at the kitchen clock. 6.42. We always have dinner at 6.30. It must be the optimum time for family interaction. My wife makes a strange snorting noise as she eats a forkful of potatoes. I picture a claggy bit of tatties stuck in her pink throat. At least my daughter Amber is actually expected this evening. She moved out six months ago but my wife insists on leaving her

7

place mat set. This annoys me. If you move out then you move out. And you don't just turn up when you want and expect a plate of food to be put in front of you.

'Peter's a dick', says the Boy.

I can almost hear my wife's hackles rise. 'What did you say?' she asks. Why do people say that when they've obviously heard?

'Peter. The *fiancé*. He's a dick.'

'That's your future brother-in-law you're talking about so you better get used to him.'

'Might be my brother-in-law but he's still a dick.'

'Stop saying that – '

'Down the hall doing wheel spins in the car-park. He's near thirty!'

'Leave the table.'

The Boy carefully, ever so slowly, places his cutlery on the plate and leaves the kitchen.

My wife is staring at me. I count the beans on my plate, seven.

'You need to talk to him'

'He's just being protective of his big sis.'

'He's a poisonous wee shite is what he is.'

I don't disagree. But the slam of the front door distracts her attention and means I don't have to respond.

My daughter Amber breezes in with a breathless hello and drops some packages and post on the table. 'They were in the porch. Do you ever check your mail? What's for tea, I'm down to bare cupboards and Peter's out.'

'It's in the oven love, stew. We were going to have chicken but your *father* forgot to take it out.'

'Dad!'

I'm struck again at the similarity between my wife and daughter. It's not really physical, my wife is short and dumpy, Amber taller but with a developing belly. More in the personal choices, the clothes and the groom. Both have highlighted blonde hair and favour a militaristic use of make-up. Similar scents too, loose fitting tops and Ugg boots. My wife looks like a tubby, overly-made up Eskimo. If Amber isn't careful she'll end up living in the same igloo.

They talk about the wedding. Why February? I still don't understand it and they better hope this snow lets up soon. Amber wasn't happy when I asked what the hurry was. I said she'd only been with that fanny Peter for seven months and should just tell us if she's pregnant. Ok, the 'fanny' was left unsaid but my wife still hauled me up. *They're in love, they don't want to hang around waiting, can't you just be happy for them?* I can't, not that I've tried too hard. And I'm still not convinced she isn't pregnant. *Only a few weeks to go*, my wife says.

In a short second I stop listening. Like some quantum fluctuation I come across myself at the bedroom window three and a half hours later. It happens more and more these days, maybe I'm gradually slipping out of existence. Up at the distillery the Filling Store lights go off, the back-shift straggling across the bridge. Someone glances up and I raise a hand as if I just happen to be skulking in the dark and haven't been standing here for a lifetime.

The packages were for me, all from Amazon. *Blue Collar, The Killing of a Chinese Bookie,* and the best movie ever made, digitally remastered just for me, *The Deer Hunter.* That perfect ambiguity. I could remake it, change Vietnam to Iraq, the steel plant to the distillery, blast furnaces in cold air to the mash tun, the stills. I need a score, something to catch the melancholy. Sad strings and slanting rain, walking home from the Still-house, hands in the pockets of my boiler suit. I've got this Oscar-winning script in my head. I just can't get it out.

I crank up the laptop and check the web history. My wife's been at the bingo and probably won again, she always seems to win. *Yahoo* reveals I've got three unopened emails. Two of them have the same oddly appealing information about how to increase the size of my cock.

The third email has remained unread since 1st January. It has <no subject>. I've never had an email from *vinales2004@hotmail.com* and I don't know if the address or the attachment worries me more. The paperclip icon has been burned onto my retinas. When I glance away it lingers, on the white walls, the carpet, a stain on my vision. It's like *Alice in Wonderland*, we've all got rabbit holes to scurry down if we're that way inclined, if we have the right strength and curiosity. I position the cursor over the email and ask myself again whether I do.

* * *

Favourite kinds of seafood. A classic morning tea-break conversation. I can't handle it. *Ah like squid,* O'Neill says in the Glasgow accent everyone knows he exaggerates. Something fishy about those eyes right enough. *Mackerel for me,* says Ronnie. His lips are too red, too moist. Must be all those fish oils my wife's always on about, whatever they're called. Flash of childhood, a teaspoon of cod liver oil coming towards me. My wife had it mixed with milk. *To disguise the taste*. A memory to make you gag. O'Neill's beady eyes mock me as I walk away.

The stacks of worn-out barrels have become flat-topped white hills, the drifts three-feet deep alongside the top warehouses. The snow's left the world empty, like childhood's open book. As a boy I read so much it worried my father. I would have immediately discovered Eskimos, fur trappers and Grizzly Adams in the snowy mile stretching from the other side of the burn up to the spruce plantation. That imagination, it's so far away now, inaccessible.

I lean against a blackened warehouse wall. What's the name for the staining caused by alcohol? Fish oil, alcohol stains, am I the only person who can't remember the names of these things?

Jack had been on about the strike again, another reason to flee. He's had a permanent boner since someone at head office passed him a confidential briefing about changes to terms and conditions, short-time working scenarios, full-closure . . . The suits went into full-spectrum denial and spooked the union into balloting for a one-day stoppage to get them round the table. Jack's convinced the end is nigh and is on a glittery-eyed 'yes' crusade. What an opportunity to continue our education! Last week I overheard him talking to Camp Gary about Gramsci. Gary said he wasn't a fan but he'd liked that song *Killer*.

I hear an engine and look back the way I've come. The Land Rover's creeping across the bridge over the burn and I've missed my lift to 10. Fourteen puncheons needed, with any luck they'll be done by the time I mosey on down. I hate the hydraulic loading plate, twenty feet in the air and wobbling like a fucker *before* you roll on a half-ton puncheon. Certain death if the platform buckles, and almost eccentric, something you'd notice in the papers. I'll wait a bit, and the sub-zero walk is better than being stuck in the Land Rover with Jack.

I flick my fag butt into the snow drift, watch the smoke disappear. When I look up I see a figure in the far distance at the top of the field. The farmer out checking the sheep most likely.

Now I look closer I can see the mucky yellow daubs scattered here and there across the white. The farmer walks slowly along the line of the fence. As the terrain climbs he's suddenly silhouetted on the horizon line. The sheep notice him and begin bleating. But the farmer just stands there and I get the sure feeling of being watched. From this distance the farmer could in fact be anyone at all, a stranger appeared, Clint Eastwood in *High Plains Drifter*.

Before dinner we decide to have sex. The boy's out somewhere. My feet are cold and I want to leave my hiking socks on. My wife pauses in the awkward clamber into her red and black basque and says a simple but definitive no. I take my socks off and lie naked on the black duvet. I can smell the horrible floral scent of one of those plug-in room deodorisers and the string of my wife's thong has disappeared up her arse crack, perhaps for ever. No way I'm going in there looking for it. My big toe, the left one, still has that infection, fungal most likely.

Afterwards she can't wait to get off me. 'Clean yourself up,' she says, throwing me a clump of pink toilet roll.

I spread my arms and legs wide, into a star shape. What it would be like to sleep like that every night, right in the middle of the bed and no-one to jab me in the ribs? And no coitus to interruptus. I heard the phrase on a TV show a while ago and think it's just as applicable for an almost non-existent sex life as pulling out before I come. Tonight's event was almost miraculous. I put it down to that book she's reading. *The Power of Now*, sounds self-helpy.

I sit up and put my socks back on, wobble my flabby belly. I can't really blame my wife for wanting to get away. Not that she's anything special herself. I'm always slightly alarmed by the way she squeezes into that basque. But I'm a professional, able to rise to any occasion.

'Can you nip down and check that soup?' she shouts from the bathroom.

I think about going as I am but decide to get dressed. The Boy's odd enough without bumping into his naked father in a pair of threadbare hiking socks, face flushed in a post-orgasmic glow. But when I glance out of the little window at the top of the stairs I see him across at the shed.

A metal pole is sticking out the top of the door. The Boy has unravelled the lead from the shed light and tied it to the pole so the light hangs down. One of the barrels Malky's always promising to cut into flower planters has been upturned, a mobile phone propped against a log on the top. I watch him check and re-adjust the angle between phone and shed. After three deep breaths, eyes closed, he suddenly leaps under the light, dropping into a ninja pose and doing a few high kicks, bunching his fists and giving short sharp punches.

My wife appears at my shoulder and we stand there in silence, watching our son film himself doing crappy karate moves in the snow.

'Have you checked the soup?' She sounds distracted.

'I was on my way.'

'*Never mind then.* It's your fault you know.'

I move aside as she shoves past and down the stairs. 'I said I was going to do it. What do you mean it's my fault?'

She turns at the kitchen door. 'What do I mean, what do you think I mean? Your *son*.' She jabs a thumb over her shoulder.

'How's it just my fault, why's it not yours too?' I pick up the post from the lobby table.

'Just try thinking about it.'

There's another letter from the residential home. My wife never opens them although they're addressed to us both. Never mentions them, and wouldn't a normal person be curious? I finish reading and stare into the mirror above the table. It's a fact of nature that no news from a care home is ever good. I lean forward and raise my chin so the skin tightens. Not quite as saggy as my father but getting there. I open and close my mouth, like a dying cod.

'You know I'm going out tonight?' she shouts from the kitchen.

I blow out my cheeks, cross my eyes and *sieg heil* the mirror. She's right about the Boy, it is my fault.

'You hear me?'

'I heard you.'

'Vari's having a party.'

'A party, on a school night?'

'What's wrong with that?'

'Nothing at all.'

'It's an Ann Summers party, seeing as you're so interested. Amber's coming too, she thought she might get something for the honeymoon.'

The leering face of Amber's fiancé looms out at me.

14

Peter the Chip they call him. *Carpenter extraordinaire*, he boasts, although he has done me a shelving job that was surprisingly finessed. Malky once told me a filthy tale about Peter, an Englishwoman needing a job done on her holiday cottage and a home-grown courgette. When Amber first took him back for dinner I was haunted by the images for weeks. 'Too much information Kate.'

'Don't be a prude, it's just a bit of fun.'

She's wearing a short denim skirt, black leggings and red pumps. In a way I admire this mirroring of my daughter's style. She can just about pull it off, still on the safer side of desperation. But if I started wearing skinny jeans like the Boy? She'd be guffawing into the middle of next week.

'Jack was on the barrels the day.'

'Aww, you're embarrassed, quick change of subject there. When's the ballot, what was he saying?'

My afternoon had not gone to plan. I took my time getting down to warehouse 10 but some problem with the hydraulics on the geriatric lifting plate meant the puncheons hadn't been unloaded. Just my luck. It meant half an hour trapped with Jack in the tea-hut. 'He's the world's first perpetual motion machine, never gets tired of repeating the same old shite.'

'You read the memo from the Glasgow office.'

'Yeah. Jack's *mole*.'

'But they didn't deny it.'

'No way they'd shut us down.'

'How do you know? They won't even sit down and talk about it. They haven't denied anything.'

'You're paranoid.'

'Look Jim, we're going to be paying for this wedding for years. What if you lose your job?'

'I'm not going to lose my job.'

15

'But you might.'

'What the hell do you want me to do about it?'

'Stand up for yourself for Christ's sake!'

'There's a union meeting tomorrow.'

'You're going, yes?'

The kitchen door slams open. The Boy stands there holding his mobile phone, gasping and sweaty-faced.

I call it 'the Den' but she says it sounds too American. *Why can't it just be a cupboard?* A cupboard is too small in my opinion. Cupboards mean racks of clothes and shoes, old magazines and dust.

The Den is lined on three sides with floor to ceiling shelves, filled with DVDs and videos I haven't got round to upgrading. I'm being sold my collection all over again but so what. It means a continuous stream of packages for months and a chance to re-watch old favourites. There's a 60 inch plasma TV on the wall opposite the door and room for two armchairs. I've long since put one of them in the shed because only I ever come in here. I can sit for hours, a few feet from the huge screen, like being in the front row of a cinema. No-one to annoy you, no-one gibbering away. Or coughing, I want to strangle people who cough in cinemas.

Has there ever been anyone more menacing than preacher Harry Powell in *Night of the Hunter*? That scene in the bedroom, Mitchum's open-faced deception with the little girl, trying to wheedle out the secret of where the money's hid. And the angled shadows as the preacher sings that eerie gospel song, horse and man silhouetted on a pale sky, the horrified boy watching him ride closer to the barn where he and his sister are hiding. *Don't he ever sleep!*

I switch off the DVD. I think I hear the Boy in his bedroom but can't be sure. He's a secretive bugger and I don't really care what he's up to. *Leeeaning, leeeeaning,* I quietly sing, like Harry Powell, *leaning on the everlasting arms.* I walk slowly along the landing to my bedroom, the darkness and snowy skylight glow like being in my own black and white movie.

In the gloom the laptop is barely visible on the desk. Just the green blink of the standby light. I resisted getting a computer for years but now I can't imagine a life without one. Strange how quickly we forget that we once got by without something. Like that unread email, still waiting. Until 1st January 2010 I got by without it. I still could, you can get by without most things. All I need to do is delete it. We only make a fetish of the things we want to.

Preacher Powell would have no hesitation. He'd slump like this as the laptop boots up, studying his *love* and *hate* tattooed knuckles. *You still scared son, still scared of what you might find out, even now, after all these years?* And then a nod of the head, indicating the inbox. He's a mocking bastard, that cynical curl of the mouth. Well fuck him, I can deal with the hollowness in my stomach, the dryness in my mouth as I open the email from *vinales2004.*

Like the subject line, the body of the email is empty. The pdf attachment is titled *Helen's Journal 1.*

Havana Cuba, 23/3/1999

If you are reading this then I am dead. It is strange, to write those words yet still be alive, to know you have now been sent this journal . . .

17

What do you think? Does it work? I have tried dozens of openers and found them wanting, slow-burning build-ups and oblique head-scratchers, contrived twists and artless contrivances. In the end I got bored and went for the default dramatic intro. So, does it work? Come on, I'm on tenterhooks! Are not the most effective openers simple and direct, immediately piquing the interest? Is this not what we have been taught to expect, to demand, from a narrative, a story? But I know so little about you, I have no clue to your expectations. You may be the ultra-pragmatist who stops halfway down the bottle. Or you may be quick to shock, to anger. If you are anything like me, poor thing, then you are both, often simultaneously.

I can write a thousand words and feel it all pour out, the bile and guilt of a lifetime written brutal and true. Then, as the cockerels start to crow, I will re-read, almost embarrassed, not believing a damn word. The exaggeration I can conjure is almost disturbing. So when everything is arbitrary and ambiguous then the dramatic first line, any line, means nothing. But which one of me is talking now?

We all need a bit of mystery. You are no different from anyone else although you may think so. How many times, truly, have you stood and looked at yourself in the old speckled mirror and thought 'is this all there is?' We can all plod on. I have done it myself, so, so often. But plodding is not living because true living is living the different. Take this journal as my gift of mystery to you, and like all good mysteries it should be open to multiple interpretations. But those interpretations depend on you, by how, and if, you choose to engage. You see, it is mysterious already!

Where I live the street kids play baseball from dawn till dusk, every day of the week. Perhaps you can picture me, a thin, white-haired woman hurling a curveball into the middle of another of your mundane days. How will you deal with it, take the strike or try and make the hit? I do not know what you look like but I can imagine you considering whether to read any more of this or throw it in the trash. I must seem so calculating. Others have made the same observation. I am simply offering the experience of difference. At the very least you should be glad I have drawn attention to the plod.

I will stop, for now. I have never really seen the point of introductions anyway. Just get on with it! Anyway, if, as I suspect, we are all characters in the same ever-repeating story then there is no need for a prologue, you cannot introduce something already known. Equally, you could make the case that there is no need for the story itself, there being nothing new under this ancient sun.

Of course, such a statement establishes a philosophical, if not a dramatic, context. Or, to put it another way, an intro-duction. Ha! I told you I was unreliable. So, to read or not to read. A balanced decision is impossible because true objectiv-ity is a chimera in most situations, never mind one as fraught as this. It is really about deciding your terms of engagement. Maybe you really are the arch pragmatist, in which case I look forward to keeping your company for a little while. If not, you will have stopped reading already.

My motives, do they matter to you? If so, as a starter I offer guilt. Yes, yes, so tediously obvious, I know. So I also sug-gest fear, the fear of forever being a stranger. Is that better? Humanity has been around far too long, all our themes are so terribly hackneyed.

Two

'I have in my hands a piece of paper.'

Chamberlain lives ... Something tells me appeasement won't be Jack's strategy. It's excruciating, the way he milks it, pausing for effect, surveying the audience before continuing.

'A letter!'

Murmurs in the crowd. Jack's done a good job of getting most of us here. All the warehouse boys, two mash-men, and the coopers. I'm the only one of the three Stillmen. Rankin's on holiday and no way you'll get Stan to a union meeting, Stan who'd once tried to get the union de-recognised. There's junior management too, a couple of lads who've worked their way up from the warehouses and still feel uncomfortable with the grubby white collar.

'Came in this morning from the Chief Exec. I'll pass out copies and put it on the noticeboards. First acknowledgment of that leaked memo boys. They're trying to influence the ballot.'

'What do you expect?' says Malky.

Jack pauses a moment and scans the crowd. 'Respect. I expect respect.'

Fuck me, he's so *earnest*.

Jack again holds up the sheet of paper. 'So for those of you who've haven't caught up with today's little admission, here we go: "Dear Mr Kennedy. In the interests of good workforce relations and given your position as shop steward I write you this letter. I cannot deny the veracity of the memorandum you came to have in your possession. It is my unfortunate responsibility to confirm that, given the financial situation of the distillery and the current economic climate, the options listed are indeed being actively considered by management. The management is willing to discuss these options, but not in the context of industrial action".'

'That it?'

'That's it.'

'Sounds like a threat.'

'Aye. "Do what we say or the deal's off".'

'They won't listen anyway.'

'Like with the pensions.'

'Not this time. This time *we* make the running, *we* show *them* how serious *we* are. All out boys, all out on the 4th!'

'Fuckin right!'

I stop listening. Snow is falling beyond the big cooperage doors and it's all so peripheral, this drama. The walls of warehouse 4 stretch into the mist, the red wooden strips below the gutters becoming invisible. Endurance is a dour characteristic but the mist will always lift, eventually. For the distillery to close the world itself would have to be mothballed.

Jack's arms flail, a dramatic crumple and throw of the letter. A few claps.

'Handy with the words eh?'

'What's that?' I say.

'Your man there', Camp Gary points at Jack. 'Fire one across the fuckin bows, see what they make of it.'

'That so.'

'Yeah Jim, that's so.'

The ballot came in the post this morning. Soon as I'm in the door my wife hands it to me. *A conscientious man*, she gravely states when I tell her Jack'll be doing the rounds to make sure we all vote. *Bit too intense*, says I. *Least he cares*, says she. The Boy moves his head from one of us to the other as we speak, making a whoooosh noise like a car zipping past. I tell him to stop but he doesn't and after a while we lapse into silence. His work now done the Boy leaves the kitchen. He pauses at the door and does an oriental bow, hands clasped at his chest.

If Jack says he'll be around at 7.45 then at 7.45 he'll appear. I'm in the bedroom on the internet when I hear the door. I can get *McCabe and Mrs Miller*, *M.A.S.H* and *American Gigolo* from Amazon for five quid. Not a bad deal. After my wife shouts for me I click on *Wikipedia* and spend the next fifteen minutes reminding myself of the plots. There's a barely audible rhythmic noise coming from the Boy's bedroom that I don't want to think about.

When I go downstairs they're sitting close together on the couch. My wife's put on eye-liner and lipstick. It looks as if they're already on the second dram. I chuck a log on the already blazing fire and settle back on the chair beside the hearth. I can never figure out if Jack is good-looking or not. Maybe it's his seriousness. Maybe women like the strong, serious type.

'Bit early for the drams, thought you had ballots to collect?'

'You're the last.'

'Course I am.'

'You get yours?'

'Aye. You get yours?' I glance from my wife to Jack. She shifts slightly, holds back a smirk.

'I'll post it for you. Not saying you'll forget, I just want to make sure we maximise the response.'

'Makes sense.'

In the hallway I take a biro from the phone table, scribble all over the ballot and seal it in the envelope.

'Thanks Jim. I was just saying to Katie that we're going to get a solid "yes" on this, lot of anger today.'

'Hmm.'

'Jack says he's been in these kinds of negotiations before. He says it's really, really tiring.'

Jack settles a strained look on his face. I think he's going for fortitude. He takes a slug and settles back, his leg touching my wife's. 'The tiring bit's getting them to the table in the first place. Least then you can get them one to one, try and appeal to the human in them.'

'I wonder about the human in them,' my wife says.

'We've got to give them the benefit of the doubt! Oh, while I remember, I've got something for you Jim. A film, *Matewan*.'

'You shouldn't encourage him, he watches enough DVDs as it is.'

'Something in keeping with the mood. About a miner's strike in Virginia in the 1920s and the attempt to unionise the workers. Cracking film. I know you're a big movie buff.'

A movie *buff*? 'I suppose I am.' I take the DVD.

'Make sure you watch it before the 4th, get yourself fired up!'

'4th's no good for me, did I not say that? I'm on leave, my father's annual check-up at the home.'

My wife looks at me carefully, a slight narrowing of the eyes.

Jack looks surprised. 'That's a shame. A real shame. Will we see you on the picket line at all?'

'Depends.'

I don't tell them I stopped into the office on my way home. Coleen, our sad-eyed HR officer, was playing computer Solitaire. She checked the dates and pencilled in my leave, 4th February.

'Here's to victory,' I say, and raise my glass.

'Victory,' agrees Jack.

We chat away. The whisky flows. The room's crematorium hot but I keep lobbing more logs on the fire. I want to know how red my wife's face can get and if Jack's hair gel will trickle down his forehead. When I come out of the toilet I hear them laughing and take a detour upstairs.

My email page is open but I'm sure I left it open at *Wikipedia*. Shouldn't the screensaver have kicked in, I've been away long enough. The chair too, would I have left it neatly tucked under the lip of the table like that? I stand at the door for a minute or so. Silence from the Boy's room, a burst of muffled laughter from downstairs. I should get back down there, dam the sexual tension before it overflows. Instead I re-open *Helen's Journal 1*. This is the third time I've read it. I can see her, sitting in the still, burning heat of blue Havana. Such imaginings have always come too easily. Tonight, my one hope is that I won't dream about her again. A harsh laugh from downstairs, as if in reply. I feel suddenly exhausted and decide to let whatever is going to happen down there happen. I'll go to bed instead, the words of the journal jumbling and tumbling, daring the dreams to come and get me.

* * *

Chipper. It's the kind of word Camp Gary would use. For reasons I don't care about, today my wife is chipper.

'It's a mystery to me,' she's saying. 'A real mystery.'

I have a twitch in my lip.

My wife slurps tea. 'Why do they keep on employing the same daft lassies as manager?'

I pull the duvet up round my neck and stare at the radiators. They're crap, no discernible effect on this crypt-like cold. I press a finger against my lip, trying to stop the twitch.

As with her eating there's a sound-pattern to my wife's tea-drinking. A slurp, a slight sticky noise as she pulls her lips apart and then a short, satisfied *aah*. I look at her surreptitiously. *They couldn't organise the proverbial*, she says, *next time I'll apply for the bloody job myself.* She won't, and wouldn't get anywhere near it if she did. That doesn't stop her periodically nagging me to *go for an office job, get out of that bloody Stillhouse so you can work normal hours like a normal person.* I nod, the vaguest sign I can muster to prove that I'm listening. It's 7.23am. I'm fixated on my twitching lip, the terminal disease it might signal.

I put on a dressing gown and open the curtain. Still dark, will be for at least another hour. The snow falls soft, sentimental. I half expect to see Jimmy Stewart cavorting across the bridge.

'Do you think the road's closed?' I say.

'Chance would be a fine thing. Soon as you're past the

25

distillery the road's clear. Council's finally got its finger out.'

'It's not the council anymore, road servicing was privatised.'

'Ok *Jim*. Bit too early to split hairs. The thing is the road's clear.'

'Just saying.' I watch Malky on the road outside, swinging the tractor and snow-plough round in a big arc.

'You're always saying.'

I need the sun. No-one should live in this preternatural dark. Endurance must be balanced by celebration, no much wonder the pagans went mental with the return of the light. Trust the Church to burn the fun. Now only endurance remains. We wait for the sun, we wait for winter.

'Do you think we should have sent the kids to Sunday school?'

She pauses as she gets dressed. 'You feeling all right?'

'Imagine they were right and we're the ones who got it wrong. All this snow could be a punishment for not believing in God.'

'Do you really think God would send snow as a punishment?'

'Why not?'

'Cause it doesn't seem like much of a punishment. Thunderbolts and lightning is more his style, isn't it? Throw me that skirt.'

'Only it if doesn't stop.'

'What doesn't stop?'

'The snow. If the snow never stops then we'll all eventually suffocate under it.'

'I'm suffocating right now! I haven't got time for this.'

'Just saying.'

'Can I get the skirt now?'

I hear the crump of tyres on snow and look out the window. A red van has pulled up outside the house. *Peter Davidson*, white lettering on the side reads, *Carpenter and Craft'sman*. When I pointed out the apostrophe my wife called me a snob and reminded me I failed O-level English. Now Peter's marrying my daughter the apostrophe no longer makes me smirk.

The Boy ignores Peter, but then the Boy ignores everyone. My wife fusses around. She's running late but nothing is too much of a hassle for Peter and Amber. If my wife insisted on being late for her work to make sure I got my breakfast I'd be checking under the car for the ticking bomb.

I've been trying to decide for a while. Today I'm convinced. Peter does have a big nose. I stare at it as I drink my coffee. It isn't immediately noticeable, more a question of the right angle and light. Actually, it seems the dimmer the light the bigger the conk. But only if he's in half-profile. In full profile the nose seems normal-sized. Strange, I would've thought that full-profile and full light would be the optimum conditions for the revelation of a big nose. Apparently not, I stand corrected. Still, I suppose it goes to prove that there's also something peculiar about Peter's nose, beyond its size. It'll be an ongoing source of fascination and the thought's quite encouraging. If I can file Peter under entertainment then his presence may become tolerable. Doubtful though, can a comedy nose alone sustain a man?

My wife, daughter and Peter are having a grand time. Jolly, it could be called, eggs and square sausage being scoffed. It takes a while for the conversation to seep into my consciousness. I'm not mistaken, they are indeed talking about having an ice-sculpture at the wedding.

'Can you imagine how *classy* it would look?' my daughter gushes.

Peter flashes me what he must've wanted to be a conspiratorial smirk. *What are women like*, the look tries to say. *What about me getting into your daughter's knickers*, the look actually says.

My wife cocks her head and says nothing, as if objectively considering the idea. I know she's already sold, that this is a charade she feels, as a critically supportive mother, she has to go through.

'What do you think, Daddy?' Amber beams in my direction.

I think, *Daddy?* I'm always unnerved when she drops into the little girl routine. 'Where do you get the ice?'

Peter forks in the last of his sausage and leans back in his chair. 'Reckon I could do it maself,' he announces.

'Oh get away with you,' says my wife, smiling.

'*Whaaat*,' says Peter.

I wait for the sneaky little wink in my direction, a raise of the eyebrows. Neither is forthcoming.

'Big block of ice, no bother. Been freezing for days and I can get the chainsaw and cut it out of Loch Cluanie. Be a footery job with the carving mind but I've got the tools. What would you fancy, a swan or something?'

My wife glances at Amber and both look at Peter, who looks at me. *I'm having a laugh! Don't worry, I know fuck all about ice-carving and hahaha did you all really think I was going to do that?* That's what I want the look to say. *Have confidence in me 'father'*, the look actually says.

My wife places a hand on Amber's shoulder.

28

Opposition is now futile. The inevitable end will be a malformed ice-swan, melting on the dance floor. I notice the Boy standing in the doorway, slack-jawed but somehow smirking. He's wearing headphones but he's heard everything.

I'm out getting logs when they clamber into the van, all but the Boy that is. *Mother and daughter in a workman's van*, Peter said when my wife accepted the lift. *Remember that you both 'came' of your own free will. Peter Davidson*, my daughter exclaimed, mock-offended. I tell myself I just imagined Peter's sleazy emphasis on the 'came'. No-one shouts a goodbye but Peter gives me a salute. There's nothing mocking in this, he isn't imaginative enough.

Unlike the Boy. Something's coming. He's standing in the middle of the road watching the van turn. When it faces him he doesn't budge an inch and Peter's forced to stop, right where the road dips into a hollow. The Boy's judged it perfectly, it'll be a swine for the tyres to get any traction in the snow. A few hoots of the horn but still the Boy doesn't move. Then suddenly he's bending down, scooping snow and hurling snowballs at the van, *viciously*. I think he's shouting *die muthafucka die* but maybe I'm making that up. As the van door is flung open the Boy starts running, suddenly hurling himself in the air, floppy-bodied, like a soldier caught in an explosion. It's impressive, *authentic*, he doesn't even put his hands out to break his fall. Time and again he surprises me, I really should be more supportive.

I listen to the revving van, staring into the snow. I don't want to leave this place but little would persuade me to stay. I half-close my eyes and the grey gloom becomes a Cuban beach, arc-lit by the sun. The Boy has disappeared into a snowy haze become shimmering heat, a young woman emerging in his place. I'm fixated by the brown body, the slow swing of the hips. She's smiling, her nipples erect behind the black bikini top. I saw so many beautiful women over there but it's a long time since I allowed myself to follow those memories. It's *Helen's Journal* of course, taking me back, that bold statement of time and place. Havana, Cuba. Over five years have passed since I was there, over a decade since the journal was written.

Another email came yesterday, another attachment. Now I've let her in once the next time will be easier. I didn't read it straight off. To rush is to lose control, to let her dictate the terms. I've waited until now and I'll wait some more. Another cigarette first. This creeping uncertainty. I don't think I want it to become familiar but I can't be sure, I can't be sure at all.

Havana, Cuba, 26/3/1999

I was always a poet. If you're always a poet then it's always a problem because poetry is about truth and the truth can hurt. You have to learn to let go. It is mainly women who realise this, I think because they recognise the maternal nature of creativity, as nurture and release.

My first poem, lost and good riddance. I was fifteen and it was called 'A Vision'. You may think it egotistical, an early and unsurprising manifestation of a character trait soon to be definitive, that a teenager, whose horizons were so narrow and whose life so innocent, could believe herself capable of anything as formidable as a 'vision'. But are many mystics not young, naïve, as if wisdom is more easily graspable

without the burden of time and the dictatorship of experience?
It is telling that I can only remember the first lines of this
'vision', the rest of the message, my lesson, *edited out by a*
mind now defined by a cynical disdain for simple answers
which blithely and irresponsibly ignore the multiplicity of
cause, effect, and perspective, in short, all the dimensions that
came to crowd, pester, and define our lives. Yes, the vision is
now gone, reduced to echoes- not of a great universal truth
but tedious adolescent banality.

Autumn rain
all the umbrellas of the world fight for airspace
but never are we dry.

At the time, naturally, my message was important enough to
send to the Grantham Review. They hated it. I still remember
their letter as clear as day. My words were 'lacking in form
and formality', my subject-matter 'over-exposed', whatever
that meant. But this was the 1950s, a time of conservative
consolidation and much closer horizons. Girls were expected
to stay put, keep the self well hid. And definitely no literature.
We were expected to like poetry, yes, especially the romantics,
but not write it. I had a male English teacher, who once asked
us to compose a poem. He took great pleasure in ripping mine
up in front of the class. I am glad he did, or I might never
have allowed myself to indulge the possibility that I was doing
something right.

Apart from one or two who went away to train as nurses (and
came back to the local hospital soon after) not one of the girls
from my year left the town. University? You have to be joking.
We trudged into secretarial or shop work. I spent two years
counting the hours as a grocery assistant before I escaped.
Husbands and babies, it's all my friends talked about. I was
terrified by the thought of having a baby and was convinced

31

there was something wrong with me. Do you know what my ridiculous parents put it down to? 'Nerves'.

Thank heavens for my cousin Morven. Without her I'd probably be living in that dingy little northern town to this day. She had moved away and I adored her. It seems absurd now, but only men were expected to go wandering, the surname-forenames like Anderson or Farquar, so many dour Presbyterian administrators still desperate to make their civilising way, nostalgic for the dying Empire. A few of those jobs were still available then, placements in Hong Kong or Penang if you had the right linen-suited connections. We forget how brave women like Morven were, to have the strength not just to imagine another life but to actually leave the old one behind. She and I shared that pressing need to get out. Who knows from where it came. I think our soul-soaked malaise was simply random, an intangible disaffection.

By the mid-50s Morven was working in the office at Fountain Brewery, Edinburgh, the legendary McEwan's. She put in a word for me and off I trotted in February 1957. 'They'll call you a bumpkin,' such was my parents' farewell warning at the train station. But it was true! Clichés, the world is regulated by them, they have followed me for sixty years. These days at Leonardo's café I'm the identikit red-nosed gringo woman, sweating her way through another impossibly blue day. I see the laughter in their black eyes. They think I'm the drinker but these Cubans would break your arm for a bottle of rum. The Edinburgh boys, they could take a scoop too. 'The only difference between us is the colour of our skin.' Ah, those clichés again . . .

Have you seen old photos of Edinburgh? It is the red and white corporation buses that stand out in my memory. That livery was called 'madder' and it always intrigued me. What was the original madness, what was it madder than? Morven and I lived up near the Meadows and I often got the Number 16 down Lothian Road. There was an advert on the back of the bus that burned itself onto my memory. Then as now I have no idea what it was advertising, only the tagline interested me; 'Have a good run for your money'. Present tense, telling me to seize the day, every day. I was 19 then, an existentialist without knowing it. When I read 'Nausea' it was like Sartre had climbed inside my head and plagiarised everything I had ever thought. As for Paris so for Edinburgh. So gloomy. Dark clothes and buildings. Dark people. I decided to make that advert my mantra, I had to make sure I had a good run for my money.

Did you know I once worked in a brewery? Lo and behold the drink got you too. Soon as you started at the distillery I found out. I know you've been there ever since because I know all about you, see, but I will not tell you how. Perhaps it was no more inescapable that your occupation would mirror mine than it is that one day we all empty the final bottle. Ask yourself how much is coincidence, how much pre-programmed?

As soon as I started at the brewery all I wanted to do was get out. I hadn't expected Edinburgh to wear off so quickly. I was young, selfish, why should only men be allowed to follow their dreams? I wanted to write my way around the world or die trying.

Melodramatic, yes, but back then it was a serious frustration. Even other women mocked me, told me to take my nose out of the air and stop dreaming like a wee lassie. I was desperate to prove them wrong and that is how I came to teach English. It was ok for a woman to teach, or to be a nurse. And there was no way I'd be wiping bums to the end of my days so teaching was the ticket, literally. It allowed me to travel the world, but I'll come to that.

I want to stress that my choices to keep moving should in no *way be read as a judgement on your decision to remain at the distillery all these years. I only wish to understand why you have never strayed. Has the stoicism of the father transferred to the son? I have no way of knowing. My hope is you are not haunted by having 'settled'.*

What arrogance, I hear you shout, the mother who played no part in my life criticising me on my choices made! Perhaps, but there will be no apology, I have avoided them my whole life. Disappointments I can talk about for hours but not apologies, apologies require regrets and those I never allow. I learned that lesson in Edinburgh, walking those sodden streets under glowering skies to a freezing office where I copied letters all day and fantasised about killing my Neanderthal boss and stowing him in a warehouse.

There was no way I was going to allow myself the distress of staying, I simply had to retain my integrity. What are we if we lose that? I tell you this because I picture you as an honest man. The world needs an infusion of honesty, does it not?

In reality, of course, I have no idea about you. You may be the biggest bastard who ever lived, beating your wife, abusing children. It could be my fault for bringing you into the world. Not that I believe such nonsense for a moment. You are cut from your father's cloth, not mine, you will be an essentially decent man with an essentially decent family. It is too much to hope, I know, that you might believe the same of me. No, I am certain that when you think of me it is with anger alone. Indifference is perhaps the best I can hope for but what are we without hope?

I live in Cuba after all, a country that still knows how to dream.

The pages have been scanned from a written source into a pdf. The outline of punch holes is visible in the margins. My mother's writing is tidy and compact, the ink blue and nowhere smudged.

Helen's Journal 1, Helen's Journal 2. How many more? No-one stops a journal after two entries. That need to know, it's stalked me since I was a little boy. The healthy reaction is to let go *right now*, delete all the emails and any others that might come. But that familiar feeling of self-loathing curiosity . . . I know I'll give in, that I'll read whatever I'm sent. I've thought about my mother so much but she always demands more. Even after death she wants more.

I know who's doing this. I understand the reference in *vinales2004@hotmail.com*. What I don't know is why. It isn't the first time I've been sent emails from Cuba. August 2004, a Cuban lawyer called Rodriguez emailed from the digital ether. His prose was ponderous but the information clear-cut. My mother was dead, a substantial estate left to me. No-one had heard from her in years, perhaps it was inevitable the next contact would be the final.

I was more shocked by my reaction than the actual news, the lump in my throat when I would have expected apathy, or frustration at best. The lawyer wrote about Cuban law and the need to *personally come to Cuba to fix the death matters in two months* or the estate would pass to Fidel. There was no mention of what 'substantial' meant and his replies to my questions only brought terse *you must come personally to organise* ultimatums.

My wife still knows nothing about where I really went. I told her my mother had died in Torremolinos, Spain. Clever boy. We'd been there, three awful holidays in a death-trap timeshare tower-block. If I'd said it was Havana she might have wanted to come. Flights

35

on credit card, true, but I've hidden plenty with paper-less statements and online accounts. Anyway, there was no way she'd go snooping, the mere mention of Torre-molinos brought down the shutters.

There's secrets and then there's *secrets*. Even JC thought I'd gone to Spain to sort out my mother's estate. He had a beer with me at the airport before I flew to Glasgow for the onward connections to London and Havana. It was quite a thrill, sitting there knowing that no-one in the world apart from a stranger on the end of an email knew where I was really going.

All those faces, boldly outlined by that ever-present sun. I have to squint as I look back at them. The colours are intense, like paint that won't quite dry, so much more gloss than the Rorschach monochrome of the warehouse walls, the Chinese gloom of the barrel racks. My mother in time-stilled Havana. *Vinales2004@hotmail. com*. Ever since I returned home it's been rushing back towards me like the wind on the moor. Time is a fickle mistress. Five years have gone by, in many ways I'm unsure what I remember actually happened at all.

Once Upon a Time in the West

She was sitting at the bar. The barman flashed me a look from behind the counter and gave her a slight nod.

She didn't acknowledge me and no wonder. I was sweating, wiping my forehead with a little green towel. I didn't want the free Mojito offered by the hotel, just whisky. The barman poured a large one and I knocked it back, asking for another. I drank the next one more slowly, trying to relax into the surroundings. She shifted on her seat and I think she caught me glancing at her long brown legs. Who am I kidding, she did catch me, outright. But her only reaction was a tired smile. Just another leering man. *They all look, sooner or later they all look.*

Three Johnny Walkers later I offered her a cigarette and bought her a drink. Man she was pretty. The barman held my gaze a moment too long when he placed the drinks down. And no smile this time. No worries hombre, I wanted to say, just a lonely traveller passing through.

Like sick. Warm sick. I lay naked on the bed, staring up at the decrepit air conditioning box. The brain-jarring rattle I could take but not the smell it was pumping out. The thought of the balcony was even worse. No fresh air out there, just heat, the oily pressing heat that hit me as soon as I stepped off the plane and hadn't let up since. I'd just have to imagine the scene behind the grimy white curtain, the rusty Ladas and cannabilised American classics, Pontiacs and Plymouths, the smell of diesel and hot dust, the grand, crumbling buildings of cavernous blacks, sudden yellows. How many families crowded behind those requisitioned walls?

Hotel Inglaterra. I guessed there wasn't a Hotel Escocia. Not that this was a concern. This was a time to step up, leave chauvinisms behind. To feel sentimental after less than 24 hours in Havana would be absurd. The guidebook was right on the money, the hotel did have a *superb location on the lively Parque Central*. I was particularly taken with the ornate lamp-posts and the classical figures lining the facade. The long columned arcade was also impressive but the best feature of all the neon sign. *Inglaterra* in vertical white letters on a blue background, a horizontal t-bar at the top with *Hotel* printed in white letters on red. It just needed a couple of letters shorting out, a femme fatale smoking in the shadows.

A stocky man in a loose-fitting brown suit had met me at the airport. He was around 30 and greying at the temples. The details stood out, as if I was being encouraged to memorise them. Probably just anxiety at being far beyond the recognisable. *Red Cuba*! Brown Suit was called Basilio and I hadn't known he was coming. The email simply said that once I checked in at the hotel someone from the lawyer's office would be in touch. But here was Basilio with my full name neatly printed on laminated paper. I felt slightly self-important as I guess most people probably do when met at airports, but no-one paid me any notice at all.

Basilio drove the yellow '57 Dodge very fast. Red fins, polished chrome. I bounced on the sprung leather seat and tried to understand the billboards. No flash cars and pouting models of the Global Village, just Che and Fidel, block letters and bold colours of a puzzling certainty, *Fieles a Nuestra Historia . . . Viva Cuba Libre! Socialismo o Muerte*, said Basilio, banging the steering wheel and laughing. I stared at the bus queues, fruit stalls, and ancient Soviet trucks, the hundreds of smiling schoolkids in white shirts and coloured scarves.

I invited Basilio for a drink but he just smiled, clapping me on the shoulder. *Welcome to Cuba, I return 9.30 tomorrow morning.* An old man with a horse and trap emerged from the black cloud left behind by the Dodge, waving at me and pointing at the nag. I ducked inside.

It took me far too long to realise the woman at the bar was a prostitute. Even a few hours later the thought was excruciating. But I'd never met a hooker before so why would I make the assumption? She let her skirt ride up her thighs and seemed so interested when I started burbling on about mountains and lochs. I only got rid of her on the stairs. *Wheech room, wheech room?* A young woman in a black satin dress passed us with a look of utter contempt.

The air-con unit had started wheezing like an old asthmatic. If it conked out I was sure I could get another room. Hotel Inglaterra seemed almost deserted. *Faded colonial grandeur* indeed. I counted thirty-three ceiling cracks and wondered about the large water stains. The J&B sank a little lower. The prostitute, Basilio, and the staring barman, none of them knew anything about me, not a damn thing. Here, if I chose, I could be anyone I wanted.

* * *

I was late. Rodriguez was annoyed but doing his best to hide it. Smiling, but the fists clenched by his sides. I'd be tense too, working in this dingy office with its peeling plaster and smell of piss.

The lawyer's mood probably wasn't helped by the crumpled specimen standing in front of him. His eyes flickered with amusement every time I wiped my forehead. The sweat was pouring out of me, a combination of last night's booze and the heat. I'd managed to get sunburned too, despite having been in Cuba for less than a day. And most of that was the night. I wasn't in the mood for his carefully rehearsed exposition of welcome and condolence.

I apologised for being late. I'd slept in and kept Basilio waiting for half an hour. As soon as we left Parque Central the streets started to disintegrate. Off the main drag they got rougher, dirt tracks in the middle of a city. Bad for a hangover. Ancient Athens must have looked like this when the Gods fled. Columns and rooftop balconies scarred and peeling. Washing strung in front of ten feet high shuttered doors. Old women brushing their teeth, skinny husbands sitting at street tables playing dominoes. Basilio glanced at me in the rear-view mirror, probably wondering why these Europeans got drunk as soon as they arrived. He wouldn't behave in the same way if he ever made it to London. London with those big red buses.

Your mother taught English in Havana for sixteen years . . . a well-liked figure in the community . . . a friend of the Revolution who worked with the Cuba Solidarity Brigades and helped organise visits to schools and farms . . . many, many friends, Mr Drever and I have been told she knew how to enjoy life . . . she will be missed. I tried to let the lawyer's

40

words slip quietly past and failed. This need, I hated but indulged it, the greedy soaking up of the details of an unknown life. I felt like a little boy being told a story he couldn't quite understand.

'Your mother was like the trogon bird,' said Rodriguez, 'a rare breed.' Then silence. The three of us looked at each other. The lawyer seized the initiative and broke the awkwardness. He was in his element. 'Get some glasses Basilio, we must drink a toast to Mr Drever's mother.'

And he was off again. Like a rent-a-minister who didn't know the deceased, delivering a eulogy that had the congregation wondering who was inside the casket. Even if half-true it was still too much. I didn't want my mother humanised to any extent. My father, back home by the sea in his neat little cottage, I'd go to him if I ever wanted the truth.

'Then there is the legacy.'

I nodded. Basilio re-filled my glass.

'The value of the estate is not . . . *insubstantial*,' said Rodriguez. 'Even by your British standards.'

But he wouldn't tell me how much. There were 'complications'. I smiled, there always were with lawyers, a species that even the Cuban revolution hadn't managed to eradicate.

Apparently it would take some days for the final amount to be calculated. Rodriguez hoped this was not too much of a burden at such a difficult time. Perhaps I could take a few days to see the Cuba my mother had loved so dearly. She lived above a *casa particular* not too far from here. He could arrange for one of his mother's friends to meet me at a café. We could visit her home, begin the sad necessity of packing up her belongings.

41

The suggestion chilled me but the whisky was beginning to do its job. I could handle that, 'course I could.

Four more drinks at the café followed. A head full of booze made it easy to decide I could like it here.

I sat at a corner table with a view of the teeming street. The barman leaned on the bar, hands on his chin. Each time I interrupted his dozing he didn't bother making eye contact, just poured the drinks. That suited me just fine. To be the anonymous drunk. To brood in the half-light, staring through the bright doorway into the street. To my left was a beaded curtain, a darker room. Every now and then a raised voice, once when I looked up a thin-armed man. He'd smirked at me and barked something at the barman, who gave a dismissive wave.

My mother, did she come here, sit at this very table with its scratches and scorch marks, brushing away the same flies that circled the sugar bowl? I crushed one against his wrist and studied the black smear. Another one landed. They had no choice, just following instinct. I envied the simplicity. In a life determined everything, even death itself, would seem like a victory. My own triumphs were rare but if you avoided the risk then you avoided defeat. I knocked back another whisky. Yes, banality trumped humiliation any day of the week.

What about this friend then, Adelina? I tried to picture them. Gossamer night and melancholy red wine, pouring out the heartbreak and fears of lives turned to years. She must have seemed so exotic, my mother. She could have told Adelina anything she wanted, any exaggeration or embellishment the old phoney could muster. And no-one to challenge the narrative but herself, looking back guiltily from the occasional mirror she

42

couldn't avoid. That was the thing about being an exile, the inflated ego. Only those back in the homeland would be able to smell the hokum. My mother must have come to the same conclusion as I had the night before. That here, in exile, she could be anyone she wanted. It was an uneasy realisation.

'Are you Mr Drever?'

The woman was silhouetted by the light streaming in the doorway. 'At your service,' I said, standing up. I winced inwardly. *At your service?* What, like I'm some colonial fuckin gent?

'I beg your pardon?'

Now I felt like a total prat. 'I mean, yes. I'm Jim. You must be Adelina.' She ignored my outstretched hand and put her arms around me instead. I tensed, keeping my hands by my side.

'It is good to meet you, so good.'

'I thought I was in the wrong café. Took me long enough to find it.'

She stepped out of the light. I realised there was no particular reason why Adelina should be the same age as my mother. Mid-thirties, I reckoned, long black hair and slightly chubby. Plain. A large mole on her left cheek which I noticed and then couldn't stop noticing.

'You want a drink? I'm on whisky.'

'Yes please Mr Drever.'

'Just Jim.'

'Ok. Jeem.'

The barman began to pay more attention. Thin Arms appeared at the beaded curtain without the smirk. The gringo was with a *local* now, his assessment shifting to something yet to be defined. What's the story then, is the girl a prostitute, a friend? Thin Arms seemed keen to know and gave me an inscrutable wink as I crossed to the bar. Adelina wanted neat whisky too. I liked the way she called me *Jeem* but not her affection for my mother.

When I came back from the toilet I saw she'd primped herself up, tugging up the top that had slipped down her shoulder and revealed her bra strap. I wondered if she'd got dressed up, if she'd thought it fitting. I had no idea what she might know about me. Over-exposed, that was the feeling. Was she comparing me to my dead mother, looking for parallels in the mannerisms, the patterns of speech? She was as nervous as me. I pictured her putting the phone down after speaking to Rodriguez, not sure at all about meeting Helen's son.

We drank. I fidgeted. She filled each silence with a question. I answered and tried not to ramble. I picked at the *bocadillos* she ordered because the booze had ruined my appetite.

'She was a good woman.'

'But what does that *mean*?'

'Just that. She was always there for me.'

'So good means being there.'

'Among other things, yes.'

I nodded.

'You were lucky to have a mother like her.'

I held back the anger and was surprised by the sudden tears in my eyes. Adelina must have thought I was going to cry but instead I started laughing, emphasising my words, saying she was so *right*, my mother was a *fine* woman, a *rock* in my life. When I had finished she stood up, a bit unsteady, and led me to the café doorway, pointing vaguely down the street.

'Do you see that?'

'What?'

'That balcony.'

I could see balcony on balcony, in fact there were ornate, crumbling balconies everywhere. 'Sure.'

'She lived there.'

'Did she now?'

'Shall we go?'

I thought about the 747 sweeping down to Cuba, the Florida Keys so clear I could see cars on the causeways. One to the next, the islands like a join-the-dots challenge. Let go, cut loose. I looked at her closely. Her smile. It more than made up for something I couldn't quite place.

Three

Didn't someone once describe a distillery as a *meditation in machinery*? If my own characterisation is equally pretentious I don't care, no way I'm ever going to tell anyone. The distillery has always been *alive* to me, see? The end of closedown is like a beast coming out of hibernation.

Two more days of warehouse purgatory. The first mash is due on Wednesday night. The weekend for fermentation and Monday morning I'll be ready in the Stillhouse for the first distillation. Camp Gary can now be viewed as novelty rather than punishment, the lorry drivers a passing amusement. I don't care about pulling my weight anymore. It isn't expected anyway.

So check off the hours, doze in the dark. Dream the storyboard. A montage, naturally, homoerotic but don't tell, something out of Cronenberg, Kenneth Anger; the crop-haired young Mashman in blue boiler suit, checking the grain hopper and cranking the lever, a close-up rub of the hands as he steps into the Mashroom, the sci-fi control panel and periodic checks down the mash tun hatch, that vague urge to jump in, what would it feel like? And the music? Melancholy, like the opening credits of *Twin Peaks*, fading into throbbing machine hum, the fuuuush of the fermentation room and the wort spurting into the washback, the Mashman's flexing muscles as he empties in a ten kilo bag of yeast and those long gleaming pipes, imperceptibly swelling as he slowly, rhythmically, rubs a cloth along them.

Slinky materialises at 8.01 Monday. Site manager and secret collector of Hummel figurines. He's about five feet tall and that yellow safety bib makes him look like a preening canary. Sounds like one too, twittering about the *significant improvements* made to the Stillhouse over the closedown. I don't see much significance but I'm glad they've roped off the area around the spirit safes. I always feel uncomfortable with the tourist groups. My fellow Stillman Rankin loves it. He's the go-to man with VIPs. *I talk a lot of shite but the suits haven't got a clue.* He puts his arms round the pretty ones who want a photo, lets his hands wander.

'Impressive, eh?' Slinky says.

'If you like. Must have cost a few quid.'

'Speculate to accumulate and all that.'

'Bit of an expense when we're in the red.'

An exhibition has been installed at the far end of the Stillhouse in front of the redundant stills. Until the 1990s there were fifteen stills in operation, eight wash and seven spirit, one of the bigger distilleries in the country. Now there's five wash and four spirit. Changed days, but why sup the mythical *uisghe* when you can get pished on cheap Polish voddie?

The blown-up images are all that remain of the glory days, the turning of the malt, peat burning in the big kiln, the august distillery patriarch. Modern set-pieces evoke the past in a melancholy homage; the thoughtful-looking manager nosing a dram, the granite-faced cooper, three laughing warehouse boys. Anything to keep the heritage flowing, the tourists smiling. *The local is always the authentic,* the glossy leaflets will declare, something like that.

'Hard times right enough but you're right to say "we".'

'Not with you.'

'Well it's not going to be just *me* or just *you* who's going to sort the problems out, it'll be us. *We'll* sort it out.'

I stare at him. Camp Gary's right, Slinky really does look like someone who has a permanently itchy arse.

'That's why this strike is a . . . disappointment. A real disappointment. Wouldn't you agree?'

'The vote isn't in yet.'

'No. But you're on leave that day anyway.'

I hold his gaze. 'Had it booked for a while.'

Slinky holds my gaze a moment too long. 'Yes . . . So Colleen told me.' Then he smiles.

That *smile*. I can't rid myself of it. It ambushes me. I see thin curling lips in the turn of a water pipe or the sag of the security rope, the swan-like curve where the top of the still becomes the Lyne Arm. If I could see inside the condenser the thin pipe would twist and snake like half a dozen of Slinky's unctuous smiles, round and round on themselves ad infinitum. When I can't settle to *Paper Moon* on Tuesday's night-shift I switch off the laptop and find myself in front of the mirror in the Stillhouse toilet, trying to re-create that *fuckin* smile.

It won't do. The night-shift is a near sacred space. I check the hydrometers and clamber up to the walkway behind the spirit stills, walking along to the three filthy armchairs left in an empty space between machinery as a make-shift rest area. Hardly any light leaches up through the mesh metal floor from the Stillhouse below. Preacher Powell would not have my problem. Javier Bardem in *No Country for Old Men* would not have this problem.

'And neither the fuck will *I*,' I whisper in a slow American drawl.

'Neither the fuck will you what?'

'The FUCK is – '

'*Whoa* pardner, calm the beans!'

'JC. You fucker, scared the shit out of me.'

A small man with full beard and thick curly hair emerges from the gloom. He's stifling his laughter, offering me a near-full bottle of whisky. 'Nice, I thought you were going to go Chuck Norris on my ass.'

'What are you doing creeping about? It's 3.30 in the fuckin morning.'

'Just back from a gig. Dundee. I saw the lights and figured you might be on nights.' Then, mimicking my American accent. 'If it'd been Rankin or Stan I'd have melted back into the shadows, man, *disappeared*.'

'You're off your head.' I grab the bottle from him. JC plays accordion and writes melancholy, beautiful ballads. Such a delicate voice. The critics love him, use words like *genuine*, *haunted*. He's been on the cusp of breakthrough for a while and his latest, *Gold Mine*, might just do it. He runs a micro-label and musical collective called *Gate*, full of outlaw troubadours, Krautrocky noodlers and alt-doodlers. If I played I'd want to be on *Gate*.

JC slumps in an armchair. 'S'up dude?'

'Same old.'

'And that loving wife of yours?' He's smiling again.

'Wedding fever.'

'Don't be such a miserable fucker. Looking forward

49

to playing by the way. Got Pepe lined up for the drums, Aileen on guitar.'

'Least that's something to look forward to. You will not believe what Amber and Peter want to do. Actually, you might.'

JC looks expectant.

'Ice sculpture. Of a swan. Maybe doves. He's going to do it himself.'

JC nods, mock-impressed. 'Now that . . . is . . . *class*.'

The hangover will be a bitch. JC leaves just before six with not much left in the bottle. I must be reeking of whisky and eat a whole packet of chewing gum, load up on coffee. At the change of shift I make sure I keep a careful distance from Stan, wouldn't put it past him to grass me up.

Grass me up. Something I might have said back in high school. But this place *is* a continuation of school, with thinner hair, bigger waists and 24/7 internet porn rather than hidden under your dad's bed. All the envy, hate and social psychoses remain as well, set hard.

I'll never rid myself of them. Half the buggers here got the same school bus until we all left at 16. We'll all die together too, attending each other's funeral until there's nobody left. Who'll be last man standing? Only JC escaped. I envied him this, a bit, but then he came back! Three years of playing his way around Australia and NZ and back he eventually trotted.

So what's the point? The same dismal patterns will eventually re-establish whatever shore you wash up on. New York, Beijing, Skegness . . . I would've ended up with different children and a different wife but they'd have been just as peculiar as the ones I actually have.

It might have been my daughter doing karate moves in the snow, my son demanding an *OK!* wedding.

JC's right, I'm a miserable fucker. I stare at the sky and stumble into a bank of snow. If my wife's looking out the window she'll be shaking her head. She'll know I'm pissed if she gets close enough so I'll hide in the shed until she buggers off. That leaves the rest of the day. The hangover will stop me sleeping. I'll end up re-reading the journal emails, I know it. I told JC, who was intrigued. But he's an *artist*, he's supposed to be interested in life's little melodramas. As for the question about me believing my mother's story? Shrewd bastard. And of course he asked who's sending the emails. No idea, I said. No idea at all.

* * *

'How are you Mr Drever?' asks Nurse Ratched.

'Doing fine. Had better days.'

'I'm sure. But some have better days than others. You know how it is, you've been visiting your father for a long time.'

'Aye, it's all relative I guess.'

'Indeed.'

'Like everyone here.'

'I beg your pardon.'

'All the residents, they're all relatives. Someone's father, mother, sister.'

Her glare flickers between contempt and confusion. Ratched isn't really her name but she was straight out of *One Flew Over the Cuckoo's Nest*. She'd set the ECT clamps with glee. 'Very droll.'

'Not my best. Bit tired, must be needing a holiday.'

'A lot of our residents would bite your arm off for a holiday.'

Bite your arm off? Like a Hammer horror, the old folks as the undead, ripping off limbs. I persist with the levity. Unwise. 'Not a bad holiday here though eh, sitting around all day.'

'That . . . I doubt.' Her look has very definitely decided on contempt.

'I'm only – '

'Take a look around Mr Drever. We do our best to keep everyone amused and active, but the best stimulation always comes with . . . independence.'

'Of course.'

'Which is why changes of routine are so important for the residents. It's been a while since we've seen you.'

'I've been busy.'

'But at least you remembered. And that means you've got more in common with people here than you realise. All our residents are remembering, it's what they do. They sit. They remember.'

I can only nod. I hate coming here. Nurse Ratched is always immaculate, not a mole-hair out of place. She's in her late-forties and the 1940s is where she truly belongs. The primness I don't mind. It's the self-righteousness and moral superiority that make my skin crawl.

That and the smell. The odour of sagging, failing bodies. It followed me from the centre of the village where I'd parked, out the single track mile to the care home. Rather the sub-zero walk than getting the car stuck in a snowdrift. That smell, my father's carried it for years. Is that why my wife slaps on more and more of those lotions, a futile attempt to mask the inevitable? *Disdain*. The word suddenly drops into my mind, cold

52

as witch's tit. It's disdain I feel for old people. For their physical decline, for not being young, for allowing themselves to be locked in this Victorian prison, half-invisible behind the snowy fuzz, the whole place and everyone in it slowly fading out of existence. I know this camouflages a deep-seated fear of old age, I'm not that deluded. Even the Ego of Drever acknowledges death.

Nurse Ratched leads me into the conservatory. I'm glad of the heat after the freezing walk but give it three minutes until the itchy sweats. There's half a dozen residents, sitting alone or sleeping in chairs. Most of them have books and newspapers beside them though nobody is reading. And no-one is watching the flat-screen TV blaring down from a gantry.

My father's sitting in one of those hydraulic chairs. He's cleared a patch on the steamed-up window and is leaning forward and staring outside, very intently. Every time I visit I try to feel nostalgia, empathy, kindness . . . Every time I muster only guilt at failing to feel what I think I'm supposed to. Nurse Ratched told me he's had a bad couple of nights and obviously expected me to enquire further. I didn't, why bother going through the motions of concern when she's got me pegged as a sociopath anyway? She said I should make sure not to upset him because he seemed to be 'getting more emotional these days'. *These days.* The insinuation was obvious and she's right. If I visit more often I'll be better able to make informed observations about the patterns of my father's daily life, what his mental state is likely to be given certain circumstances and therefore how long I should stay, what I should say.

I'm surprised by the warmth in his eyes. He turns slowly when I take his hand, like he's known I was there all along. There are a few brief moments of recognition before his gaze clouds. When he places his hand against my cheek it's like he's been told to and can't quite remember why.

Little I say will be remembered. That's the thing about dementia, nothing sticks. I could take his hand and tell him I've been sent some emails (*they're like letters dad*) from my dead mother, remember her, your wife who left us decades ago? I could drop in questions to test her story; where did she work and did she have a cousin called Morven. Maybe he could reassure me that the emails were full of lies and I should go back to thinking of her in the way I've always tried, as someone who doesn't matter because she's never existed.

I get back to the car just after twelve-thirty. The dashboard display says minus 9. Even as I look it drops to minus 9.5. The cold is vicious but I leave the heater off, punishing myself, I guess, for being able to leave that place and the envy that hides behind his clouded gaze. My footprints stretch back across the narrow bridge and up the single-track. Time and again for years I've been coming here and always the same emptiness. No signs of life and in the absence of colour no more ambiguities. Just never-ending white, an oppressive, unmoving nothingness.

Which is still better than the home. The manager intercepted me before I escaped. If a fit lad like me can't make it what chance for the inmates? Again he wanted to offload his guilt about the home's looming closure. Again he was *sorry it had come to this state of affairs*. Again he reminded me that *a transfer home is keeping a space open, but it is becoming critical that you sign the necessary documentation.* Needless to say he *could facilitate the matter, help out in some way, at any point, just . . .* He let it trail off, whatever he was going to say left unsaid, so how could I know what he was actually offering, if anything? Just par for the course, I usually leave the home perplexed, as if my father's dilapidated mind has somehow affected my own.

I close my eyes, try not to think about the confused old man who stared at me blankly but was happy to let me hold his hand. I don't want to think of his sudden tears, or Nurse Ratched ordering me to just *go now*. I don't want to stand again in the conservatory doorway, watching her cradle my father's head and rock him back and fore with such gentleness. We had been silently sitting. I've no idea why he became hysterical. I hadn't mentioned anything about my mother, even though JC suggested I did. I should have stuck with my first instinct and stayed home. There's the lesson. Staying put, maintaining sweet ignorance.

If only.

Another email's waiting. Synchronicity, you can't do anything about it. Still <no subject>, only the attachment.

Why did my mother decide not to send her journal back in 1999, leaving it to *vinales2004* to send it now, over a decade later? I can see her razoring gaze, watching with amusement what she's set in motion. This *not wanting to remain a stranger* is a scam, the journal never intended as a mea culpa for my benefit but a catharsis to soothe her conscience. If not she would've fuckin sent it. Am I really supposed to believe the alternative, that the ego-monster spent years agonising about sending or not sending before death overtook the decision? Seriously?

The more I read the less sure I am how to react.

Not that there isn't plenty of choice. I've spent so long obsessing about her that there's no emotion, no variation on any theme that I haven't dug up, raked over. I could've tracked her down, sure, but I don't understand people who go searching for the parents who gave them up for adoption or whatever. Was the fact of the abandonment not a vague clue? Why track the bastard down to be traumatised all over again? There are far too many seekers out there and seeker sounds just like sucker.

Better to obsess on your own terms. Better a range of options than the truth. And this journal can reveal no truth because I don't believe any of it. How much can we ever believe anyone's story?

Havana, Cuba, 4/4/1999

Goodness me, those last few pages! I should be more sensitive. The problem is it has never, ever been a strong point. But I should be able to project, as I tell my pupils; to master English you must step into the world of an English speaker. Some of them are very good at it, they know instinctively how to play the game, how to lie.

However, I can't begin to imagine what it would feel like to read my dead mother's journal, knowing that she was alive when she just wrote this sentence. I should be able to empathise, to understand that this is your first connection with a mother who left your life a long, long time ago, that woman without a face who has suddenly reappeared in your life for no apparent reason other than that she is dead.

There is another reason, of course, there usually is. I want you to know me, James. I realise you have no means of engagement other than these few words and I have considered how you might react. In my maudlin midnight drunks I imagine your wretched pain at a rapprochement that will not now happen. Then, come dawn's bleak hangover, I have heard your screaming derision. But whatever your reaction it will not be in the face of my physical presence. It must be very frustrating to know that you cannot have the last word.

What about my presence? I am not tall, I am not short. I am average, but I do not have an average temperament. Average would have kept me in Edinburgh with you and Edward. It was expected, certainly, but it would not have been right. And my face? It is lined now, furrowed like the fields of Caithness, tanned a deep brown. When I first met the tropical sun I thought I would never get used to it. Just biological panic, within six months I wanted it hot, hotter! I am 61 years old and who knows how I made it. Sometimes the bottle winks, like it knows the secret. I can never decide if booze helped me get this far or blocked a different, easier path.

What else? Some have told me I am swift to anger but quicker to forgive. It is an unfortunate combination, it being difficult to maintain relationships on the see-saw extremes. They have come and gone, those relationships, and mostly they are gone. It is not my intention to appear self-pitying, but I have no control over your conjectures. Leonardo in the café has told me that that after six shots of aguardiente I look like Paul on the road to Damascus, just before he sees God. Leonardo, he has such respect for my journey, the struggle to follow my own star. Note, however, that I resemble a biblical patriarch, not a matriarch. And perhaps my femininity has indeed been a casualty of struggling against so many supercilious men for so long.

These nights are ever more muddied. I did not think the act of writing a journal would be so complicated, such a minefield of doubt and projection. These connections with a previous self can be so difficult to find. I have spilled my drink and the writing pad is sodden. Ten minutes on the balcony is all it takes to dry out. Maybe I should try it myself! Did you grasp what Leonardo said? That I look like Saint Paul just before he sees God. Such is my luck, to always be on the fringes of the revelation. If I had been paying more attention I would not have chased it all around the bloody world but probably found it in the rain bouncing off an Edinburgh corporation bus, heard it in the wind slicing up Craig's Close.

That was where I first saw your father by the way. Craig's Close, December 1957. I had been down Rose Street, the usual Friday evening at Milne's Bar and the Abbotsford. You have heard of the famous 'Rose Street Poets', yes, MacCaig, McDiarmid, Robert Garioch, Tom Scott? Shabby old Milne's was the place to be for a budding poet like yours truly but intimidating as hell for a woman. Today it has probably been tagged with something horrendous like the 'Poets Pub'.

Morven had known for years that I wrote poetry and she took me to Milne's Bar my first night in town. Straightaway I was hooked, the atmosphere so vibrant. I had never heard such conversation, the politics and the passion, the smoke and the shouts. And the men, the men!

I was intimidated to begin with but such a groupie, everyone deferring to Comrade MacDiarmid when he deigned to drop in, MacCaig holding court like a sardonic head teacher, Mackay Brown's ancient, unreachable sadness, sucking at you like the tide. I had a little crush on George but he was no looker, I tell you that. Morven said never to let on that I wrote, no matter how good it might be. I was just a woman, tolerated as possible inspiration, more useful for fucking. Even Sylvia Plath would have been laughed out the door, her inferiority predetermined by her sex. So I kept quiet, looking forward to the day when I could reveal myself as the mysterious 'Samuel Davidson' whose poems had become a publishing sensation.

If only! Because no journal published my work, under that name or any other.

Those men, they were like none I had ever met, sharp and cruel, full of imagination. They were so attractive but I was still so green, I didn't have the self-confidence to take them on. That is why I gravitated to your father. He could not have been more different, he reminded me of the men in my home-town, not much fun but gravely reassuring. Morven said he would make a 'great project' and gave me six months to cor-rupt him. But I was protective of Edward, he always seemed a bit bemused by the modern world, like he'd fallen asleep in 1895 and wakened up 50 years later. He was always blinking, does he still do that, like everything is a bit too bright?

Your father, yes, your dear father. I was amused by his haughty, militaristic bearing as he marched down the steps of Craig's Close that first night. He was wearing a long black coat and carrying an umbrella, mud splattered on his well-pressed trousers. The close was narrow enough but I was tipsy and decided to make it more so, making sure he had to squeeze past me. As he did I regaled him with an off the cuff sonnet. He hesitated, then stopped and turned. After all, what man can resist a poem recited by a beautiful woman? His blush was a beautiful rose pink but he accepted my offer of a drink and off we trotted to the Grassmarket.

What a story that would have made! Truly we all crave romance and if you are an emotional pygmy who swallows the lumps in his throat then I pity your underhand need to keep it hidden. In truth it was another projection, the romantic life that could have been mine among that coal-stained Presbyte-rian stone. I did regale him as he passed but his look, his look, it was cold as Greyfriars kirkyard.

A more tranquil mademoiselle would have let it go with a light-hearted bow and onto the next bar. But I brooded about

that face for days. So disdainful, the way he almost shook him-
self down after turning away, like settling his feathers back
in place. Clearly the religious type. I would not have believed
he worked in the brewery warehouses. He came across more
as a minister-in-waiting, sorry, a priest. Edward, I am quite
sure, remains as Catholic as they come. Here in Havana I see
so many like him, so many. They each have those invisible
stigmata, hidden but indelible.

I stop reading and rub my eyes. My wife's left one of her face-creams on the computer table. Geranium, maybe lavender. It smells like one of her oily baths. I rub a little bit on my finger, then my face, making sure I do those gentle circular motions under the eyes like I've seen her do.

That's three entries so far. The old bitch is getting into it now, moving up the gears. Is she making up for lost time, or maybe she knew she was running *out* of time. I never did find out what the terminal cause was. Cancer, heart failure, liver disease. The Big C is probably the most likely. All it takes with cancer is the socially mal-adjusted specialist telling you to wind the clock to three, four months and start counting down. The shock must be stunning.

How do you begin to deal with a deadline like that? I mean, it's not like waiting to see who your football team signs in the last minutes of the transfer window. This is a *dead*-line. My mother might have spent her entire life in some smug Zen present, all that *Dead Poets Society* carpe diem bollocks. But last orders please and here they come a-tumbling, all the repressed fears and tears of a lifetime, her essential nature finally laid open to the pitiless light.

I scratch my balls, trying to establish the themes of my unexamined life. Nothing comes to mind. I'll be the grinning death-bed fool. Just keep that sweet morphine coming nurse, not to kill the pain but erase my ghost-faced wife sitting there sneaking peaks at her watch.

I close down the computer and open the curtains. The rubbish wagon has left wide circles in the snow. The bright green bins are out of place, the Stillhouse glowing yellow under the wet paper sky. I can't remember the last time I saw blue. It's snowing, it's always snowing. I watch the hunched figure in the brightly lit weighbridge booth. Ronnie most likely, tallying the weight of this week's grain lorries. His big nose will be running, it's always fuckin running.

My wife must've cleared the bird table in the garden and put out some fresh nuts and seeds. The thickening flurry's beginning to bury them but no bird swoops down for a last peck. Nothing's moving but the snow. I've never watched the mysterious way that snow piles up without me noticing, even as I watch it. Snow just happens. More exactly, *piles* of snow just happen. There it is, life examined! That's as serious as the analysis should be. I'll refuse my mother's confessional soul-twitchings, better piles of snow than pangs of conscience.

I see her now, clear as day. She's on a beach, staring at the quicksilver Caribbean, the sand white as the snow falling beyond the window. The surf's whispering something she can't catch but the words will come to her later. That's what the seething Cuban night is for.

'Are you up there!'

Of course I'm here mum, I always have been.

'Jim!'

Waiting, just waiting for you.

61

'*Jim!*'

But it's not my mother, of course it isn't.

'You deaf? Your dinner's out!'

I still can't pick out the reason I didn't tell my wife about Cuba. Was I leaving open the option to re-mould myself? Like I'd turn up in Havana, claim my mother's dough and disappear into the great blue anywhere, a skip in my step and a Panama hat on my sun-burned bonce. Or did lying just seem the simple option? Maybe more than anything I wanted something I wouldn't have to share. I felt it was my due but even now, years later, I can't say why.

Cuba. It crowds closer the more I push it away. This terminal winter, the white fogged moor. There's all kinds of shapes out there, faces I recognise but am not willing to acknowledge, not fully. The courage to look has to be forced upon me, it's always been that way. But are you telling me that anyone would willingly choose their own haunting? It's hard to believe five years have passed. Talk about a story . . . I knew at the time it would have me lost in the mid-distance, a close-up shot as I look back on bold memories. *Havana*, I'd say, after the requisite dramatic pause, *it's one of those places*, a slight frown as I finally return your gaze.

Saturday Night, Sunday Morning

The skinny old guy's name was Luis. The owner of the *casa particular*, he'd rented the top floor to my mother for the past thirteen years. She'd tried with minimal success to teach him English.

'I very, very, sorry,' he said and shook my hand, big rheumy eyes open wide and watery.

'Thank you.'

The old man's face suddenly cracked open in pain. He dropped like a stone to the doorstep, clutching at his left foot. Adelina crouched down and put an arm on his shoulder as Luis gritted his teeth and pulled off his sandal. He spent the next five minutes patiently pointing out each scab on his swollen left foot. Occasionally he'd look up, the very picture of self-pity.

It should have been difficult. But it felt more like a role. The person wandering through my mother's apartment was not me but an actor. I opened a wardrobe, pulled along the hangers. Identikit cotton trousers, size large, long boho skirts. She favoured purples, dark greens, now and then plain white. I held a shirt against my face. Patchouli, the standard hippy scent.

Adelina didn't follow me. Maybe she thought it wasn't fitting. She leaned on the balcony and looked across the city. There I was in my dead mother's apartment, rapidly sobering up.

The flat-roofed bedroom was no more than twelve feet square. About the same size as the Den back at home. Even in the eight pm dark it was hot. During the day it must have been unbearable. There was barely enough room for the single bed and bedside table, a squat wardrobe and small bookcase making up the rest of the furniture. The bed was still mussed up from my mother's final night. Had she learned to sleep easier over the years? Maybe if I stared long enough her head might re-emerge from the indentation it had left on the pillow.

Among the paperbacks and textbooks on the bookcase were several larger, bound volumes. Photo albums, like the ones my wife kept. I didn't know what to do, my desire to open them almost perfectly balanced by disgust. This wasn't something I wanted to do alone.

'Adelina.'

'Jim?'

'Can you help me?'

Hobbling Luis appeared with a tray of coffee. He hovered for a while, staring at the opened photo albums. Where is this? I asked Adelina. Who is this person? When do you think this was taken? She could only help with the photos from Cuba and Peru. Nothing prior. It seemed my mother had said very little about her life before Peru. So much for her 'best friend'.

'You must not be sad.'

I felt more angry than sad. 'I'm glad my mother had such friends here.'

'What is the word you use when something sounds embarrassing because it is so obvious?'

'A cliché.'

She smiled. 'Then I apologise for this cliché. She was like an older sister to me.'

I put the albums back on the shelf and lifted a sandal from the floor, running a finger along the dark, sweat-stained indentations. I opened the jewellery box on the bedside table, lacquered rings and silvery chains, endless sundry beads, carved bone pendants. The clothes and jewellery, the bodily odours. Rodriguez's eulogy came drifting back to me, out of the night.

There was a little shelf under the bedside table. I reached in and found another box, a smaller, wooden one. Inside were more pictures, twelve in all. I went through these more slowly, aware that my heart-rate had picked up slightly. I recognised myself as a child but hadn't seen any of these photos before. Myself in a coach built pram. In the arms of a stern old woman. On the shoulders of a proud looking man, my father. Hand in hand with my young mother. And a man I didn't recognise sitting at a desk. He had black tousled hair, troubled eyes.

I stared at the wall. 'I've never seen these before.'

'It must be so difficult.'

'No. It's what I was looking for.'

'There is so much we don't know about our parents.'

'You're not wrong there!'

'Have I said something out of turn?'

'You mean you don't know?'

'Know what?'

'Really?'

'I'm afraid I am a bit confused.'

'Did she ever say much about me?'

'Helen? Well not a lot. I mean, no. Nothing.'

'There was a reason for that.'

'I'm not sure – '

'She abandoned me, left when I was four years old.'

'I didn't – '

'She never got in touch.'

I looked out the doorway onto the balcony. The concrete floor was painted burgundy, the walls a light lime green. Large tropical plants in terracotta pots had been placed here and there. I imagined my drunken mother staring across Havana's crumble in cotton trousers and a cigarette-holed shirt, listening to the hoots and shouts and sporadic drills, consumptive Ladas. Her bare feet would be scorched by the heat-baked concrete and she'd lift one foot then the other, moving to the rumba from the café 20 metres below. I hated her.

'I want you to tell me about her. I don't know anything about her, not a damn thing.'

*   *   *

7am, the noise from the air-con unit an enervating rattle. Another hangover. Hard white light was already leaching round the blinds. The previous night had receded to an improbable distance. What had seemed so obvious now didn't fit. I picked up my mobile phone. No calls. The only text had come from my wife just after I landed. *Good. Take care. Sun cream!*

The sycophantic waiter who cleared my breakfast table said it was a beautiful day and asked if I was taking the tourist shuttle to the beach. *I sure am*, I said, surprised by my sudden decision. Back home there was no way I'd have gone on an organised tour. But the more I considered it the more I wanted to go, despite the painfully white creature in lime-green swimming shorts peering back from the full-length mirror and begging me to reconsider.

'Hi there,' said a young man in shades when I got on the bus.

I sat across the aisle. Thierry had a pretty girlfriend, Monique. I told them I was the manager of a Scottish distillery. Out the lie popped, just like that. I had them hanging on my every word.

Playa de Guanabo was 45 minutes from Havana. I had my first proper look at the city, the winding sea-front shatter of grand buildings, the desert-like expanse of Revolution Square with the memorial to Che, the huge Korda portrait. I remembered growing up in the late 1970s, the news reports from the Soviet Union and the shorthand images of hatchet-faced leaders and khaki parades. Here, the stereotypes had never been moth-balled. In Cuba there still was revolutionary graffiti and 1950s American cars, old dancing men with cigars.

The beach was heaving. The Inglaterra tourist gaggle huddled together on a carpet of inter-locked beach towels, as if for safety. We stripped down to our bathing costumes and glanced warily at the bands of wiry young men who roved up and down the sand ogling the women.

This wasn't the Varadero promise of empty paradise beaches. This was Cuba central, reggaeton pulsing from the wooden beach hut, screaming kids and shouting mothers, strutting, laughing men and sun glinting from bottles of Havana Club. Afterwards, we would say we loved it. We'll say it was 'authentic' and ignore the nervousness we were all trying to hide.

The bullshit flowed. It's so much easier to talk to strangers when you're someone else. My wife would have been astonished. I imagined that *look*, hands on hips at the appraising distance she measured so well. I told everyone I was on a three-month tour of Latin and South America to source new grain supplies. *It's all about sustainability of supply, Thierry.* I'd set up a meeting in Caracas with one of Chavez's advisers about a possible oil deal, apparently.

'Viva la revolucion,' said Thierry.

'Viva Chavez,' I said.

A passing Cuban in dubiously tight black trunks stopped, breaking into a broad grin. *Chavez, Chavez, Fidel,* then a long burst of excited Spanish. I waggled my bottle of rum and the man sat down, beckoning over a few friends. Ordinary Jim would have retreated somewhere safer, like the other tourists who smiled politely but buried their heads in books. They fired off questions about Scotland, most impressed by this man who made the famous whisky.

The bus got back to the hotel just after three. Thierry was drunk and Monique horny. She kept tugging at her boyfriend's t-shirt and whispering in his ear. The lucky Frenchman was in for a fine afternoon if he could get it up. I'd told him about Adelina, how we met on my first night and *you've got a girlfriend Thierry but man you should try the Cuban women!*

The concierge called me over as we walked through reception. 'Mr Drever. A man has been waiting.'

I turned to follow the pointing arm. Basilio was dozing in one of the leather sofas beside the tourist desk. He had a rucksack at his feet. The concierge tutted and hurried across the foyer, roughly shaking Basilio awake. Basilio reacted angrily, shoving him away and for a moment didn't seem to know where he was. When he noticed me he immediately calmed down, settling a look of compassion on his sleep-swollen face as he approached the reception.

'My sympathies. Again,' he said, offering me the rucksack.

I hesitated for a moment, looking from Basilio to the bag, then unzipped it.

'Your . . . mother.'

I placed the urn on the concierge's desk, who quickly crossed himself. Thierry's sunglasses had slipped down his nose. Monique put a hand to her mouth. Everyone looked at the urn, then me.

I reckoned it was made of pewter. Polished to a fair shine and then tarnished by my fingerprints. I set the urn down beside the TV. It had condensation on it, like the Cristal beer I'd just opened. How was this possible, had it just come out of a fridge, were the ashes still *warm*?

Silence seemed appropriate so I didn't turn on the air-con. The heat rose and everything sweated. Urn, beer and me. I finished the Cristal and cracked another, watching beads of water slowly slip down the neck of the urn, round the shoulders and down the body as it tapered in and then out again at the base. I decided I didn't like it by the TV and moved it to the low coffee table on the other side of the room. It looked much better there, I decided, in the same instant realising I'd just aestheticised my dead mother's remains. Like an ornament, I was trying to make her *best fit*. The thought spooked me and I went for a shower.

When I came back to the bedroom the urn didn't look right anymore. I moved it to the bedside table. But the thought of waking up in the night and seeing the shadow of my mother skulking in the half-light made me move it to the floor.

What now? Was the protocol gravely to consider death, all the family members who'd disappeared as the years passed, all the traumatic illnesses and slow declines. But none of those deaths would come, no ghost-faces loomed out at me. I rolled over naked and looked down at the floor. Yep, my mother was still there, the closest I'd been to her in over forty years. I felt nothing. Even pre-urn she'd been dead to me all this time. It was unacceptable to compare her to other family members. I moved the urn back to the coffee table.

'Adelina?'

'Jim? Yes?'

7.03pm. She'd told me I could get her on her home phone any time after seven. 'I hope I'm not bothering you Adelina. I've had a bit of a strange day. I hope yours was better?'

'Are you ok?'

'I am, yes.'

'It is ok to tell me the truth.'

'I don't suppose you're free tonight?'

'Tonight? Yes I – '

'I mean, I don't want to put you out.'

'Put me out, but I am inside?'

'No, I mean I don't want to cause you any trouble, if you are busy.'

'You have not seen Cuban television, no?'

She was there within the hour. She was obviously choosing to ignore the object on the table until I decided to mention it. Instead she was friendly, talking about her day. My monosyllabic answers soon silenced her. It wasn't conversation I wanted, just her simple presence.

We sipped neat rum. I had put on Bermuda shorts last worn around 1990, the palm trees and surfer dude long faded. I wondered when my skinny legs had got so hairy. Between us the ash-tray was almost full. She asked me why I didn't put on the air-con and I shrugged. She was wearing a knee-length denim skirt. I noticed her slim legs but didn't stare.

'Do you think the dead belong in the same house as the living?' I asked, pointing at the urn.

She glanced at the coffee table and looked a bit nervous.

'Must be strange to think that your friend has been reduced to something that fits in such a small container?'

'Jim. It is very difficult for – '

'Back home some people make a feature of these things. They turn it into a shrine and surround it with photographs and candles. Imagine you dropped it, imagine looking down at the mess of white ash and seeing something? Like a tooth. Or a toe. Imagine seeing the toe of your dead husband in the middle of the carpet? You'd never expect such a horrible thing to happen. But it might, surely even crematoriums have technical problems now and then?'

'In Cuba we don't really have these . . . containers.'

'What will I do with her?'

'Her?'

'Yes. Her.'

'There is no *her*. Not in there. She is everywhere, *anywhere*, but not there.'

'It may as well be full of manure for all that I can connect with it. You know manure?'

She shook her head.

'Shit. Cow shit. Horses. They use it as a fertiliser on the fields to make things grow. I want to take that urn full of shit and throw it in the sea. Do you think she'd like that? Did she like the sea? Would she like to be floating free and dead in the Caribbean, slowly dissolving? 'Cause that's what she was like for me, a slow dissolve from the age of four till nothing was left, nothing left but the smell of shit that I can still smell coming out of that fuckin urn.'

Adelina put a hand on my arm.

'Do you have psychiatrists in Cuba? Have you heard of "closure"? Apparently everyone wants closure but I got closure when she closed the door one day and pissed off. Why would I want her to explain herself, like sure, I understand, water under the bridge and all that. Fuck *closure*.'

She took her hand away. She looked as if she was going to say something then changed her mind.

'Go on then,' I said.

'What?'

'Tell me.'

'About Helen?'

'You said last night that you'd tell me about her. So I'd like to know. Tell me something.'

'I do not think this is the right time.'

'Come on, *tell* me something!'

'Jim, you are drunk. Please.'

'Of course I'm drunk, my mother's sitting over there in a fucking urn.'

'I will go now Jim and I think you should sleep.'

'I dreamed about her you know. On the flight over. For the first time in years. We were both on this amazing long beach, nothing for miles in either direction. And she's talking, talking, *talking* but I can't hear anything. She's saying all these things and I can't make out a word. When I woke up I felt so claustrophobic, like there was a hand on my throat.'

She got up then and walked to the door. When she turned round her gaze mixed pity and contempt, like she'd expected better and again been disappointed. 'You can phone me, Jim. But never shout at me. I do not know you. Your mother was my friend. Not you.'

Four

Apparently my chinos are too short, they come too far up the ankle when they should fall across the bridge of the foot. My wife sent me up the stairs to get a pair of jeans, to *compare*.

'Right. Take your slippers off.'

'Katie, don't you – '

'Stand there!'

So there I stand, bare-foot on the freezing lino, top lit like a baddie in a German expressionist movie. *The Cabinet of Jim Drever*. I need some heavy eye make-up, exaggerated gestures.

'Right. Now put the other pair back on.'

I do as I'm cold.

'*Seeee*,' she shrieks. 'They're *much* shorter!'

I look at my chinos and wiggle my toes, which seem to be taking on a blue tinge around the tip. The length still looks fine to me. I'd be more inclined to single out the fact that I still *wear* chinos, last fashionable in 1988, or that they've been over-washed into a sickly marbled green. But no, she's picked on the fact they're too short. When they're obviously not.

The worst thing is that she's being playful, which annoys me even more. Our arguments are usually heated and often vicious, every word targeted. It throws me off kilter when she picks on something that I'm not meant to take seriously. But invariably I do, can't help it. I counter-attack, singling out the pot of lentil soup she's made for dinner and managed to burn.

'It tastes like embers from the fire.' Hardly a biting insult, granted, which is probably why she laughs. She's heading for the high ground, trying not to let the situation degenerate into a shouting match. She even chuckles and shakes her head, like *oh Jim, why do you always have to take everything so seriously*. Yep, she can be disciplined when she has to be.

And now Amber appears, her mother immediately enlisting her help. I have to take off my slippers and stand up again. Amber takes an appraising step back, angling her head. *Yes*, she agrees, *they're definitely half-masts*. The look of savage triumph on my wife's face is almost medieval. The worst thing is that as I sit at the kitchen table listening to them gibber on about tomorrow's wedding-dress fitting I can feel a draft on my ankles. It can only mean one thing, my trousers have ridden up because they are too short. They are indeed half-masts.

'She's going to look lovely,' my wife says later.

'She will do.'

'Did you see how excited she was?'

'I did.'

Amber's been excited about her wedding since she was four years old. I wonder if this says anything about me. Did she realise early that her father was such a distant presence that he couldn't ever be relied upon to be the manly rock that every daughter needs? Maybe she projected outwards, yearned for the day when her Donnie Juan would appear.

Round here you get what you can get. She probably wasn't too fussed when Peter appeared not on a panting steed but a transit van smelling of stale fags and chip suppers. Expectation is relative. For Amber, this was Mary Mastrantonio meeting Kevin Costner in *Robin Hood*.

My wife's dewy-eyed, a troubling prospect. We'll either end up talking about the kids all night or have sex. If I'm unlucky it'll be both. 'I've never seen her like this, she's really blossomed. Do you remember that Goth phase? I always knew she was more feminine than that.'

I'd actually liked the Goth phase. Well 'like' is maybe a bit too strong. But the rebellion was surprising and I'd admired it. I'd never have had the balls, even if I'd wanted to whitewash my face and huddle in a basement with angst and acne-ridden teenagers. Like that time when we were teenagers and JC wore a pair of leather trousers to a pub in the Town. The classic Jim Morrison phase. We barely avoided a kicking for being a *couple of fuckin faggots*.

With Amber it was actually the shock on her mother's face that I liked more than the rebellion. *I tried to understand Jim, I really, really did.* But in the end she put it down to drugs. Drugs! Defeat by any other name. You can't understand your teenager so you put it down to drugs, the *evil* of drugs (she actually said that). In the past it would've been the devil, Amber burned at the point overlooking the Firth, my wife nodding grimly, *it's for her own good.* 'All we need now,' I suggest, 'is for the boy to find himself a girlfriend. It's just what he needs.'

She's appalled but amused at the same time. 'God, can you imagine it?'

'Maybe the McAllister lassie from up the glen.'

She gives me a nudge in the ribs, a guilty smile. 'Stop it, that's awful.'

'What!' I protest, like I'm serious. The McAllister girl, Anne or something, has learning difficulties. 'He could do worse.'

'Stop it.' All of a sudden she looks appalled.

I can hear the usual thrash metal pumping out from the Boy's room upstairs. A few years back I asked Malky how his kid was doing. *He's fourteen now, at the wanking.* I take the glass of wine my wife hands me and swallow half, trying to obliterate the image of my masturbating son. That's the trick about being a parent, honing the strategies to deal with the horror.

She's looking pensive now. 'Do you think there's something wrong with him though?'

'He's just a teenager.'

'I know, I know, but some of the things he does are just so weird.'

'I'm sure you were a bit weird yourself at that age, weren't you?'

'But that's the thing,' she whispers, all conspiratorial. 'I don't think I *was*. You weren't either, I remember. What do you think happened to Gonzo? I mean, really what do you think?'

Gonzo was our cat that went missing about 6 months ago. 'The cat? The cat was about 15 years old, she just crawled away to die. Who do you think's skulking up there, Ted Bundy Junior?'

She nods vaguely then suddenly seems to make her mind up about something, face brightening. 'You're right. Amber turned out ok. I'm sure the boy will too.' She smiles, reaching across the table and putting a hand on mine. 'We drank an awful lot of wine that night too, when I got pregnant with her, do you remember?'

'How do you know the exact night?'

'I just know.'

'But how?'

'Oh for Christ's sake Jim.' She snatches her hand away. 'Can you not just take my word for it? Call it woman's intuition.'

'How come there's never any man's intuition?'

'You really are determined to spoil this aren't you? Well I won't let you.'

I didn't realise I was spoiling anything. Now she's all playful again, coming round and giving me a shoulder massage. I close my eyes. She's actually quite good at this. She starts on about Amber again, the wedding preparations, how the final number for the meal is 65, that the menu is sorted. And the Dress, the *Dress*, she's more excited than Amber about the Dress.

'You can give me a hand when you come back,' she says when I get up for a pee. 'I said to Amber we'd have first go at the place settings, who sits with who. Oh come on Jim, it'll be fun to do this together.'

'Mmm.'

I spend a long time in the toilet. I even brush my teeth. She doesn't really want my help so why the pretence? I open the bathroom window. Breathe, breathe the cold air. The kitchen window is directly below me, casting a vague yellow glow on the white frozen ground of the back garden. In the middle of the glow is a darker patch, something blocking the kitchen light. My wife, she must be standing at the window too. Someone looking at our house from a distance would see the two of us standing alone at our different windows, staring out.

Mean Streets has almost finished when she opens the door to the Den. She stands behind me and I feel myself tensing. Then she tousles my hair, like I'm a little boy. 'You're such a prick,' she whispers.

She's right. She goes to work the next morning without a word. Ambiguity. I can't help it. I sit in my purple pants re-reading my mother's journal and realise she's the very opposite. Straight down the line. No *subtlety*. I should be grateful for that small mercy, I suppose. It would have been upsetting, *cruel*, to be given the impression that she wasn't sure about her choices.

Nope, she locked on to the target and never deviated. *For better, for worse*. Like the grim-faced words of the minister on our wedding day. I repeated but wasn't sure I meant it. But you can't hedge your bets when the congregation's crowding, alert to any err or umm, any verbal slippage that might reveal a nagging doubt. That's the whole problem, we repeat without thinking, trusting that happy certainty will forever prevail if we say something often enough.

Not me though. Never have. Some might call this a failing. Certainty, after all, is the mother of belief in the beardy man in the sky, the Red Flag or the swastika, even a football team. Ambiguity can only lead to disrespect. Like the kids at school who changed their allegiance based on who'd just won the league. I'm sure Man United didn't have half as many fans back in the 1980s when they were pish. And no doubt they'll all melt away when the success starts to dry up. Then we'll be mocking the fair-weather fans, their disloyal *ambiguity*.

I never had any certainty in any of it. I can imagine a God and not imagine a God, it just depends, on whether

I'm constipated, drunk, how heavy it's raining . . . Football? You can fuck right off with football. Imagine the utopia we'd be living in if the loyalty and absolute belief that people show for a football team was mirrored in politics. Only the fascists seem to manage it, never the lefties. But it's easier to be a selfish bastard than a saint, the bovine herds happy to believe the default system we're left with is the pinnacle of human achievement.

Course it is! Who wouldn't want 25 brands of cornflake, who wouldn't want a cabal of interchangeable wet-lipped deviants long to rule over us, who wouldn't want to fly, fly, *fly* to sweaty-arsed places where we do everything we do at home but wearing fewer clothes? Even today, as the system collapses around our penny-grubbing fingers, we can't bring ourselves to imagine that there might just be an alternative. It's because we can't function with ambiguity. Except me, which is why I find it hard to garner enthusiasm. About most things.

Take last night. I feel a bit embarrassed. It's unnecessary in most cases, perhaps even all, to pick a fight about lentil soup. It's probably also wrong, being a father and husband, to be so obviously uninterested in my daughter's wedding. My wife was in a good mood. I should've been able to indulge her for just a little while. I should be able to reminisce without cynicism. But I'm not convincing enough to lie properly. My wife hates my ambivalence. *Why can't you ever say what you mean, why do you always have to twist things?*

My wife gets home early, mood improved by the latest appearance of The Dress. She, Amber, and the dress fitter bunker down in the living room, the Boy and I under strict instructions to stay upstairs. To reinforce the point we were both brought bacon rolls and a coffee.

I close the last journal entry. Although I only got the email a couple of days ago the thought of not getting another is vaguely disappointing. Outside the world remains buried in white. Nothing moves. I click to Porn Hub but can't manage an erection. How many middle-aged men are sitting in cold bedrooms as the snow piles up, idly watching an Italian orgy?

A sudden thump and I instantly close the site. Amazing how fast I can move when I think I'm going to get caught having a tug. A true gift, discovered age twelve and honed ever since. Amber's shouting. The slam of a door followed by frantic knocking, my wife's raised voice and words I can't make out. Sam Spade would conclude that Amber has locked herself in the bathroom for an as yet unknown reason. Now would be a good time to take the interest I so spectacularly failed to show last night. I step onto the landing and peer down the stairwell.

'Everything ok?'

In a moment my wife's face appears below me. She looks worried and puts a finger to her lips.

'What is it?' I half-mouth, half-whisper.

My wife glances round warily then quickly puffs out her cheeks, patting her stomach at the same time. Then she's gone. In a moment the knocking on the bathroom door starts. *Amber honey it'll be ok, don't worry.*

When I turn round I see the Boy at his bedroom door. He gets more pasty-faced every day. I see a screen flickering behind him. Maybe Bruce Lee's face, he's obsessed with the box-set I got him.

'What's wrong with her?' I can almost *feel* the glee waiting to burst out.

'There's a problem with the dress.'

81

He suddenly looks triumphant. 'She's too fat, isn't she?'

'No she's – '

'She's too fat.' Then he runs to the stairs and starts shouting. 'Who ate all the pies, who ate all the pies?'

My wife's face is back in an instant. 'You, back to your room. *Now*. Jim, why can't you keep your mouth shut?'

No point answering. No point protesting. The afternoon feels suddenly heavy and I decide to escape. The Boy's evaporated. At times he's almost soundless. Maybe my wife's right and there is something wrong with him. She looks at me with loathing when I come downstairs. Amber's still sniffling away in the bathroom. I pop my head round the living-room door and see who must be the dress-fitter sitting on the couch. She's trying to figure out what she should do, pretending to read one of my wife's magazines, trying to not to be there at all.

Peter's the last person I expect when I open the back door. He looks excited, expectant.

'Well?'

'Eh?'

'How's it going in there?'

'Fine.'

'Does she look good?'

'Looks fine.'

'She'd look beautiful in a sack,' he grins.

I hesitate for a moment, looking for the piss-take. 'What are you doing here Peter, isn't it bad luck or something.'

'You believe in all that shite? I just wanted a peek but they've shut the living room curtains. Must've known I'd sneak along!'

'I'll see you later Peter, just going for a walk.'

'Mind if I come along?'

I do but he comes anyway.

We head up the hill running parallel to the house, following the single-track as it swings towards the village, three miles away. No tyre-marks, just the criss-crossings of deer and hare. We follow the forestry track into the woods. The pines and spruce are packed so dense that even after so much snow there are occasional patches of brown needly ground under some.

It takes twenty minutes before the burbling begins. Like he was being respectful. Now and then I glance at his big nose. Sometimes a line of snot hangs there, would it freeze if he left it alone? Like an icicle, a *snoticle*. He's telling me that all he wants to do is make Amber happy, that he knows what some people say about him but he's really a changed man since he met her. *That's good*, I say, and *uh-huh*. He's looking for reassurance, desperately hoping that I'm going to say something like *sure son, you'll make a fine husband and son-in-law*. I don't, naturally, and he gets increasingly nervous. He should understand that this is what a father must *do*, reserve his judgement. He must be able to project himself into my position and understand the wariness. He must come to understand my *ambiguity*.

We head onto the moor. A hare bolts out from under my feet and I watch its zigzag escape into the milky void. The wind skries, conjures up a blinding spindrift. I take care not to reveal to Peter my delight in these moments. We take shelter in a decrepit grouse hide, sitting in silence.

'I really do mean it Jim.'

I decide to take pity. 'I know you do.'

His hug is unexpected. Like his relief has suddenly overflowed into this inappropriate show of affection. I let him hold me for a couple of seconds. Fat snowflakes settle on the sleeves of my waterproof jacket. What it would be like to die out here on the moor, behind this misty curtain with the afternoon light fading faster and faster? My last thoughts would be about my warm breath in the cold air, how it fogs less and less as my body heat gives gradually out.

But I forget. Peter's here. No chance of a dignified end with Pete around. He'd have me on my back, pumping my chest and giving me the kiss of life. You must be a bit confused when you come back from the brink of death, a tad disoriented to say the least. What would you make of coming round to your daughter's red faced fiancé straddling and snogging you?

He's saying something about climbers being killed in the mountains. They didn't have the proper gear, froze to death twenty minutes from the car park. *Can you believe it? Couple of fuckin idiots* .... The more I ignore him the more panicked he gets, one of those people who fill gaps in conversation with any old crap. Every time I see Peter he's moaning about something, an old fart before his time. Soon he'll start on about his ailments, how he's *struggling by*. He'll become like Luis the building superintendent back in Cuba. Why did he insist on showing us his swollen, scabby feet before he let us into my mother's apartment?

* * *

The temperature rises. For a day or so the snow holds out. I hear it first, a slow dripping from the gutters.

84

Then the burn, rising in volume as melt-water swells. Peaty water eats away at overhangs of ice which detach soundlessly. The snow-plough carves black scars into the white.

Then the crows appear. I see the first on the wooden platform of the bird feeder in the garden. It's so ravenous it doesn't even look at me as I stand there watching it peck furiously at the withered nuts. Something on the fringe about crows, the blue-oily feathers that catch the light. It clambers skywards and gives a harsh scrawk, proper crow vernacular, *what the fuck are you looking at?* I follow it to the top of the dark grains plant. There's a whole murder crowding up there, silhouetted against the silvered sky, still others above the Stillhouse.

The temperature drops, freezes everything solid. Five days the crows remain. I pass under their monitoring gaze as I walk between my house and the Stillhouse. We start discussing them, surprise giving way to a vague unease. Malky says he chased off half a dozen ripping at his bin bags. Camp Gary says he flung a stick and was chased by a whole gang. *Clawed in the fuckin head*, he says, but who's going to believe Gary? No-one remembers so many crows and it's inevitable that we'll talk about them for years. It'll be called the Winter of Crows. *Remember the Winter of Crows? Must've been the weather.* We'll all have our stories and we'll all remember differently. *Must've been a coupla hundred of them, eh?*

But I'll remember more, black huddles along telephone wires and rooftops, squatting on our shed roof. I hear them cackling in the dark as I gather logs, see them briefly in headlight beams of the new-model Audis sweeping down from the distillery offices and past me.

The heads I glimpse in the green-lit front seats are

darkly identical, once the glow of a cigar, maybe a turning face. The emergency board meeting called in response to the 19 to 5 vote in favour of a strike must be over. Jack will be on the phones. The laughter from the shed roof suddenly swells, like *what difference can it possibly make?* Then a low ruuush ruuush that takes a moment to grasp. The beat of wings, the crows on the move into black magic night.

In the tea-hut on Monday morning I think about passing on what I know. How the crows followed the suits out of the distillery. How their cries had merged with the low roar of high-powered engines. How all had gradually faded into silence. But I don't. The supernatural runs close enough to the surface in this place without encouraging it. That'd be an *omen*, lucky or otherwise, and I can't be bothered with all the frowns and questions and incredulous looks and *are you sure it wasn't one of your weird films*? Instead I listen to the crow stories, the speculation about what the management is going to do and the endless football banter, waiting for Rankin to pop his head round the door so I can take over in the Stillhouse.

The atmosphere changes immediately when Slinky appears at the door. He's got a big red zit in the middle of his forehead. It's almost boil-like and he knows we're all staring at it. This is guaranteed to unnerve him. Slinky's too vain to realise that his ever-immaculate appearance only provokes mistrust. He's avoided, like late-winter ice on Lochan Dubh.

'Morning boys.'

A couple of grunted hellos.

'Robert's on his way.' Slinky waits for someone to look at him. 'He wants to pass on what was said at the board meeting.'

I swear there's a little gleam in Slinky's eyes. He backs out of the door, deferential, and if he was wearing a cap he'd probably be doffing it to the tubby, red-faced man who comes into the tea-hut. Robert Burns (no joke) started with me in the warehouses years ago when we were both 18. If you want an identikit 'Good German' for a war movie then Rab's your man. He's got the proper buzz cut and the gloomy jowls, the darting gaze of a man permanently in the midst of an existential dilemma. But he's a decent man, whatever that means.

'All right lads. How's it going? See those crows finally fucked off.'

The response is better this time, Rab's got the respect Slinky can only dream about. He's worked himself *up*, see?

'Not going to piss you about lads. The board was pretty disappointed with the strike vote. I was too, as you know. But that's your right, I know that. I can understand why you're angry. These are tough times. Not just here but all over. No one likes to be constantly wondering if their job's going down the shitter.'

It's an act, of course, the concerned manager keeping it real. Slinky's letting the side down. He's barely able to contain his contempt, impatiently fidgeting, waiting for Rab to get to the point.

'I want you to know that I did my best to keep your interests to the fore during the meeting. And I'll be brutally honest with you, we talked short-time, we talked about redundancies, but we also talked about substantial investment from the corporate centre. All options were on the table. And nothing was decided. But I tell you boys, the strike's not in your interests. We'd like a delegation from the workforce to negotiate directly with representatives from the board. All the options. But you've got to call the strike off. You've got to take this – '

'Where's Jack?' asks Camp Gary.

'He's due on at 8.15, shouldn't he be here?'

Slinky's smirking now. It's only 7.55, Jack's probably still driving.

'But he's not here, is he? You should be taking this up with him Rab, he's the shop steward,' says Malky.

Rab gives his glasses a dainty polish and settles them back on his neb. 'I thought I'd come straight to you boys, you don't need Jack to be holding your hands, do you? It's not my fault he's not here.'

'You should've waited,' says Camp Gary.

And then Jack appears. 'Bloody right you should've waited. I'm the designated liaison. This is bang out of order!'

Jack's always been one conspiracy theory away from David Icke but this might have him buying the turquoise shell-suit. He shoves past Slinky who shoves back. Then Camp Gary steps forward and shoves Slinky, who looks genuinely scared. Before you can say righteous mother-fucker they're on the floor and Slinky's got a cut above the right eye.

No-one says anything. It's like an intense fight scene in a Jack Palance flick, the seen-it-all-before cynics look-ing blithely on, *the way it's always been boys, the way to settle things*. There's even snow beginning to fall beyond the cooperage doors, a script you wouldn't believe, big flakes blowing around the two men wrestling on the wet floor, breathing hard, their feet kicking up water. Rab and Jack have disappeared and I wonder briefly where they are. It's just me and Malky watching the silent fight, then Rankin appears at the Filling Store door on the far side of the cooperage. He's got this big, shit-eating grin as he leans against the wall and lights a rollie. A fine idea. I roll myself a fat one and hand the baccy to Malky.

All day long I'm sought out. *Did you see the fight then?* They know I did, of course. *Who started it Jim, what do you think'll happen next?* I have no answers to these questions and my lack of interest disappoints some people and annoys others. So little happens round here they can't understand why I don't want to talk about it. I'd rather listen to the pot stills. You get more sense from them. Each one's an individual, always something different to consider.

Today there's a pissed off fizzzz in number two spirit, a cool huuum in four. Imagine how the tastes would differ if the spirit from each still was separately matured instead of being mixed together? Imagine the taste of different emotions; anger, happiness, uncertainty, singularities that everyone can identify with, none of that 'hints of fig and banana' or 'choco-peaty top note' pish. The taste of fifteen year-old contempt, that's what I want.

Camp Gary appears at lunchtime. He's got a cut above his lip; *see that, it's like a little 'z', like Zorro!* He's been on a celebratory tour, showing off his wound in the cooperage, visitor centre, warehouses . . . An easy win, I can't think of anyone apart from Stan who likes Slinky. And no-one likes Stan either. Gary takes the laptop from me before I can complain.

'Have a read of that.'

'What?' He's opened the website of *The Sun*.

'My stars, Libra. "Today you will be the centre of attention. People will seek you out to congratulate you and it will seem like you can do no wrong. Today is a day you will feel rightly invincible." What do think of that eh?'

'Amazing.'

'I've been wanting to hit that little fucker for years and all this time it was written in the stars.'

When Gary leaves I read my own horoscope, Taurus. *With your antenna on red alert right now you're suspicious of your family when their stories don't add up. Try not to jump to conclusions because their secret may involve a nice surprise.* If I had coffee to splutter it would've just been spluttered all over the laptop. Babs Cainer was on fire today, first Camp Gary and now me. My wife has a near-religious devotion to Ms Cainer's delusions and if I mention this there'll be a triumphant *I told you so!* But I'm a fair man, mostly, sometimes even charlatans deserve their due. Another email arrived late last night. I haven't read it. But when the universe, the *stars* goddammit, tell you to do something I suppose you have to listen.

I settle back on the chair and click to *My Documents*, where I've saved *Helen's Journal 4*.

Havana, Cuba, 9/4/1999

'You can't run forever!' Because running is running away and running away is bad. That is what they say, yes? Like all such platitudes it is nonsense. You can keep on running for as long as you like. That is the key, the liking. As long as you enjoy running then you are going to keep doing it and why not? Only when you stop enjoying it does the switch flick, the running become a bad thing.

You can't, you shouldn't . . . wherever you go the Morality Police are at your elbows (keep them sharp!). Once or twice I have watched people change in front of my eyes, people I respected, the decision arrived at in the middle of our conversation (maybe it's me!). Out comes the permanent marker and the arbitrary stop line. It is like a religious conversion, stripping away remembrance of all things past. They refuse, suddenly, to see the series of decisions that led them to here, to this point. If they had not made their own choices, if they had not decided to run, then they would not have even arrived at where they are now, they would still be in the same boa constrictor-like town or village they were born in. Those are the ones I distrust the most, the ones with cold bunker eyes too scared to ever leave.

Look at it this way, if it had not been for John Tannehill then I would not be here now. What's this, who is this John Tannehill I hear you ask? I will come to him soon enough. Two more shots and I would have been straight off on that tangent. Luckily I am relatively sober. It has been raining, you see, and I feel cleansed.

This isn't the kind of cold, morose rain that you are imagining and I remember. This is the hurricane's rain, hard and warm. I run to the balcony when the first thunder comes, I love to watch the sky darken, the street below me emptying, the chatter and shouts as people make a dash for shelter. Leonardo always comes to the door of the café and looks up, gesticulates for me to get back inside, 'la lluvia,' he shouts, 'la lluvia!' I feel like Christ, I am Christ when I take my clothes off and spread my arms wide and lean back, face to the angry sky, those drops heavier, heavier on my face, my chest.

There is no feeling like the tranquil aftermath. Stripped bare and cleansed, the mind clear. It is the only clarity I get these days and in those moments it is always John Tannehill I

*see. As he is meant to be seen, not as I will remember him half
a bottle later.*

*As I say, I will come to him soon enough. It is hard to
keep the thread of these words. How I have managed to keep
teaching for so many years. My pupils must be completely
bewildered. I pass them all but God only knows if they take
away more than a smattering of English.*

*Let us back up a little. I was talking about choices. My first
major one was my flee from the Northlands. A flee it most
certainly was, I did not mention that I had been targeted by
the local bank manager, a fastidious forty year-old with a bald
head and tiny cock (my apologies, but one must call a spade
a spade, or a tiny cock a tiny cock), who was desperate to get
married. But if I had not run away then you would not be
reading this now because I would not have met your father.
Ergo, the running away was not a 'bad thing'.*

*However, I have lately been wondering about the greyness
that surrounds 'choice'. What if our life's outcomes really are
as pre-programmed as the priapic bishops claim and we are
ever-destined to meet who we are ever-supposed to, regardless of context? Like an ongoing, interlinked re-working of an
incredibly complicated pattern. Perhaps if I had chosen to stay
in my hometown your father Edward would have made a decision to move there, or maybe he would even have lived there to
begin with. Or vice versa, or both. In any case a rearrangement
would have somehow happened, placing Edward and me in the
same context at the same time so we could meet each other.*

*Maybe the older I get the more I believe that. I am not
stupid, I realise it is the proximity of death, searching for patterns,* meaning, *hoping we're not just making it up as we go
along. I have spent far too much time in Catholic countries.
Some people think God is dead in Cuba, but I have never been
anywhere he is closer.*

An old woman gets religion, what a bore! Even if I had come up with a wise new universal truth you would have dismissed it out of hand as egotistical nonsense, the same old reconstituted crap. Are there any original thoughts left? Thousands of years we've been bumbling around, the narrative possibilities must be exhausted by now. Here I am holding forth like everyone else who thinks they have got something important to say. I don't, I am silently screaming like the rest of us, hoping someone might decide to listen.

It is getting hot again. I sit here sweating in my little shack-like structure on the third floor of a crumbling building on Brasil, just up from Plaza Vieja. It's actually a casa particular, like a bed and breakfast for tourists. Luis has rented me the top floor and I have the red-painted balcony all to myself. The heat, I am grateful that it sometimes numbs all other considerations. Can you imagine your emaciated, white-haired mother lying naked on her lumpy bed, trying desperately to sleep? That is me. That is what I have become.

Please do not get me wrong, I am resolutely not looking for compassion. I stand by my choices and I would make them again. Being faithful to a chosen desire is the only truth. If that has yielded loneliness then so be it, but I shall not apologise for the truth. There, make your own judgement. You will have your own long nights. It does not matter whether they occur in a baking, corrugated iron hut in the middle of Havana, or a Georgian mansion in Edinburgh.

I close the laptop. John Tannehill. I haven't thought about him since Cuba. Although the uneasy feeling is familiar, the suspicion of an impending *something* has swollen, become tangible. I walk to the end of the Stillhouse, past the new exhibition and demonstration spirit safe.

It's much colder in the old Mashroom. The rusted iron vat still squats in the cold, long since replaced by the Lauter Tun. Someone walks above me on the walkway, shadow sliced into little pieces by the mesh flooring. I can't move. I have to let the deep hum of machinery shut out all else. There's the usual smell of electrics, something fused maybe, burned out. I feel trapped, caught in the electro-magnetic grid with nowhere to turn that won't shock. *Just breathe, son*, my father would say. There's nothing that can't be managed, in time.

I kept a diary too, once. I was eleven and filled it in religiously, every night. But I didn't write it for me. I'd been pestering my father about my mother again. *What was she like dad, why did she leave and never come back?* And the same evasive, monosyllabic answers. So the diary was for her, as if I could write her back into our life, conjure her presence from my father's vague, irritating clues. He must've thought of her, maybe still does, alone and stupefied in memory's locked house. I'll see him forever, sitting in his little living room and staring into the fire. Did he know John Tannehill, did they meet, shake hands?

I hate her. My father's a decent man. He endures, she's dead. Yet her spectral presence still mocks, his endurance more evidence, somehow, of his inadequacy. They're so different I can't imagine them together, existing together. It's surreal. But no-one ever truly knows another. I came close with my wife, a long time ago. Now we're utterly changed. We've stopped even warily circling the strangers that emerged over time and become simple objects in the other's life, chipped ornaments you can't bring yourself to throw out.

Although we too may endure. Unlike my diary. I

ripped up the pages and scattered them into the North Sea from the pier along the road from my father's cottage. Almost a year I'd kept it up. My mother wasn't coming back so what was the point? I was so angry then.

I'm hooked. I admit it. I wait for the next email attachment, I wait for the optimal time and conditions to sit down and read. I know I'm creating a melodrama, like I want to be trapped by my mother's story. It's probably why I didn't delete the first email as soon as it arrived.

But I'm obsessing about the journal for another reason. It stops me wondering why *vinales2004* is sending me it in the first place. Maybe I should look for clues in the PO Box, the letters that must've accumulated since I stopped checking. But I've no more intention of doing that than I do of skipping naked into the snowy gloom with a spruce branch up my arse.

My first instinct has always been to stick instead of twist. Better to let the present re-assert, the reassuring mundanity of the present. But the more it fills with my mother's story the more unsettling it makes the present. What does she expect me to do with this new knowledge? There's so much information pouring down, sooner or later we have to admit we're saturated. I put the brolly up early, settled back to watch the waters rising round every other sucker. If I've missed out on a whole series of existential insights then so what, I'm the one in charge of the remote control and that'll do me. The distillery doesn't allow for change and neither do I. Here things have always moved to a geological beat. But this new knowledge, I'm not sure of it, I'm not sure of it at all. I don't know how to deal with it.

My mother comes so readily to mind these days. It's a soft dusk, pink towards the horizon. The day's indigo darkens and the bottle of Havana Club slowly empties, the first of the evening patrons arriving in the Obispo café. She's mid-story, another story she's been telling for years. Leonardo sits across the table and listens intently. His wife died five months ago and he's lonely. He might hold a flame for the white-haired British woman but it's so long since he felt these emotions he can't be sure. He seems so sorry about something and she can't follow enough of his heavily accented Spanish to be precisely sure what.

Angels with Dirty Faces

Flashes. Flashes of what I'd said. No detail though, just the pressing sense of something bad.

It was all about degrees of intensity, the boozy enjoyment inversely proportionate to the depression of the comedown. Not that I remembered enjoying myself all that much. No headache though, just a lingering light-headedness that meant the alcohol hadn't flushed out yet. And that despite the sweating, the soaked sheets. I'd forgotten to put on the air-con the night before. I felt guilty. At home I would've shrugged it off, as per usual. *Just the drink talking,* the convenience of cliché, its ever-reinforcing determinism. *Just the drink talking*, like, what do you expect, what can be done? But this time I didn't want to shrug it off.

I found the urn in the shower cubicle. No memory of putting it there. The shower had been dripping on it all night and I wondered if the water had leached inside, turning my mother into grey, gritty soup. She had to go. No way was I leaving her here to return to every night.

Thierry and Monique looked at me warily in the breakfast room, probably wondering what was inside my rucksack. I wanted to go over, quietly point out that there's weirdness in all of our lives, what's yours, what are you hiding? Instead I laid out the photographs from the wooden box I'd found in my mother's apartment. I studied the snapshot faces as I forced down a plate of scrambled eggs and pseudo-frankfurters; my mother's smile, my own chubby toddler face, my happy father, the man with the thin face and dark hair who was not my father.

Adelina didn't answer her phone. Nor Rodriguez. Beyond the lobby doors it was raining hard, an actual curtain of rain. I sat outside under the covered arcade that ran the length of the Inglaterra.

I understood why the expatriate life could be so seductive. Everything was new, the shape of the palm leaves in Parque Central, the pattern of the traffic. Even the rain, the way it exploded from the asphalt like tiny creatures throwing up their hands. Freedom also came with novelty. But it seemed sad to be ever on the outside looking in, your homeland drifting too, those ever briefer return visits to more and more you don't recognise, new judgements based on misunderstood impressions and fainter memory, your opinions tolerated by people who don't trust you anymore because they don't see their lives as a series of vignettes.

You'd romanticise it, of course, your homeland, when you were back under these colonnades as the rain fell vertical and the smell so different and the heat so welcome and your friends asked *what was it like being back* because they wanted a guide to their own return. *It's changed, but it'll always be home.* And there would be nods of sympathy but no-one believes you because they too know sweat-tossed tropical nights when you again watch your roots wither and die, one by one, and you know that even if you wanted to return you can't.

I ordered a coffee and remembered that first step off the plane at Jose Martí. How did my mother handle the tropical heat, did it made her think about how far she was from Edinburgh?

At home the rain was no doubt falling. I saw myself hurrying across the distillery bridge, anxious for the warmth of the Stillhouse. Did my mother remember rushing along Princes Street or Lothian Road, collar up against the drizzle? Did she turn to her lover in moon-dappled Caribbean night and whisper in sweet melancholy tone how the streetlight would shatter into a million pixels in the rain spray from the passing Hackneys? Or was it all long forgotten, or never even remembered in the first place because it had never been valued?

The heat rose as the rain eased. Soon the traffic was picking up again, the road already beginning to dry out. The sheltering guests of the Inglaterra began to venture out, guidebooks to hand. I stepped into a watery sun that brightened with each step and was hot and blazing by the time I reached the long and winding seafront promenade, the Malecón.

I tried Adelina again and this time she answered. She listened to my apology with a patient understanding that brought a lump to my throat. I could meet her, sure, but she'd be busy this afternoon with a kids' baseball team she helped coach. Unless I wanted to come along?

In the guidebook I found the area called Vedado straightaway. I just had to follow the ever-stretching Malecón westwards and look for a little park off a street called Paseo. I felt a bit less paranoid although the guilty anxiety remained. A long, dreamless sleep was the only cure. I hoped Adelina would know what to do with my mother. I took the urn from the rucksack and placed it beside me on the sea wall. The two of us sat there, listening to the sea.

She was embarrassed when I gave her the flowers. 'Where did you get these? What will my boyfriend say?'

I felt unsure for a moment until I realised she was talking about the seven year-old boy holding her hand.

'Arturo will be *sooo* jealous.' The little boy squinted up. There were about ten other skinny boys and girls with grubby faces, standing around the baseball diamond marked out in the corner of the dusty park. Some of them were giggling, pointing at the man with the flowers.

'Adelina, I – '

'Jim.' She placed a finger against my lips.

'No. Please listen. I feel like a fuckin idiot. It's bizarre, this sweaty guy appears from nowhere and tells you that his mother, your best friend, abandoned him when he was a child. I didn't even bother to think how you'd react to that. I mean, it must have been a bit of a shock.'

She looked at me closely. 'I didn't believe a word of it. Why should I?'

'I can understand that.'

'You know what finally made me think you were telling the truth?'

'What's that?'

'Your anger, I can't believe that anyone could pretend to be as angry as you were last night.'

'I'm sorry. It's just that you knew her, Adelina. You knew my mother. That's more than I ever had.'

'I can only tell you about the person I knew here, in Cuba. She did not speak of her past.'

'I know that.'

'And that is ok to you?'

'You're going to tell me she was a gentle person, a good friend, all that stuff?'

'If that is what she was then that is what I will tell you.'

I stuck out a hand. 'Then I'm ready.'

She smiled and shook my hand. 'Tell me, have you ever played baseball?'

'Well I – '

She shouted something in Spanish and a bare-footed boy sprinted over. When I pointed at his head he handed over his cap. I tried to squeeze it onto my head but it perched there like a pork-pie hat on a cartoon character. That set the children laughing again. I puffed out my chest and settled myself at the plate, wiggling my bum like I'd seen in movies.

'Vamos!'

The pitcher hurled the ball much harder than I expected and I had to duck. The next one I missed completely and the third whacked me on the hand. I dragged the bat behind me and returned to Adelina with a hang-dog expression. 'Think I've got it in me for the Big Leagues?'

'Who knows what we could achieve together,' she said, standing up and clapping her hands.

Just a throwaway remark but I still wondered what she meant. I watched her with the kids. She was good with them, natural, they listened closely to all her explanations. I remembered the one and only time my father came to watch me play football. First-year trials at high school. I was so nervous that I might as well have been on a different pitch. No-one passed to me and the only time I won the ball I miskicked the cross and put it out for a goal kick. I wanted my father to clap my hands like the other dads, like Adelina. *Chin-up son, eyes on the ball, track back.* But he just stood on the touchline looking awkward, as if placed there by mistake.

'You got kids?'

She tensed, momentarily. 'Yes. Do you?'

'No. Do you just have the one child?'

'A boy.'

I was more surprised by my disappointment than my lie. A child meant a father, which meant a husband.

'He is called Floriano.'

There was a cheer from the kids as my nemesis pitched another fastball. 'That kid's got a rocket of an arm.'

'A what?'

'A rocket.'

'I don't understand.'

'Like in space. 5-4-3-2-1, *boooooom*! "Houston we have a problem". A rocket.'

'Ah, *un cohete!*'

She repeated the word in a shout and the boys started making *whooshing* noises, throwing their arms in the air. The pitcher smiled broadly, dropping into his stance and aiming the ball at me.

'You don't need to feel bad, Jim,' she said when they were packing away the baseball gear.

'I do. You've gone out of your way to be friendly. I'm sorry Adelina, I don't know how long I'm going to be here and I can't get through to Rodriguez. I feel like I'm chasing a ghost.'

'There are no ghosts Jim, just people we don't yet know. I told you I'd tell you about your mother.'

'Talking about my mother.' I bent down and opened the rucksack, taking out the urn.

'You've been carrying that around all day?'

It was my turn to look embarrassed. 'I thought you might know where I could scatter the ashes.'

She looked perplexed, as if wondering whether this Scotsman was completely insane.

'I can't keep her in my room. Have you got any ideas? Maybe just over the sea wall and into the sea?'

'You can't do *that*. There are rules. I think. You might need permission.'

'Who's going to find out?'

'I don't know, someone might. You should make it official.'

'How long will that take?'

She studied me for a moment then shrugged. 'Sometimes we can live with a little more excitement than usual.'

'Can you can think of anywhere? She's weighing me down, who'd have thought the dead were so heavy?'

'Don't say that!' And then she was laughing, which set me off. It was a relief, she could easily have fled from this lunatic with his sunburned face and skinny, painfully white legs. And his dead mother. In a rucksack. 'Help me take these things home and then we can go there.'

'What about your husband?'

'I don't have a husband.'

There wasn't much evidence of anyone in Adelina's apartment. She lived on the third floor of one of Havana's ghost mansions, the memories of a lost prosperity still visible, almost, in the stained, peeling columns and the ornate, rusting balconies. Where aloof ladies once fanned themselves, lines of washing now stretched from one grand shuttered door to the next, the appalled spectres tut-tutting the ham-hock women shouting to each other across the street.

She'd shared the flat with her grandmother, who died a few months back. *I am packing her away, it is so sad.* I waited as she took a shower, wandering the echoing rooms stacked with boxes. Only the small room which opened onto the balcony contained any clues to life continued; a mirror and a sideboard with beauty products, a shelf of English-language teaching materials, a huge TV-set. I couldn't shake a feeling of sadness, a pressing weight of life examined and found wanting. I was glad when we were back out in the baking streets.

'Your mother walked everywhere you know. In the department she was called The Wanderer. It was the boots she wore, she got them when she climbed Machu Picchu, you know, in Peru?'

I nodded.

'I can imagine her now, striding along. She had long white hair down to her waist, as white as sand.' She looked at me, searchingly, as if trying again to find an echo of my mother.

We headed back into the city. I watched my feet, saw a pair of battered old hiking boots, the rustle of a long skirt and maybe a quiet song, my mother humming as she angled through Havana's mess, always knowing where she was going, always smiling, yes, she was someone who smiled at strangers, who waved and bent down to talk to children, an eccentric and respected for it, for living in Havana, for matching the old domino men shot for shot into blue dusk, her white hair a lantern lighting the wasted concrete canyons of fast-falling night, the old men staring and some held a flame but she'd never responded to any of them.

I may have glimpsed her then, a suggestion in sun-dazzle on white stone, there on the edge of vision, turning the corner ahead but gone when we got there. The rucksack began to weigh heavier and I remembered my father sitting me down when I was fourteen. *You're a man now James.* And then he told me about my mother and when she had left. But not why. He never had anything to say about the why and I despised him for his arrogant refusal.

'Did she have a good life?' I asked.

'We have lots of lives Jim.'

'I mean your grandmother.'

'My grandmother? She had lots of photos, hundreds and hundreds. In the last few years she spent so much time looking at them. Was she trying to return to a time of happiness? Or was she looking for the clues for where she went wrong? The truth is I don't know. She was a good person, I know that. If that is the measure of a good life then that is what she had.'

'She sounds like my father.'

'Was he a good man?'

'Was? He still is. So good that St. Paul better up his game when my father gets to the Pearly Gates.'

And into Havana, city of movement; an intricate, free-flowing dance making the steps up as it went along. European cities were staid, self-conscious in comparison. I understood why my mother walked everywhere, her gaze moving like mine from the young men eyeing me from little streetside booths to the chrome-sparkle of a passing '56 Plymouth and the looming mansions with their decrepit, leaning *cailleachs*, the dome of the Capitol on immaculate blue, the marble-white columns and undulating balustrades of the Grand Theatre.

The buzz of traffic I'd expected but not the pulsing reggaeton, the Buena Vista old men replaced by skinny teenagers busting moves to choppy electronic beats, sometimes on the wrong side of cool, friends with big smiles clapping them on. They still had ghettoblasters here, chunky boxes in silver and black. They still looked cool. We passed the Inglaterra and down narrow, crowded Obispo, past the 10 peso pizza stalls and the Bucanero bars, the queues outside electronics shops, the white-cotton tourists who walked slightly faster. I didn't expect the bookstalls at the end of the street, the sudden quiet of Plaza de Armas.

'Your mother would come here every lunchtime. We'd browse the books together. Not that we bought many. It was a quiet place to come. The students in language schools can get very noisy.'

'You think this is the best place?'

'I can't think of anywhere else.'

The plaza was more of a garden, the trees muffling more of Obispo, the cafés now a low murmur. Carlos Manuel de Cespédes, a nineteenth-century hero of Fidel's, peered down from his marbled plinth, the only witness as we crouched at the foot of a Royal Palm. I took the urn from the rucksack and we scattered my mother on the dry ground beneath the tree, an endless stream, it seemed, dusting the hot air as I spread her around, scuffed her into the earth.

'She would appreciate this,' said Adelina.

A light breeze ruffled the palm fronds into a flickering shimmer. I brushed my mother from my shoes and rubbed her between my fingers, trying to dredge up some emotion.

'I'm thirsty,' I said.

'It's a hot day to be out walking.'

'So where did the old reprobate drink then?'

She looked grave. 'Your mother drank in a lot of places Jim. She drank an awful lot.'

'Did she now? Did she have a favourite place?'

The Castillo de Farnés was back up by Parque Central, a streetside bar crowded with ever-changing locals stopping in for *empanadas, bocadillos,* a quick beer. Adelina told me that my mother had lived in Havana for over fifteen years. Before that she'd taught in a provincial town in Peru whose name she couldn't remember. *Did people really like her?* I asked. *They did,* Adelina answered. *Both colleagues and students.* I admired the skill with which she was easing me into my mother's life. Just the right amount of detail. I was grateful.

'What about you?'

'Me?'

'You know so much about me but I don't know anything about you. I mean, are you from Havana?'

She frowned and looked away, into the street. But when she looked back she was smiling. All through her childhood in rural Cuba and her move to the big city in '91 she kept on smiling.

'So you're a bumpkin like me then,' I said.

'A what?'

'A country-bumpkin, a farmer, salt-of-the-earth.'

'Oh I see, well, yes I suppose I am.'

'Where I come from we've got our own language that hardly anyone speaks anymore. Gaelic, it's like Irish.

107

Anyway, there's a name in Gaelic for people like us. *Teuchter.'*

'*Chook*-ter.'

I raised my beer. 'Here's to us then. To the old women who are no more and the two *chook*-ters!'

Again that smile. She seemed happy, being with me, although I wondered if I was being indulged.

The boxing match on the TV-gantry babbled in Spanish and if I didn't already smoke I'd want to. I liked it here, the chrome topped bar, the twitchy barman and the three shelves of spirits, J&B, Johnnie Walker, *ron*. Even Che Guevara was relaxed, smiling down from a portrait above the bar. A sign outside the toilet told me that Che, Fidel and two *compañeros* stopped in here for a meal back in '59, just after taking Havana. The victory was won, it must be why Che looked so playful. An impossibly handsome man, ideals to match and never any smugness in the eyes. What must it be like for a whole society to grow up in his shadow? Was he was still a presence for the ghettoblaster kids, an inspiration or impossible myth?

'I always preferred Camilo Cienfuegos.'

I looked back at her. 'Who?'

'You don't know Camilo! You've been in Havana three days and you don't know Camilo. Shame on you Jim!' She wagged a playful finger.

'I will go to the Museum of the Revolution tomorrow, I promise.'

'Good! Camilo always seemed more down to earth, lots of fun. What woman could ever live with a God like Che?'

'Or man.'

'To Che, then.'

'And Camilo.'

'To Camilo and Che!'

We tipped back our bottles and Havana flowed, blue into black, the gummy old men, the hip-hop Ladas that made sense only here, the cheap tables and frayed cushions, the hopscotch asphalt leading here, leading there, the verandas of bars too many to count, the whirr of the fans and the drumming, the strumming, Adelina's sweet fired eyes, the bottles and beats of Obispo, O'Reilly, the catcalls and slick walls of endless jazz night where the stones keep their heat, the smoke and the light, my ghost-flicker mother somewhere just out of sight.

Five

I'll never know them, not now. We exist together, no more. I have little desire to interact. What's the word, *gregarious*? If it was my mother just finishing this killing night shift she'd be moaning in the tea-hut about the fucker of a problem in number three spirit and ripping the piss out of Camp Gary's fishing story. *It was this big*, he's saying. *Like that guy in the bog at the Station Hotel eh Gary*, she replies, *another big one you reeled in*. Malky would love her, she had the proper bolshie bullshit. If she'd stuck around I might have turned out the same.

I cross to the warehouse and lean against the wall, looking into the turbid sky. Nothing, no great revelation streaks across the grey, no clouds to conjure dreams or nightmares.

Back I go towards the Stillhouse, taking care to keep to the footprints I've just made. The fresh snow's already becoming hard as the cold slips below zero. There's sadness in seeing snow scarred by track-marks. I want maximum emptiness, still trying to convince myself that my days are a blank canvas to fill how I choose. Or maybe disturbed snow just looks messy. Whatever. Back and fore I'll go, perhaps forever. Sometimes I do a little jump and skip one of the footprints, sometimes I hop the whole way. Sometimes I hover on one wobbly leg.

O'Neill appears. Says he's been watching me from the

machine room door. I'd noticed it was slightly open but thought nothing of it. I mean, who'd suspect there'd be some cunt there, lurking in the dark? O'Neill likes to challenge the world but his passive aggression is such an obvious act I wonder why he wastes everyone's time. And he's a swine to shake. I wander towards the stack of old bourbon barrels behind the cooperage and he silently follows. Makes me nervous, I have to glance back to make sure he hasn't drawn a knife.

Then Des appears from another side door. Too many doors in this place, you can be ambushed at any time. Now it's two of them following me as I walk along the line of barrels, scraping the snow from the top of each. At the end of the row I turn and face them. In any other context this would be awkward. Not here though, as with so much it's beyond embarrassment.

Des frowns, opens his mouth. He's in re-entry phase, returning from whichever distant star system he's been visiting. O'Neill and I watch him closely. *Snow*, he finally says. Certain comments stop time dead, making already mind-numbing situations exponentially worse. Like someone going on and on about a traffic jam when you've been stuck in it for two hours and counting. Or saying snow when it's been pouring with snow for weeks. The more meditative among us might be shocked into a state of instant enlightenment by such stark obviousness. Not me, I fear an immediate nervous breakdown, violence I won't be able to hold back.

'Snow,' agrees O'Neill.

'Snow,' says Des.

'Always the snow.'

'Always the snow.'

'Least Amber'll get a white-wedding.'

O'Neill's grin is mocking, he's looking for a bite. He tries again, adds a question.

'The fuck's she getting married in February for?'

I just nod and he reverts to his default sneaky snigger.

'Snow,' Des repeats and I take my cue to leave.

I've worked with Des and O'Neill for years but we'll never know each other. In our ignorance our conversations have corroded to coldness tinged with malice. The fault may very well be mine. I may be a fool but I'm not an idiot. I'm well-aware of all the psycho-babble about how abandonment makes relationships difficult. Why some people need to spend a hundred quid a pop to be told the obvious by some yoghurt weaver is beyond my pay-scale.

It's not always been like this. I remember less alienated times, which suggests there might be an element of choice in my indifference. Maybe I'm just jaded. What did Al Pacino's detective say in *Sea of Love*? *I have done some desperate, foolish things at three o'clock in the morning.*

Like one night when I was seventeen, hopelessly in love with my future wife and she was away visiting her granny. I was alone, gibbering pissed on Export and Thunderbird. *Fuck it*, says Young Jim, *I have to see her.* So I charged the battery in the old Leyland Princess that had been abandoned in my father's back garden for almost two years. I was fifteen miles down the road before sanity returned and I turned the car around. I never lost control like that again.

I peer through the kitchen window and watch my wife bustle around. These emotions, events, did they really happen? They seem less like memories than memories *of* a memory. Like the affection in my wife's eyes as I rush inside and pull her towards me, give her a long cuddle. She remembers we used to do this and that's enough to halt the rushing routine that would normally brook no interruption. Where's she been transported to, what moment long-forgotten has suddenly re-emerged blinking into the light? But I've long realised that unless you replace old memories with new the more questionable, corrupt, the originals start to appear. That's why she's pushing me away, looking at me with an appraising eye.

'What? Can't I give my wife a cuddle?'

She folds her arms across her chest. 'You choose your moments. I haven't got time for sex Jim.'

'So if I give you a cuddle you think I want sex?'

'Don't you?'

It's a trick question. If I say *no* the ramifications could be huge. *Yes* means that she's right. Either way I lose. 'I was just thinking about that time I was going to drive to your granny's to see you. Remember that?'

The eyes soften again. 'Course I do, you bloody idiot. You could've got the jail for that.'

I last knew my wife when we were *in love*. And if you want to keep knowing someone you better make sure and stay that way, otherwise the interest fades and before you know it there's some stranger lying in your bed scratching and farting where you wife used to be.

'I hope they make it,' I say.

'Who?'

'Amber and Peter. I hope they make it.'

My wife takes my hands. She strokes my cheek, like her touch might remember something long forgotten. *I do too*, she says. I think of my mother, lying alone in

113

a Havana shack. When did she realize she didn't love my snowbound father with his opaque memories? I'll be seeing the old man today. The manager of the home had phoned. He'd received the letter I sent a few days ago and wanted to meet *as a matter of urgency*. So back I go to that vision of my future and the vanishing father I have never known, that ghost of a ghost.

'Mr Drever.' The manager holds my gaze and frowns as he grips my hand, piling on the concern. I suspect his mannerisms are overcooked in most scenarios: bereavement, celebration, sex.

'Always a pleasure.'

I immediately regret the choice of words. It sounds sarcastic when I meant light-hearted. He's too self-important to shrug it off and the slight narrowing of the eyes is unmistakable.

'I'm sure.'

I need to lighten the tone and notice he's one of those people with photos of his children on his desk. 'Nice kids.'

'Thank you.'

Why does he have these photos here? Is he worried he'll forget what they look like? It'd be horrific to have the mocking eyes of the Boy follow me around the Stillhouse all day. 'How old are they?'

'Ten and six. Mr Drever, can we cut to the chase?'

'Sure. Let us cut.' Why do I say these things?

The care home is the only one in a fifteen-mile radius. It's full of local oldies and used to be family-owned. Some corporate entity bought it a year ago and within six months decided to shut it down. *We care because we all have to*, their brochures say. They advised it in good time, true enough, sent information and had people contact me from three alternative homes. With power of attorney all I had to do was choose and sign.

'Are you fully cognisant of the challenges of caring for your father at home?'

'It's only temporary.'

'There is still a place open at – '

'Can you recommend a nurse?'

'I can, but that really isn't a long-term solution.'

'It's *temporary*.'

So. The old man's coming home. My decision, even though I don't want another stranger sleeping in my house, even though he was difficult enough when *healthy*. Contradictory, sure, but it's the classic recipe: complacency, laziness and guilt. Ignore the quantities, just pour and mix. And what can I possibly prove to myself or my father by bringing him home only to ship him out a few weeks later? The hate for my mother is sudden, swelling. She should be the one dealing with these fuckin issues. It should be her looking after him, not me.

Nurse Ratched takes me to the day-room. The old man's sitting in his usual seat in the conservatory. The windows are steamed up and the temperature tropical. He's *compos mentis*. This makes me feel even more guilty. It's so much easier when he's away with the fairies, less disquieting than to be reminded of the person he once was. When do I tell him he's got to leave this place? The matron told me that today's been a good day, so why not now?

'You're looking pale, son. Been on nights again?'

He's wearing a tatty green tank-top with white shirt and tie. His brogues are polished to a shining mahogany.

115

A bible sits on the arm of his chair and if I half-closed my eyes he could be back in his neat little seaside cottage. In front of him on a small table is a *Scrabble* game set for three players. But no other seats. 'You doing ok dad? You winning?' I point to the board.

He gives that now-familiar unnerving smile and taps the side of his nose. 'Easy when you know how, eh?'

'I suppose it is.'

'Easy when you know how.'

I expect the mist to quickly descend but it doesn't. I'm struck again by how he endures. He asks about my wife, Amber and yes, he would very much like to come to the wedding.

An essentially good man. I've never measured up. He never imposed his values but his quiet moral decency and generosity were pressure enough. I've always felt like a twelve-year old in his company. Then the dementia began to set in, Lewy body they called it. When he had to move into the home it was his suggestion that I take on his power of attorney. It would make things easier to manage, he said, as he got more and more sick. But it seemed like a test, a last opportunity for the son to redeem himself. Bastard. I've watched his disappointment at my inevitable and ongoing failure swell and ebb on the inconsistent tide of his illness, my guilt magnified by an inability to do or say the right thing, now when the challenge is greatest and my need to succeed, in both our eyes, is the most urgent. The appalled relief I felt when he was diagnosed has long evaporated. Despite his dementia, I remain the child, he the man. Is that why I decide to ask about John Tannehill, this shaded presence in my mother's journal. Am I looking for cruel revenge, a haunted memory, perhaps, that will play on endless loop on his malfunctioning mind?

'Who was John Tannehill, Dad?'

He stares at me, says nothing for a long, long moment. 'I haven't heard that name in years.'

'Mum knew him?' Time presses harder when my father's rational, insisting that I get my words in quickly.

He places his hands on his lap, the quiet pose I remember from a million Sundays sitting beside him in church. 'John Tannehill was a troubled man. Your mother was a troubled woman. The world is full of people like them. I don't suppose you need to look very far in your own life to find other examples of two troubled souls finding solace in each other.'

'Solace?'

He reaches across and takes my hand. 'Yes son. *Solace.* We all need solace.'

'I want to know about him.'

'Jim.' His voice is warm, almost a whisper. 'What does it matter? The sun rose today, didn't it?'

He's a master of defusing tension and I almost smile, reaching out for his feather-light hand, the almost translucent skin. I've noticed on several visits the clump of cotton wool held in place by white surgical tape on his left wrist. But I've never asked about it, another reason for Nurse Ratched's lacerating disdain. I see her out of the corner of my eye, bustling around some of the other residents. She's still watching though, she's always watching.

'You were lucky son. Your mother would not have been good for you. She was a child of changing times and I couldn't keep up. There's nothing particularly new about feeling you've been somehow misplaced,

117

dumped in the wrong era.' He glances up, suddenly forlorn. Are those tears in his eyes? My father never cries. 'I was never as adaptable as other folk. This was a blessing, I think, when your mother left. It meant I wouldn't do something daft like go chasing after her, it meant I'd stay put and do my duty to you. I loved her, yes, and I grieved as I should. But a deeper part of me was relieved, God forgive me.'

I can't think of any time when my father has spoken so openly. It's a moment I should rise to, a bonding opportunity that might never come around again. But much as I know I should hug him I won't. As much as I feel the swell of a thousand questions I won't ask them. I've long been his alter-ego, too self-aware. Too weak. 'The wedding's coming up.'

His gaze softens, the eyes betraying familiar disappointment at my expected failure. I'm sick of his forgiveness, his superiority. 'Yes. The wedding,' he finally says. 'She's a good girl, Amber. I haven't seen her for a long time. I hope she's chosen well. Is he a good man, Jim?'

'Peter? He's got potential.'

'*Potential*.' He's suddenly anxious. I notice Nurse Ratched straighten up. 'But can he *provide*?'

He isn't talking about money. Peter will have no problems on that count. It's the deeper provisions, the invisible intangibles in their all-weather manifestations. Like he always provided and I've never been able to live up to with my family. But I can't give him that assurance about Peter. Why not? I've lied to him my whole life. He's always been a secret worrier and this mind-fracturing disease might be making it so much more fevered. What's fuckin wrong with me, why can't I lie to

118

reassure this decent, ailing man? 'I'll have a word with the matron. She'll get you ready on the morning of the wedding and I'll come and get you.'

'Yes, yes,' he whispers, left hand on mine as he taps with the other. Anxiety flickers again in those blue eyes, a cloud coming in. The unnerving, child-like smile returns. Still he taps my hand. My time is almost up. But today is not the day I tell him he has to come home with me.

* * *

Havana, Cuba, 11/4/99

I had no idea your father worked at the brewery. But there was Edward one grizzly morning, rolling a barrel past when I was dropping off a note to the warehouse foreman. I asked if he needed a hand and he stopped in his tracks. 'I beg your pardon,' he said and gave a snooty little sniff. He looked good out of the priestly garments I had first seen him in, very well-muscled (those upper arms . . .) with a cross round his neck. I decided there and then I wanted him to screw me, I wanted to watch that crucifix bounce as he screwed me.

I hope that doesn't shock you. But it always starts with lust, does it not? And my, oh my I certainly had a lot of lust. I started waiting for him at the distillery gates.

You have to understand that this was still the 1950s, such behaviour was very much taboo. Young ladies were supposed to be coy, they were the ones to be a-wooed, not a-wooing go. That didn't stop them getting shagged behind a grotty pub on a Friday night. No, it was ok to be a slut so long as you pretended not to be. Anyway, for a few weeks your father ignored me, all my winks, jokes and little flirtations. Then

119

one morning he stopped, looked to the sky and said, 'ok, you win, I'll buy you a bloody drink if you promise to leave me alone.'

It is as simple as that really, all our stories ultimately are.

Time and again I have witnessed it, a series of basic causes and effects that repeat with minor variations. Edward would see the Absolute in this and perhaps I do too. Catholicism's a dark, hefty religion, though I guess if you are going to catch religion you might as well suffer the original. I just could not get to grips with those Buddhist and Sufi wannabes I was to meet in London in the sixties. It just seemed too playful in comparison, too undemanding. The Creator has never struck me as being all that relaxed about his Works. I have often wondered if it is your father's lingering influence that makes me feel so comfortable in Central and South America.

I went to chapel with him, once or twice. These were the days of the Latin Mass, heavy on the incense. I had been brought up Presbyterian and this was very different, exotic even. There was something intoxicating about it, hints of deeper truths. Edward never knew that I once went to Confession. It was a strange thrill, almost erotic, sitting in that musty box, the shadow of the priest behind the mesh.

Sex? Edward was not comfortable with sex! Sure, he was a randy goat but it conflicted him terribly. I agreed we should get married sooner rather than later and so we did. August 1958. Morven thought I had gone completely insane but it seemed like such a great big adventure. Naturally, my parents did not come. Getting married was a good thing, but to a Catholic? No, this was not done, which made it even more exciting. I thought I loved your father too, that lust was evolving into something deeper. And the thought of a stable home, where I could have the space to write was so very appealing.

149 Broughton Road. A tiny one-bedroom tenement flat, first floor. We moved in a week after the marriage. That winter was freezing. I set a little desk beside the window and sat there for hours, trying to write. I moved on to prose, poems a bit limiting for all that I now wanted to say. I was so young, convinced I had found the keys to the universe. You need so many more words to explain all that . . .

I read passages to your father. He'd sit there in front of the three-bar fire, frowning. I do not think he ever really understood what I was saying but I had to get it out. Sometimes I would wake suddenly in the night, like someone had spoken to me in my sleep. I'd be up and through to the desk, desperate to get the words down. I think there are certain times and places when the occluded, the unconscious, runs closer to the surface. In Broughton Road it poured right out of me, like it pours out of me now, for the first time in years, now as I look up into Havana night and again feel the universe vibrate.

But no-one is listening, now as then. And if you do not listen then how can you ever truly hear what another has to say? I was part of the fringe set, beyond the Rose Street Hierarchy, a 'lesser writer'. I tried out my best work but no one got it, too many literary prejudices and petty preconceptions. Then I met an American sailor, another poet, at Milne's Bar, March 1959. He talked about this American movement, 'Beat' he called it, a revolution in words and society at the same time, tearing down received structures and letting it flow, flow, floooow. 'You've never heard of them?' he said. The next night he brought me a book, 'On the Road', handing it over like a sacred text. 'It'll change your life Helen, I swear to God.'

He was right. After that there was no going back. I realised how ponderous my writing had been and was determined to just let it all go, let the words roam. I plucked up the courage to do another couple of readings but they still wanted poetry, no room for prose, let alone spontaneous prose. 'Cosmopolitan scum' MacDiarmid called Alexander Trocchi in 1962. Such a telling comment, a neat summation of the eventual attitudes of most 'movements', Beat included; the insularity, the complacent content to replace one received structure with another.

I had more time for the Gaels. Sorley MacLean, he was more tuned to the universal than most of the Rose Street Boys. They'd shout me down, the bastards, your father one of the few applauding. 'Just listen to her you pack of jackals, listen and maybe you'll learn something.'

I gave up on the readings and started inviting people back to Broughton Street. Bribe them with a few whiskies, out with the notebooks and hey presto, captive audience! Saturday nights were a no-no to begin with, Edward wanted to be fresh for chapel on Sunday. But he soon gave in and if we had people round he would skulk off to bed before midnight. There he was next morning in his Sunday best, stepping over the bodies on the floor. That was when he first saw John Tannehill, passed out on the couch with a bottle clutched to his chest.

I see my father's quiet, Arctic fury. He picks a way across the snoring floor, careful with his new-polished brogues, impatient to re-centre himself in the morning Mass. But I can't believe it. I close the email. It's so quiet tonight. I try to fill the void with images of my father as a young man.

'You watching porn again?'

I turn with a start and see my wife leaning on the doorframe. I hadn't heard her coming up the stairs. She's all smiles and carries a leather-bound book. I make some kind of muttered response and realise I've been staring at the bamboo forest screensaver on the computer.

'Look what *I've* got.' I see now that it's a photo album. She jumps onto the bed and opens it, lying up on her elbows. I'm tired of being tested like this. I know the correct reaction is to sit down and let her lead me through the photos, letting her flush out the nostalgia. Thing is, I'm not *expected* to do that because she knows I'm completely uninterested. And because she doesn't expect me to sit down beside her I can't. To sit would appear suspicious. Then she'd be convinced that I've been sitting up here wanking. 'Remember this?'

Our wedding photos. What did my mother imagine when she thought of me on my wedding day? A strapping young man, jaw set as he faced the future with his beautiful young bride? Would she have been proud, *that's my boy, I knew he'd grow into a fine, handsome young man*? No chance. She dripped cynicism. She'd have predicted the shitty, grey white suit, flecked with bits of black cotton, like a badly harled house. It pinched at the armpits, the sleeves a couple of vital centimetres too short. I can't help staring at the photo, the cow-lick in my hair, sticking up like an antenna. 'I look like one of the Jetsons. What a state.'

My wife cackles and turns a page. There's my father, straight-backed in black at the top table, glass of water in front of him. No booze for father. Poor bugger could do with a few drams these days. I try and picture my mother sitting beside him. Would he smile at her as they prepared to let their son go, squeeze her hand, proudly satisfied at how they'd brought him up?

She turns another page and there's the famous shot, it surprises me more and more as the years pass. My wife and I are staring at each other in the midst of the wedding crowd, caught in a secret, gentle moment. The image is crisp and natural, the lighting delicate.

These were pre-digital photography days. You got what you got. To have a photo like this is a near-miracle. Today you can take a hundred and select the best, have it enhanced to make sure that memory's sentiment is maximised. I prefer yesterday's thumb on the lens, the over-exposure and blurring. My life, after all, has been a steady sequence of imperfections sprinkled with occasional transcendence. I can't remember the last time we looked at each other like that. My wife also seems to sense it, reaching out and placing a hand on mine.

Solace, my father said. *We all need solace.* Had he truly found it in God or was the Big Man a crutch, a means of vicarious content, like my wife and I searching an old photo for something lost?

'We need to pay for Amber's catering Jim. They want it in advance.'

I draw my hand away, thinking of the manager at the home, the final unpaid bill for my father's care.

'I checked the balance,' she says. 'Is there any overtime coming up?'

Now I'm suddenly wondering if this whole 'let's have a look at our wedding photos' is some kind of ploy to butter me up. *Look how happy we were, look at when we took the world on together and no problem was too hard to overcome. Back then you wouldn't have thought twice about putting in some extra shifts, eh Jim, eh?* 'Sure, nothing I'd like better. Two nights on and two back-shifts and then down to the warehouses on Friday afternoon. Fantastic.'

'Well I can't do extra, no extra shifts for me to do or

I'd do them.' She slams the album shut and sits up on the bed.

'I can do a couple. Not going to bring in much though.' A capitulation, yes, but we do need the cash.

'Every little helps!'

She's all jaunty again, a little victory won. I should shut up but I won't. 'A few more months to save wouldn't have hurt. They've known each other for years and all of a sudden it has to be now?'

'Oh stop it.'

'Tell me again why's she's getting married in February?'

'For Christ's sake Jim. They're in love, they just want to get *married*.'

'The whole world doesn't stop for them though, there's other responsibilities.' I glance round, watching her eyes narrow.

'What're you talking about?'

I cross to the window. Heavy snow returned this morning. I watched it come from outside warehouse 16, a purple-black band rushing in from the north. Then the scour of the wind, the first flakes. I closed my eyes, I like to feel the blizzard on my closed eyelids, the numbing cold of a world obliterated. Beyond the window the white world's slipping into night, the snow stopped, for now. Malky's ploughed it round into a big half-circle, like a crooked smile.

'Dad's going to have to move in.'

* * *

He sits at the bar, casual-like. There's a double Highland Park in front of him, mark of a man with taste. The red-head in the black mini-dress has already noticed this, and the way he turns the glass in his hand, the golden liquid catching the light. What's he so pensive about? She's intrigued and who wouldn't be. After a moment he catches her eye. A quick smile. The four-piece is playing a pulsing low beat, David Lynch-like, a haunting sax, black suits in front of red velvet drapes. He moves along the bar. 'A night for ghosts,' she says, 'and I'm going to haunt you.'

'I'd say a penny for them but you look like you'd want a pound.'

JC plonks himself down on the seat I've been keeping. I push across a whisky. He's grinning, beard its usual straggle of mousy-ginger. He's wearing a beanie hat and tatty old Aran sweater. 'See you made an effort.'

'S'what the punters expect.'

'You've been wearing that sweater since you were fifteen!'

'That's the whole point!'

I shake my head. But he's right, integrity comes of familiarity. His fans would forgive, probably not even notice, any sartorial debacle. It's the dreaded 'new direction' that would doom JC. Even the pseudo-Europop of his last single (the critics called it 'ironic') had led to some sharp intakes of breath on the internet noticeboards. 'Where's the fit groupies though? I thought with the Mercury you'd be fighting them off. It's the same old hackit lot in here.'

JC looks mock-serious. 'A nomination shouldn't change a man.'

'Course not.' He hadn't won last year's music prize but the kudos had boosted his sales. Late-career recognition, Warner Brothers came a-knocking, the gigs starting to sell out. JC soaked it up but kept it in perspective. The punters were starting to thin out again but there were still a few more than before, a solid mix of original die-hards and genuinely smitten newbies. Tonight's gig was sold out months ago. An easy win, a home-town showcase for the *Gate* label, three short sets from the roster then JC and his band to headline.

'Hard night at the ranch?'

'The usual.' I'd fled from my wife at the top of the argument's second hour. Long-standing wars like Kashmir or Gaza must be similar, ongoing skirmishes combined with the occasional brutal rocket and mortar assault ending in the tattered stalemate of the forlorn status quo. The taxi driver took some persuading to drive out in the snow to pick me up from the distillery and take me back into town for the gig. I wasn't too fussed if I couldn't get back.

'The wedding?'

'The father.'

'Eh?'

The red-head at the end of the bar suddenly cackles, her leather-clad friend snorting away beside her. The spell's broken. She swallows the rest of her pint and necks a purple-coloured shot. A little bit of liquid trickles out of the side of her mouth and she catches my eye, winking as she wipes it away, coquettish as your granny with the travelling salesman. Her crow-like laughter intersperses my conversation with JC. He's understanding but gently judgmental, as is JC's way. *Wouldn't have hurt to have told her. She's going to be worrying now, Jim.*

JC's a man who's never understood the need for secrets. He reckons that explains why we're so repressed as a nation. I've asked him many times why he uses a pseudonym if he's got so little to hide. Simple as fuck eh, sing your way to enlightenment, a clean conscience,

127

an uncompromised life! Imagine my wife's face as I stop an argument in its tracks with a little improvised tune. How we'd laugh as we realised the mind-sapping inanity of our fights . . .

I swallow the whisky and gesture to the barman for another. It's too easy to be a cynical prick. JC's one of the few people I admire and the last person I'd want to alienate. I've been jealous of him at times, I can't come close to the integrity the fans dig. He'd told Warners to piss off. I think I've always been a tad unnerved by the mirror he holds up to my shortcomings.

'I wrote a song for Amber's wedding. Thought I'd try it out tonight.'

JC's grinning again and I'm genuinely touched. 'Nice one,' I say.

'Fuckin *sound*!'

We burst out laughing, a couple of daft lads again. Few people have the ability to strip the years back to a more straightforward time. The reminder of hope, that's JC's gift. It brings the crowds, even Crowgirl along the bar feels it. Alone in her bed, three in the morning, that fragile time between drunkenness and hangover. She puts the headphones on, reading herself into the lines of a JC tune, starting to smile. I'm getting sentimental, whisky always does it. One of these days I might be the one taking the wedding album to my astonished wife. She'll probably wonder if I've just been diagnosed with a terminal disease.

The gig's tremendous and it's a pity my wife's not here. Honest. She'd enjoy it if she let herself. I'm not totally cynical, I haven't yet given up the possibility of *shared interests*, even if it gives me the shivers. But she's always been odd around JC, something in our relationship she doesn't quite get and therefore mistrusts. And she refuses to admit she enjoys his music. *That's good*, she'll say, before discovering a sudden dislike when I tell her its JC's latest.

Not that there could have been any coming together tonight. She was still coldly furious when I left the house, half-way down a second bottle of Pinot Grigio and forty minutes into a whispered phone-call with her demonic little sister in Aberdeen. *It's like he's trying to sabotage the wedding, why else wait until now?* Maybe JC's got the answer in a song.

I'm drunk when I leave the town hall just after 11.45, waiting for JC outside. There's a woman standing at the bottom of the steps, wrapped up against the cold, maybe here to pick up the porter.

Crowgirl stands a few feet away, rubbing her hands and trying to catch my eye. She's seen me laughing with *The Star*, knows she won't get near him and is happy to settle for me. I'm not yet drunk enough to forget that these are not my own eyes I'm looking through. They're Whiskyman's and Whiskyman's only ever got me in trouble over the years. A knee-trembler round the back? My poor willy would be frostbitten before I'd unfurled the main-sail. She's a sturdy lass, so slapstick at best, X-rated Harold Lloyd. Still, the thought is vaguely appealing to the sex-starved ego of a 50 year-old man and I'm glad when JC appears.

He chats with Crowgirl for a couple of minutes before she staggers off with her friend from the bar.

'You know her?'

'No flies on you eh? Shona's at every gig.'

'Have you?'

129

'Course I have! Just the once though.'

'Really. I was just thinking about it myself.'

JC starts laughing. 'You're a horny bastard. Course I haven't been with her!'

I skin up a rollie for JC and start on one for myself. There's still a few punters straggling out of the hall, a noisy group of young lads, fifteen or so, standing in the foyer. One of them gives the thumbs up to JC, who waves back. Almost all of them are wearing check shirts. Funny how the uniforms come round again, I had a red and black one just like that when I was their age. The porter leans against the shuttered hatch of his lodge. He looks asleep on his feet but is suddenly all action, rattling his set of keys, ushering the boys out the doors.

They surround us, pissed but friendly, all wind-milling arms and breathless compliments for JC. I stand to the side and smoke my fag, watching the woman come up the steps.

She's wearing one of those ear flappy Davy Crockett hats and a brown duffle coat. I turn round, expecting the porter to greet his wife. But he's locking up the doors without even a glance outside. The lights go off, leaving only a vague orange glow from the few street-lamps. The woman stops a couple of steps below me. I watch her take off the hat. Even in the half-light I know the black hair spilling across the shoulders, the deep brown of those eyes. A shiver runs down my back but not from the cold, the more incongruous shiver that comes of spending too many hours in the tropical sun, too much time in that pulsing Cuban heat.

'I thought you would be here tonight,' she says. 'You left me JC's music, remember?

Time. It can stop. Just like this.

'Have you enjoyed reading about your mother's life?'

I feel the flush creep up my neck.

'It's what you always wanted, after all. To know.'

She's still so pretty.

'*Vinales2004*? Please don't tell me you've forgotten all about Viñales?'

Soft Top, Hard Shoulder

Mid-afternoon. Havana silenced by the juddering floor-fan. My mother's little roof-hut on the top floor of Luis's *casa* had become a furnace. I walked her rooms and sat on her bed, stood at the balcony for a long time. Again the old waiter from the café on the corner was looking up.

Ornaments and books, jewellery and clothes. A life was *laid down*, I figured, a directionless trail into the tumble of our own wilderness, further and further into the mountains and mist, ever-stretching to that final day we're not even aware of until it's upon us, past us. Each trinket and object I packed away felt like a stepping-stone lifted from the path my mother had laid, winding back the years until the landscape was empty once more.

How many can say they have a plan, or have the courage to admit where they should have branched off, the moment truly ripe for the road less travelled? Mostly I just made the choice and fuck it, the best-fitting stone settled in place with a good hard stamp and on to the next, the next, the *next*, trying to outrun the doubt. It was up to others to cast God-like judgement across my works, to stand in my battered shoes and claim to understand why this choice was taken and not that and for crying out loud was it not obvious that particular decision was wrong, so why didn't I stop, just a moment's pause to take stock, weigh the options? But when was the optimum moment for reflection? Self-knowledge was ever-evolving, never complete, midnight's certainty the morning's doubt. I might as well chuck the balls in the air and see what comes bouncing back down off my empty head.

Luis appeared just after four. I guzzled down the bottle of water he offered me. The old man shook my hand again then hovered in the doorway. Maybe he wanted to make sure I showed some respect and didn't just throw her stuff around. *Did you know her, did you truly know her*? How would Luis answer, Luis who stayed and Luis who sighed and if I looked up the old man would be sure to be wringing his hands, because that's what he was supposed to do.

I went on packing and didn't notice when he left. Who cares what the old fucker thought, I was going to fling her stuff in boxes as if I was going to a car-boot sale. I picked up *Siddhartha* and a dog-eared copy of *The Dhammapada*. A folded sheet of paper fell from the pages and I read a handwritten poem called *This Night*. It was pretty good, she should have stuck at it.

The occasion demanded a soundtrack. I put in the iPod headphones and gleefully chose Talking Heads debut classic. *Psycho Killer, No Compassion, Who Is It?*, a viciously inappropriate soundscape to my mother's fast-disappearing past, the jewellery that must have meant something, the skirts worn in places that would never again be remembered, the endless bits of paper, like notes left to herself, fragments of thoughts maybe destined for a diary.

But I didn't find any diary and didn't want to. I lay back on the bed, loudly singing along to *Tentative*

133

Decisions. What would solemn old Luis make of that? I was sleepy now. Care had to be taken, I didn't want to fall asleep in my mother's rooms, surrounded by all this ephemera that might sink deeper in dream, force a more profound reckoning. I had to get out of there, back to the Inglaterra before it got too late, and get drunk and so fuckin what.

For two days I worked alone. Adelina was busy teaching. I phoned my wife, who sounded distracted as she asked about Spain, as if she had one eye on a turned down TV.

'I won't ask how you're doing because she doesn't deserve *any* reaction. Anyway, you came to terms with it a long time ago.'

I walked with my wife's words into Havana's night, through the Malecón's phantom gloom of pimps, glitter-eyed addicts and sorrowful lost, all the tired whores of back-land Cuba come to blow through the city like dust and always someone else to take their place. I thought about the terms they had come to, how my own story would compare. I felt restless, even nervous, the caricature I'd created of my mother in childhood starting to fragment. The emptier her apartment became, the more her existence was physically erased, the more she swelled in my imagination. All those belongings with their questions. Where had she bought them, where had she been all these years, what was she doing here, there, anywhere?

It was disturbing to think that in death she might become even more of a burden. The photo albums piled it on, all those hundreds of pictures. I began to see her in context, the battered hiking boots in the wardrobe worn in the photo of her with some students on a trip to the Sierra Maestra, the striped yellow and black t-shirt flung on the bed and seen in a Santa Clara bar-room snapshot. All those smiles. They chipped away at my distortions, corroborating Adelina's evidence: her popularity, the voluntary work in village schools, the political activism with international solidarity campaigns. I couldn't help but return to the photographs I'd found in the little wooden box. I studied them over my dinners in the Mercaderes restaurants, laying all twelve on the tablecloth one evening while I waited for Adelina.

'His name is John Tannehill.'

I looked up, surprised, holding the photograph of the man with the haunted gaze. 'John Tannehill?'

Adelina put a hand on my shoulder. 'Your mother mentioned him once and showed me that photo.'

'Do you know anything about him?'

'Nothing at all.'

'She must have told you something?'

'And a good evening to you too!' She picked up my glass of red wine and drank it down. 'That is your punishment.'

£quoteI smiled. 'Sorry. I've hardly spoken to anyone for days. I'm a bit obsessed.'

£quoteShe nodded at the photos. 'So I see.'

£quote'Yeah, must look a bit strange.'

'You need to get out of the city.'

'I don't want to go to the beach again.'

'Not the beach, somewhere quiet.'

Adelina wanted to go by Viazul bus but I insisted on a car. If she'd had a bit more self-confidence she might have thought I was trying to impress her when I chose

135

the black Audi A4 cabriolet from the top-end hire place in Miramar. But I was only out to impress me. I'd taken a few steps beyond myself in the last few days and liked it. I felt like taking a few more.

Imagine my wife's face, Jim in a flash motor with a pretty brunette, zipping west from Havana. *Vorsprung durch*, the suspension earned its price as the tyres crumped across the pitted sections of *autopista*. There were few vehicles on the road, the odd patchwork Lada and snub-nosed Soviet lorry crammed with people, staring at us through diesel fug.

She wore big wraparound shades and a green headscarf that flapped in the wind. When she smiled I thought she looked like Penelope Cruz. She tried to convince me that her parents would be pleased to meet me. *They met Helen a few times*. If this was meant as reassurance it just made me feel uncomfortable. I had to relax, the real Jim Drever was at home, remember? This new Jim was a distillery CEO. He could handle the weird, he hired fancy motors and empathised with his dead mother. *You will like Viñales*, she told me. *It takes its time.*

Mojotes, she said, pointing out strange limestone outcrops that scattered the valley floor like an abandoned game played by long-departed giants. Time had eaten the rocks away, leaving dark, sharp-edged hollows, trees and creeping vegetation. Hawks circled high in blue, trucks edging past as we weaved towards the village. The earth was chocolate brown here, tilled by old men with ploughs pulled by oxen. Slow and methodical, up and down, fighting back against the pine and palm that would smother everything if left unchecked.

Entering Viñales was like stepping into a scene from every movie about Latin America I'd ever watched. The

136

road stretched one, two miles and dead straight. No dirt-track these days but still the odd man on horseback clipping along the asphalt, roving dogs and fat men dozing in chairs under shaded arcades, the copper-blue cupola of the church in the main square; echoes of a past still close to hand, frowning at modernity. The Audi felt absurd, a ridiculous imposition. I wondered if this show of conspicuous consumption was more offensive to the faces following our stately drive up the main street than my assumption that because they were poor they'd give a shit. I took off the aviator shades anyway.

'I am so sorry for your mother.'

Adelina's mother Brunhilda took both my hands in hers. She was no more than five feet tall, skinny as a rake and tanned a deep brown. Only when I said *thank you* did she turn her attention to Adelina. I wondered if her cursory embrace of her daughter was made out of respect to my assumed grief. Her pot-bellied husband with bald head and pencil moustache followed her down the path from their small, blue-painted house. Again a handshake, a reassuring pat on the shoulder. I felt uncomfortable accepting their condolences when my own emotions were so ambiguous. Brunhilda's husband suddenly broke into a beaming smile.

'José,' he said, jabbing at his chest. 'No hablo inglés.'

I repeated the action on myself. 'Jim, no hablo español.'

José exploded in hacking laughter and both Brunhilda and Adelina jabbered at him in Spanish. José rolled his eyes and beckoned me towards the house, miming the tip of a glass to his mouth.

Brunhilda had put together quite a meal. She and José

looked on proudly as I surveyed the table set out on the little veranda in the back garden. She went through the dishes one by one; white bean soup with potatoes, boiled lobster, rice with black beans and crisps made out of yams.

'I hope this wasn't done just for me?' I asked Adelina.

'No. Not just for you. For Helen too. She visited a few times. She helped my father paint the balcony.'

I looked at the faded pink of the low surrounding wall. There she was again, wiping her brow as the cicadas pulsed, looking up into endless blue before stooping to dip the brush. Then José was handing me a glass of neat rum and I was looking again into his twinkling eyes.

'She doesn't come home too often,' said Brunhilda.

Adelina looked offended. 'I come when I can, I am very busy.'

'My daughter in Habana, my son far away in Santiago, my sister in London – '

'London,' I said.

'For a long time, yes. I am sent a letter every now and then. Apparently I have a nephew and a niece but I have never seen them. I probably never will. Cuban stories are complicated Jim, if you spend any time here you will know that.'

'*Habana*!' José suddenly exclaimed. 'Beeg seety.' And another explosion of laughter.

'I always hoped she would stay here, work in the little museum.'

'Mother, the museum was *boring*.'

'Ah such a disappointment to your mother that you did not stay.' A quick wink at me that Adelina didn't notice.

'*Si, si*,' nodded Jose, sadly, '*el museo, el museo*.'

'Every time, it is like this every time I come home. My mother just cannot *forgive!*'

'Did you hear that Jim! I am sure you treated your dear mother with more respect.'

I didn't answer, just nodded. The mix of Spanish and English seeped into quick-falling night. The kitchen light spilled out, glowing on the walls my mother had painted. Had she had told them anything about me, where exactly had she begun the story of what brought her to Cuba?

That evening Adelina and I walked into the little town. Few lights shone. The streetside cafés were almost deserted, the occasional patrons all men, sitting quietly in the parasol shadows, beyond the fluorescent arc-dazzle of the inside bar. I felt mildly drunk. I let the night in, let it settle.

'This is a place made for stories,' I said, and didn't feel embarrassed.

'I agree.'

We took turns, sitting in a little bar beside the cross-roads, thirty seconds each to pass on something from our lives. I told her about my work as a Stillman, how the distillery had always seemed to be alive, a huge pulsing organism breathing heat and light into the cold and dark of the surrounding moor.

'It sounds so romantic.'

I wanted to say there's nowhere more romantic than right here, right now, this dusty roadside café in old Cuban night, with its unknown beers and Ciego Montero soft drinks perspiring in the heat and the curl-ing smoke of Hollywood Blue cigarettes, the wilting mint in a glass on the bar.

But I said nothing.

'So different from here.' And she told me about her childhood in Viñales, that growing, impatient sense of somewhere beyond.

'I wanted to get away, once. But I stayed home. Anything you try to outrun will eventually track you down.'

'That makes me feel sad.'

'It's the truth.'

Neither of us spoke. Back home the barking dog in the distance would be a bleating sheep, the soft heat on my face an Arctic scour. But the same keening awareness that came with a lull in a loaded conversation, the buzz in my ears that may be the sound of my blood, the study of my hands. 'I told you I had a son,' she said eventually.

'Yes.'

'Why did you not ask where he is?'

'It's none of my business. I didn't know you, not enough to ask.'

'Do you want to know?'

'I do.'

'Then ask.'

'Ask you about your son?'

'Yes. I want you to ask. I give you permission to know!'

'Ok. Tell me about your son.'

I watched her closely, her face in profile as she looked away from me, out across the road.

'I haven't seen him since my husband took him to Miami three years ago. We had split up a few months previously and he had always talked about getting out of Cuba. I did not imagine he would take my son with him. But he did, he risked my little boy's life on a leaking

140

boat. I hate him for that. But they made it. A lot do not.'

I wanted to take her hand but didn't. I felt shamed by her openness. I'd lied to her back in Havana and hadn't told her about my wife and children. For reasons I didn't want to dwell on.

'That is when I realised your mother is . . . that she was a good person. She took me in to her apartment and she put me back together again. There were many evenings, long nights, when I thought I would go mad. She treated me like a daughter when I felt as if my own mother was blaming me for the loss of Floriano. She did not speak a lot about her past Jim and I cannot speak for her then. But I know what she was to me, I remember that kindness.'

'You must miss him so much.'

She smiled. 'I will see him again. I have to believe that. What are we without hope?'

'Not much.'

'And that is why you must listen to what I tell you about your mother.' She was animated now, leaning across the table. 'You must have the hope that your mother was different to the person in your head. Believing that is too much, I know. What if I *do* never see Floriano again? His father can tell him anything he wants, Floriano might hate me like you hate your mother. But there is always a story, a reason. You must have the hope that when you know the story you can begin to understand. It is my hope that Floriano will forgive me.'

We spoke little on the way back. Adelina kissed me on the cheek and closed her bedroom door. I lay on my bed, wide awake. I wanted to knock on her door, tell her she had nothing to be forgiven for. Instead I went

141

out onto the veranda and found Brunhilda sitting in the dark.

'Be careful with Adelina. She is a dreamer. She falls in love very easily.'

I sat down beside her and lit a cigarette. She squeezed my hand as she left me alone. I thought of my mother's belongings, the stepping stones through her life that I'd dug up and packed away. That old, old feeling, there it was again, like being a spectator in my own life.

Six

Adelina's here. No more safe memory, compromised in the re-telling. She's an actually existing presence.

I mean, sure, why wouldn't she have made her fuckin way *here*?

Makes perfect sense.

What's the old Zen mind-bender, if a tree falls when no-one's around does it make a sound? Well if I refuse to admit something's happening then maybe it actually isn't. I knew Adelina was *vinales2004*, of course I did. But now she's here I have to *admit* I knew. Deluded? Maybe. Thing is, if I'd admitted it before then I would've had to consider the bigger issue.

The 'why'.

It's swelled into a giant neon question mark. I mean, if you're one for fevered speculation then here's the Big Kahuna, Las Vegas brash, in your face like a stripper's g-string. So why? There's something else here, beyond my mother's journal, something I'm missing.

Just lie for now. Lie in bed. Shadows and milky light. My wife's an indistinct lump. She could be anyone. I want to be her, anyone but me, anyone other than this sleepless freak.

I pity insomniacs. JC once had a tenement in Edinburgh. Third floor in a narrow street. In the flat across the street, directly opposite, the curtains were always open. Day or night you could look right in. Once I got up at about 3am for a drink of water. In the opposite flat an old man was sitting in a wheelchair, his kitchen lit bright as day. I turned off the light and stared at him. He didn't move and I felt so sorry for him. But after a while I realised that it wasn't him who didn't want to be noticed. No, he was ready to cross the distance.

Details. They're so much more immediate by night. Less manageable. Like the moonlight sharping in at 80 degrees to a point on the floor beside my wife's dressing table that I can't see. I want to sit up but the slicing light-beam is somehow a worry. As if it's challenging me, asking if I really want to see what it's illuminating on the floor. I draw my foot back under the duvet before the sudden tentacle grabs it, the first reveal of the monster.

Shadows, all these shadows, I wait for the moon to shift round and obliterate them one by one.

My wife whimpers. Her foot touches my shin and I move my leg away. She used to tell me her dreams. First thing in the morning she'd roll over, momentarily bemused, unable to figure out if I belonged to dream or reality. *You would not believe . . .* More often than not I wouldn't, her dreams genuinely bizarre, a smorgasbord of ponderings for the chin-stroking shrink. She took a genuine pleasure in telling me but not anymore. Not that she's stopped dreaming, those little moans, twitches, aren't they the signals of REM sleep? She just stopped telling me and I can't remember when. To mention it would bring attention to something irrevocably lost. But sometimes I still want to know. I want to know her dreams.

She must have her own secrets. And the bigger the secret the deeper the dreams. When I came back from

Cuba I dreamed of Adelina every night. She wasn't ready to let me go, nor me her. In time the dreams came less often, a slow fade to monochrome and then empty space.

We couldn't reach each other, too much time had passed. In the reflection of *here* the memory of *there* became more and more absurd. Like an aberration. And aberrations should be quietly jettisoned unless you're deliberately looking for madness. Ok, I haven't let go of the memories completely. But long nights of the soul? That aint me. I locked it down, moved on.

Adelina.

Jim.

My name repeated three times as I hurried down the town hall steps. She grabbed my arm but I pulled away. That insistence in her voice. JC turned to look at her but said nothing.

By the time we reached the car-park she'd stopped calling my name and was just standing there, silently watching us load up the gear. Then a last, sudden lunge as I got into the Volvo. We left her alone in the empty car-park, briefly illuminated in the headlight sweep. That look on her face, like disappointment anticipated. She looked so cold, so cold and out of place. As she can only ever be in this setting, *my* setting, which will never know a molten sun.

The journey home lapsed into silence once JC realised his stream of questions weren't going to be answered. I lost myself in the engine's hum, the black furrows of the snowy road. Now and then JC looked across. But he knows me, he knows I'll eventually spill my guts.

I stared up at the house as the Volvo fish-tailed back down the road. The bedroom light was on and my wife probably drunk, sour whisky on her breath as mine. The thought of our putrid breath mingling appalled me, the ongoing stench of decay. I turned away, walked across the bridge past the Dark Grains Plant and up the track that runs alongside the top warehouses.

Night closed like a hand on my throat. Each step might bring asphyxiation closer but I'd keep on walking, barely alive come sickly morning, the morning that never relents. When I felt sleep coming on the third time I fell into a drift I realised how drunk I was. A voice said I could die there, another said so what.

Stan was asleep in his seat in the Stillhouse rest area. An Andy McNab thriller lay opened on his chest and his mouth hung open. A little bit of drool had dripped onto the collar of his boiler suit. I held the guard rail tight as I took the stairs to the level below. The Stillhouse buzzed, heat rising as I moved along the gantry that ran the length of the spirit stills.

My favourite spot is beside number two. It's almost halfway along the Stillhouse and someone would have to come out of their way to find me there. I moved round the still so I was out of sight of anyone looking along the gantry and sat with my back against the warm copper. As the heat began to seep into me I drowsed to the caramel smell, the fizzzz and swisssshh of the boiling spirit. I've always been able to feel it, *see* it, bubbling in the dark, rising as steam through the long neck, cooling in the condenser, liquid again. Nothing but truth here, the spirit agitated but untroubled, following the way defined since the barley was sown.

Coppered heat, still warming me as I lie here hours later. My wife whimpers again. Lately she's taken to bringing a teddy bear to bed. I feel its furry little body

146

pressing against my right arm and want to grab it and fling it across the room. I doubt even that would wake her. She didn't even twitch when I stumbled around getting undressed, not even when I turned the light on. Suddenly I want to embrace her but almost immediately the feeling is replaced with unease.

Adelina.

That searching look as she repeated my name, as the headlights swung. So be it, there's no hiding place for the truest spirit. I'll stow myself away in my own cold warehouse, face my own four walls. Adelina, those moments and places, they hang like jewels in this freezing dark, so close I could reach out and touch them. Her face hasn't changed. Perhaps that's the essential problem, facing up to what can never be altered. So let the head sink into the pillow, the fists unclench. I've got no choice, I can't hold them back. Not the faces, I can handle the faces, Adelina's and all the others. It's something else. Even as I try to force it away I know it's pointless. The bars of shadow on the bedroom walls shift with the moon, like a clock, silently measuring the time slipping past. I turn on my side and pull the duvet up round my head. Still I hear the ticking shadows. I let the questions flood over me.

*   *   *

Havana, Cuba, 12/4/1999

The first time John Tannehill looked at me is the one time in my life I wished I was invisible. It was a Friday night and there were five of us in Milne's Bar, the drink flowing. In all that noise and smoky bluster I could feel someone's eyes on

147

me. I ignored it for a while but eventually looked around. I saw him straightaway. He was standing at the bar, talking to his companion but never taking his eyes off me.

I was a bit unnerved. He could have been a magus reaching into my deepest core or just another bar-room lech, eyeing me up. When I found the strength to hold his gaze we could have been the only two people left in the world. It was exquisite but intolerable at the same time. After a moment I wanted to just disappear, evaporate. I wanted us to forget we had ever seen each other but knew he would be forever imprinted on my memory. Then he was walking towards me. My heart, it was beating so hard, a feeling of panic rising in my throat. I had no idea what he was going to do but couldn't wait to find out. He stood at the table until a confused silence had fallen. Then he picked up my almost full pint of 80 shilling and drained it in one.

'Can I buy you a drink?' he asked.

My friends exploded in laughter. I just stared at him in mute shock. 'An American,' was all I could think, a drawling accent like a matinee idol.

I melted there and then. The French call it 'le coup de foudre' and I hope you have experienced it in your life, I truly do. We are told that it is a chimera, of course. We are told that only silly little girls believe in love at first sight. But maybe we never fully lose sight of the twelve year-old inside of us, desperate for the fairy tale to be true and the prince to sweep us off our feet. I do not think it is purely a female longing either. We may express, rationalise, it in different ways (after all a man should be a manly man in a man's world, should he not!) but I believe it is a universal desire, to be suddenly and utterly lost in love.

The sailor-poet I told you about who gave me a copy of 'On the Road'? That was John. He was a second assistant engineer in the American merchant marine. He had a rucksack full of books and journals and said he had written his best poems while watching the 'full moon dance with Shiva on the quicksilver sea.' He really did talk like that and truly was a dreamer, the most genuinely honest man I have ever met. I would learn that unshakeable integrity can often leave you in a very lonely place, but for a long time I didn't notice, let alone care.

He was docked in Leith for five days. Then on to Marseille and Singapore. I told your father I was taking a few days off to visit my parents and John and I took the train to Aviemore, the Cairngorms.

We all have defining moments, book-ends of existence. When I watch the last fade of the Cuban light those three days still spool in front of me, as vivid as the original. When the weather cleared we took long walks. I remember Lochan Uiane, spellbound emerald against the dark moor, Cairngorm perfectly reflected in the iron-flat waters of Loch Morlich. 'You could stare for hours and be unable to distinguish the true mountain from the reflection,' John said. 'But in the end it doesn't matter at all. In fact, that's the whole damn point.' Then he was running across the browny sand, whooping, pulling off his clothes and diving into the freezing water.

I had never met anyone like him. All those moments growing up, those people with their approximations of me, of themselves, that pressing dissatisfaction I felt with your father, it all evaporated when I was with John.

On Cairngorm plateau we read our poems under candyfloss clouds, the blue you get when the universe smiles. Never once did he patronise me, not like the defenders of the poetic faith back in Edinburgh. I could have loved John for that alone. That night he wrote his first poem for me, 'This Night'. I keep

149

it in the copy of 'The Dhammapada' that he handed over the morning he shipped out for Singapore.

> *Under moon's razor glow*
> *I see all of you*
> *clear as the pine's silhouette*
> *ambiguous as the charcoal peak.*

Those words have never left me, for better or for worse. I close my eyes and watch them scroll, sometimes with sweeping calligraphic whorls, sometimes with Helvetica-type functionality. It depends on what I have emptied from the bottle, seething anger at John for not being here, for writing words that meant forever when forever was a lie, or dumb forgiveness.

> *I'd walk harder*
> *if I trusted my step*
> *dream harder if I remembered the last.*

John's uncertainty is my burden. I remember the dream, you see, I have never stopped remembering. And it will ever be mine alone, which is why I will quote no more from a poem you could never understand.

Morven was cautious. She told me not to fall too hard. I thought she was being cynical because of her own failures, or that she was jealous. Who listens when they are in love?

I thought it so thrillingly cosmopolitan when I watched John inject a syrette of morphine in the Cairngorm Hotel. 'Military supplies from the Korean War,' he said, a habit he had picked up when he was working the harbour barges in New York City. Love may be the drug, but when you put it up against heroin there is only one winner.

Not that I understood that then. What I did understand

was the deepest sadness I had ever felt when I watched The Montana steam out of Leith docks that rainy April morning. He would send a telegram to let me know when he would be back in the UK. I waved until the smirr swallowed him. Never once did he take his eyes off me.

My depression lasted months. I couldn't write, I could barely function. The head of the typing pool hauled me up for unsatisfactory work. 'I can always let it go,' he offered, and I let him put his hand up my skirt. What did it matter anymore? Your father was very concerned, he always was such a sweet, caring man. He took some time off and we spent a few uneventful days on the island of Mull.

Direction, he kept repeating, I just needed direction, *I was clearly pining for some kind of purpose. You, James, you would be my purpose.*

I wouldn't say you were an ugly baby, but you'd have won no prizes. My apologies if that sounds blunt, but it is true. You must have noticed that everyone talks so much rubbish about their babies, how beautiful they are. Let's face it, they look like grubs. Or frogs. That's what you looked like, a little jaundiced frog. They had to give you a hell of belt on the arse to bring you round.

Then they handed you over. My child. You may as well have been an alien for all that I could relate to this new creature or understand how I was to communicate. I just didn't know what to do and handed you back almost immediately. I can still see the nurse's look of utter contempt, as if I wasn't fit to be a mother. But Morven agreed with me, she appeared at the hospital reeking of booze, took one look at you and said, 'ugly little spud'. In fact, she called you Spud for years. 'How's our little Maris Piper,' she'd say.

Is this inappropriate? Should I paint myself in a more forgiving light? But if this journal has been about anything it has been about sincerity. In any case, it doesn't take pervy old Freud to tell you that the roots of my alienation from you were fixed from those first moments. As soon as you were born I realised that I would always resent you, your needs that would constrict and then consume me. I have long suspected that post-natal depression is a disease of grief, the death of individuality that comes with childbirth.

I am not offering any excuses so I will not do you the affront of apologising.

Anyway, you could never convince me that you would have wanted a mother like me, who tried but not very hard, who took an interest but not much. Edward would more than make up for my absence. I was in awe of how he adapted to parenthood, as if he had trained for a lifetime to step into the role. Catholicism underpinned it all, the creation of life as the highest form of worship. You should be deeply grateful to your father, he alone was of exponentially more value to your upbringing than he and I combined. Sometimes the sum of the parts is less, not more.

I wonder if the handwritten pages were scanned into pdfs by my mother. Or perhaps Adelina physically cut out the pages and made them into these neat, bite-sized pieces. Did she read the words carefully before deciding where to end each excerpt? Best dramatic effect and all that. It's obvious that my mother neatly copied out a rougher draft, there's not one spelling error or word scored out. There must have been edits and changes of content but I'm not going to see any of that, just this cleaned-up director's cut. I think that's what disgusts me more than anything, the effort she made to make her story as accessible as possible.

And then she didn't send it.

Helen's Journal 6 arrived at ten to one last night. It

means that as soon as JC and I left Adelina in the car-park she must have gone back immediately to wherever she's staying and sent it.

My mother and Adelina.

They're both here.

Again they crowded my dreams. Again they melted away, like snow slipping down the window. If I was hoping for respite I should have known better than to boot up the laptop. I've become their prisoner. There was a time I would have told my wife everything. We would have figured it out. That's what married couples are supposed to do. Not now though, not a chance.

I re-read the attachment, pushing back the claustropho-bia. I blame the snow, when the world's reduced to a blank the imagination gets fevered, starts adding the detail and colour that the landscape hasn't provided for weeks. I've never known snow like this. No-one even talks about it anymore, it's become a malign ever-presence. I don't want to see it again or feel it on my face. It's enough with the curtains closed, knowing it's still there, still pressing.

My wife left at 6am. She asked if I was going up to the picket line. I used half-sleep as an excuse and just grunted. She said something about making a stand, if the jobs go they aren't coming back. As usual I wondered if she'd make me a coffee, as usual she didn't. Like the recounting of her dreams this stopped a long time ago. So much time has passed, always so much time passing, so many disappearing details that I don't even realise I've forgotten.

Jack and my wife will no doubt be standing close together on the picket line. She'll have made *him* a flask of coffee and they'll be smiling at each other through the steam. It really is a peculiar thing, to watch this flirtation, this courtship, and feel absolutely nothing. I'm neither enraged nor jealous. Just ambivalent. My wife would no doubt say bingo, you've hit it on the head, ambivalence is the reason I can't be bothered to make a stand with my fellow workers. *Sometimes you have to step outside yourself,* she said to me a couple of days ago.

I can't imagine how to do that or why I would even want to. Isn't the self the last bastion against the crush of uniformity? If my essential nature is ambivalence then I've got to keep the tattered flag flying. Some would say I'm just too scared to make a decision one way or the other, that I'm paralysed with fear. I'm not sure. Take Exhibit A, the sad affair that Jack and my wife will undoubtedly have, if it hasn't already begun. The prospect doesn't leave me fearful. If anything it fills me with a certain relief. She does indeed deserve some pleasure. Just no fucking in my bed, please. Or the Den. Anywhere but my bed or the Den.

I finish my coffee and re-settle the laptop. Pornography makes its inevitable tired suggestion but I'm drawn back to the journal entries. I read for a while then come across myself staring into space. Adelina. The first time I saw her in the café. Edged in black, the sun bright in the doorway behind her. I know she will come again. The weight is sudden but I don't know what exactly is pressing, expectation or uncertainty. I'm glad of the searing heat of the 40-minute shower. I could stay here all day, all night, letting everything just stream, stream away.

'Glad you could make it.'

'I can't stay.'

Jack's not bothered, it's clear that nothing's going to shake his camaraderie and content. This is his commissar moment, Petrograd in October 1917. Today will define the emotional parameters of the rest of his life and my wife's beside him to share the pride. She stares at me with a mix of defiance and disdain. And surprise that I bothered to come along at all.

I'm a bit taken aback myself, I hadn't expected such a turn-out at the picket line, Malky, O'Neill, Des and Camp Gary, a few other warehouse boys. They've strategically placed the picket at the corner of the visitor centre car-park, blocking access to the Mashhouse, Stillhouse and the Filling Store. Malky's even made a makeshift brazier from an old oil drum. *Canna have a fuckin picket line without a brazier!* Everyone's cheery. Applause breaks out when Slinky appears, canary bibbed as per usual, on the other side of the car-park.

'You coming to join us?'

'Guy's a fuckin plum.'

'Love to have another go at him,' says Camp Gary.

'Hey hey,' says Jack. 'The argument will win boys, not the fists.'

'The fists'll win too, he's a scrawny wee cunt.'

'Let it be, boys. Keep it disciplined.'

Jack's in his righteous element, my wife's eyes shining with devotion, like a lapdog. She's a big hit with everyone, the only non-distillery worker on the picket line. *It's what the miner's wives did in '84*, she tells us, *a bit more solidarity and things would've been different.* Jack's nodding furiously, even history would start to doubt itself if it hung around with him too long. Rosa Luxemburg reborn has even arranged a 'Family Intervention' for later today. There's things we have to discuss, apparently, so many things that have tumbled past me like the burn in spate.

155

'Check it out!'

'Aw aye, here we go.'

'Spiderman's swung into action.'

The distillery Land Rover has pulled up beside Slinky. Ronnie, the warehouse supervisor, leans out of the window, talking to Slinky and gesticulating towards the picket line. Never a faster man than Ronnie have I seen scampering up the racks to check the barrels. Blink and he's twenty feet in the air. He likes that we call him Spiderman, when we're waiting for a lorry he'll say his Spidey Sense is telling him twenty minutes till arrival. He drives slowly across the slushy, gritty car-park and round towards the picket. I step back towards the Still-house door, the others forming a line across the access road, blocking the way.

'Mornin boys,' says Spidey, leaning out the window.

'Ronnie,' says Jack.

'Goin to let me through then?'

'Sorry Ronnie, can't do that.'

I see Slinky across the way. He's on his mobile.

'Not very democratic that. Man's got a right not to strike.'

'He does indeed. But you're in the union Ron, you go with the majority. Otherwise what's the point of paying your dues?'

'It's not like I'm doing much. Stan's just needing a hand with the boiler.'

'That's the whole point. Doing "not much" is the same as having everyone at work. It's either all in or all out.'

Ronnie sighs, shakes his head. 'Just get out of the way, Jack.' He edges the Land Rover forward and everyone has to take a couple of steps back. *What the fuck*

156

do you think you're playing at, shouts Malky. I've never seen my wife move so fast. She's across to the Land Rover window and slapping Ronnie hard across the face, then reaching in for the keys and throwing them back to Camp Gary. He quickly pockets them, standing defiantly with a big cheesy grin.

Ronnie looks stunned, the very picture of emasculation, knuckles white on the steering wheel. A slow hand clap follows his humiliated trudge back across the car-park. The distillery manager Rab rolls up in his big red Mercedes. He gets out with a wave across to the picket. I think he's laughing as he speaks to a beet-red Slinky, who's about to start hopping up and down like Yosemite Sam. Then he's driving off with a few long toots of the horn.

My wife's being crowded, congratulated. Jack's got his arm round her shoulder, asking if she's ok.

'Fine,' she says, 'always wanted to do that.'

Jack must have a hard-on, surely. Their eventual sex has just been given a nuclear super-charge. What a turn-on today's incident will be, Reds in the bed right enough! *That's some woman you've got there Jim*, he says, *some woman*. I couldn't agree more, no doubt she'll still be high as a kite when we sit down this evening for the 'Family Intervention'. I tell Jack it's a pity I can't stay but I've got to get to the home to see my father. He nods in sympathy and I guess my wife's probably updated him with our latest dramas. He's the only one who acknowledges me when I leave. My wife's warming her hands at the brazier, back turned.

'Shame you can't stay,' says Jack.

'Gotta get going.'

'Course. Course.'

'The old man's coming to live with us.'

'Did you vote with us Jim?'

Damn near tripped over his tongue in his eagerness to get it out. Must've been gnawing away for a while. Fuck him, I can hold his gaze all day long. 'You know me well enough by now, Jack.'

'Aye. I do.'

'So why the fuckin question?'

'Ok Jim, ok.'

I walk away. When I'm about twenty feet away he shouts out. 'You watched *Matewan* yet?'

Slinky's scurrying ahead of me, across the bridge. A big 4x4 has pulled up in the turning circle Malky's cleared of snow. A tripod has been set up, the camera pointing across towards the picket line. A guy in a long black coat is holding one of those big fluffy microphones and a pad of paper. He holds out a hand as Slinky reaches him. Slinky ignores it, of course, and his own hands start windmilling in that over-blown, self-important style peculiar to him. I trudge past and nod to the cameraman, who's got a vague smile on his face as he listens to Slinky bleating away. *This is private property*, he keeps saying. He's got no presence, never has had. *Turn it off*, he's pleading, *you can't* . . . Yes, Slinky's an easy man to ignore.

JC's girlfriend Ruth opens the door on the fifth knock. As usual I get a hug as if I've been lost in the Yukon for the last ten years. JC's always been a lucky bugger with women but even he landed sweet when he met Ruth. She's from Yorkshire, straight down the line but gentle as midsummer surf. Six years JC's had her living up here in exile. All the strange, swirling currents of this

158

place and she's still cheery. I'm amazed she hasn't been dragged under by now.

'Jim.'

'JC.'

He gives me an appraising, sideways look and holds my gaze for longer than normal. I'm here to spill the beans and he knows it. Ever since I was a kid I've been like this. It's as though I take a long time to work myself through. Others say I can't face up to things and they'd have a point. But you can only realise the truth of something when you're ready to let yourself admit it.

It's become one of our friendship's rituals, Jim's reticence and JC's exasperated patience. There's comfort in ever-repeating patterns. I know JC will move around his cosy little living room as I speak, change the music, stop me mid-sentence to clarify something, shake his head like *how the fuck have I got myself in this situation*. Ruth plays her role too, legs folded under her and hands cupped round a mug of tea. She says *Adelina sounds nice but she must have a reason for coming here, Cuba isn't an easy place to leave*. I refuse any speculation, just glad of the shelter, the crackling fire and the soft music. I want them to let me into the warm existence that they effortlessly inhabit, where all is so clear and so present.

'You have to tell Katie. I mean, she's going to find out and it's not fair.'

'I know, I know.'

'Why do you always take so long to do what you know you're eventually going to do anyway?'

'Just thinking it through.'

'But you already have!'

'Maybe. Maybe I have.'

159

'Ruth. Gonna nip out and get the mell hammer from the shed, Jim's needing a bit of encouragement again.'

I leave just after one. Too early to head back to the distillery when my wife thinks I'm visiting my father. Instead I drive up the glen. The Corsa slips and stumbles into the snow, the white void. I can't make out the edges of the winding single-track. Only the fences on each side and the drooping Sitka and pine let me gauge where I should place the tyres. Eventually I'm through the woods and dropping down to the flat bottom of the glen. The river barely moves, edging sluggishly east, a black gash in the universe.

I stop the car where the road comes to an end. There's a house about fifty yards away, just beyond the start of the hiking track that eventually reaches the west coast. The windows have an orangey tinge, smoke rising from the chimney. The house looks homely but I've never liked its almost supernatural stillness. If I crept up and peered inside I'd see hollow-eyed ghosts staring back, mocking laughter piercing me like the shrill ring of my mobile phone.

It seems apt to receive the first phone call here, Adelina's name blinking on the blue screen. I reject the call and it rings again as I'm turning the car, again when I'm driving up the distillery road.

The Boy's at school, my wife still dreaming of Jack's revolution up on the picket line. The house is cold and quiet. I shuffle from room to room with a blanket draped round my shoulders and the mobile in my hand. I find myself touching ornaments, lifting books, standing at the door to the Boy's room and surveying the mess. The wind gets up. From the kitchen window I watch the snow sweeping in again. My phone rings again and this time I have to answer.

'Yes?'

'Jim? Are you there?'

I feel suddenly embarrassed. 'Adelina.'

'I know this is a shock, Jim but we have to talk.'

I can think of nothing to say.

'Jim? Are you there? I said we have to talk. It all must seem so dramatic and I am sorry. But you gave me no choice. I did not know what else to do.'

'This is my life.'

'And I have mine!' There's a hint of anger in her tone. 'You have no idea. No idea at all.'

'This is *my* life.'

I end the call. It's wonderful to hear her voice but I refuse to let myself think about that.

I spend the rest of the afternoon wrapped in the blanket in the Den, watching *Matewan*. The film's morality is obvious, insistent. After the conversation with Adelina there isn't a better antidote to uncertainty. I'm gripping the arm-rest as the film comes to its climax. No doubt Jack sees himself in the reflection of the martyred union organiser Joe Kenehan.

It's amazing to think that people like Jack and Joe exist, men who'd know what to do when the next phone call comes. Even as I judge from my ever-careful distance and question their principles without offering any alternative I *know* they'd know what to do. Me? I'm just like you, the fearful 99 per cent, cobbling virtue from self-interest I'm blind to see, perma-bemused and trying not to stand out, to be *singled out*. Adelina hasn't phoned back but she will. I remain alone, for now, pacing these whispering rooms, refusing the heroic battles, the man

161

who observed it all, who still observes, who passes with the lightest of touch.

'It's been pretty frantic in the last few weeks. No-one's fault, but it's time we sat back and took stock.'

But my wife's steely glare at me makes it absolutely clear there is fault to be dished up. She looks away, belatedly trying not to be too obvious. 'The last thing we want is any more surprises.'

Peter sits beside me, hands neatly clasped. He's uncomfortable, probably wondering how he landed a part in this sit-com. Opposite him, Amber's face is a mask of frowning concern. She and my wife are wearing the same fluffy purple jumper with plunging neckline. Lucky Pete can ogle two sets of boobs and has the biggest tit of all, Jim Drever, right next to him. The Boy's elsewhere, staring up at the ceiling. I follow his gaze and see one of those round yellow smiley stickers stuck there. When I look back at the Boy he taps his nose and smirks.

'So item number one.'

I hold up the piece of paper; I can't believe she's typed up an agenda. 'Is this really necessary?'

'Item number 1,' she says, a bit louder. 'The Return of the Father.'

'Sounds like a film,' says the Boy.

The Boy's right. Peter tenses slightly, stifling a laugh. He's on unsafe ground here, doesn't want to do the wrong thing. He might end up on the mother-in-law's agenda next time.

'I'll be picking him up on Wednesday.'

'We know that Jim. I think we're all just a bit surprised is all.'

162

I neck my third dram and settle back in the chair. 'A surprise for me too.'

'But you've known for months,' says Amber.

'That I have.'

'So how is it a surprise for you?'

I've no answer to this.

'You might have thought to *tell* us, is what Amber's saying.' My wife's using that wheedling tone that sets my teeth on edge.

'No-one likes surprises,' Peter says.

I stare at him until his cheeks start to redden.

'Know what I mean?' he stammers.

'Where's he going to sleep?' Amber asks, but she knows that the only available room is her own.

'Yours,' says the Boy. 'Haha!'

'Shut up you little – '

'Amber.' My wife takes her hand. 'I know you're thinking that it seems you've been booted out. But you haven't. We'd all have had a bit more time to get used to this if your father had told us a bit earlier.'

'I know mum. It's just I know I'm getting married and we're going to be living at Pete's. But this is still my home. I'm just a bit sad. Everything seems to be changing so fast.'

'You big daftie, you'll always be welcome here.'

Damn right. Not a day goes past that she isn't welcomed here, seven months after she 'moved out'.

'I know it's not ideal that your Grandpa's coming here. And this goes for you too son. But it's all for the greater good.'

Christ almighty, has Jack just materialised? Even Peter's staring at her, brow furrowing, *huh*? I should say something, it's what's expected of fathers in situations

163

like this. 'I'm sorry Amber, I should've mentioned it sooner.' Peter's nodding again. Like a reward for my contrition he re-fills my glass. 'It won't be long, there's a couple of homes I need to check out.'

'Which you won't leave too long this time?'

A tremendous sniper shot from the wife. Right between the eyes. Joe Kenehan would roll with it, take the whupping and re-group. I'm the Bad Guy here. The only reason this Family Intervention was dreamed up was to humiliate poor Jim Drever. What do they call it in Red China when you have to publically denounce yourself? They're right of course, I sometimes get embarrassed by my own indifference. 'No. I'm on the case already.' Because things are better when they're a *case* are they not? More exciting. Something to solve.

'Good. So now that's out of the way we have item number two on the agenda. The Wedding!'

After an eternity of hugs between mother and daughter, dewy-eyed glances between Amber and Peter, and universal discomfort between all of us when we run out of ways to make our joy apparent, Amber pulls herself together. 'The ceremony run-through's a week Friday. Dad, have you made sure you're not on nights 'cause the only time we can do is 8.30?'

'Not a problem.' Actually it might be because I've forgotten all about it. Not that I'm going to grovel into some confession before I've had a chance to speak to Stan about switching a shift. That would not be prudent. I keep schtum as we work an interminable way through the sub-agenda. The Dress, the catering, the *ice-sculpture*. I'd forgotten about the ice-sculpture but Peter apparently hasn't. He's been working on it, *honing the necessary skill*, he says. The whisky ignites a bonfire

164

in my imagination and I'm thinking soaring doves, elegant swans, lovebirds. He looks a bit embarrassed as he admits, *I'm not sure I can manage all that Jim.*

'What about a big cock then?' asks the Boy.

The stunned silence begs to be filled, so the Boy continues.

'Can't be all that difficult. And it's all a phallic ceremony anyway, so why not a big cock? And a fanny.'

Am I more surprised by what he's suggested or that he said *phallic ceremony*? Who would've thought that the Boy had such an impressive vocabulary? Kids truly can amaze you right enough.

'Get out,' shouts my wife.

'He's only joking,' says Peter.

'It's quite funny, Mum!' Amber agrees.

The anger freezes on my wife's face then melts like one of Peter's crappy ice-sculptures. She starts laughing and then we're all laughing. All except the Boy, who looks a bit annoyed.

'Well maybe we needed a bit of light relief. How about we take the bottle through and watch a DVD?'

'Only if I can choose,' says Amber. 'It's my big day coming up so you'll all just have to put up with it!'

Peter looks confused, I nod vaguely and the Boy seems on the verge of panic. He's over-played his hand with cock and fanny and hasn't been exiled from the Family Intervention after all. There's no escape. He too must sit, again, through the premier cru Hollywood cheese which is *Father of the Bride*, Amber's all-time favourite movie. At least we don't have to talk. It might be excruciating to sit and watch Steve Martin's credibility melt from his marshmallow face, but at least no-one has to *say* anything. There's just the odd uncomfortable catch

165

of the eye, everyone except Amber eager to be released from this mawkish evil.

My phone blinks. I made the mistake of leaving it on the arm of the chair. My wife's noticed. She's looking at me suspiciously, probably wondering why I've put it on silent and why I don't answer.

I take it with me to the toilet and delete Adelina's details from the contact list. Not that this'll stop her calling. Again I search in the reflection of the bathroom mirror for shame, embarrassment, *something*. Nothing there. Nothing but the usual gormlessness. I close my eyes, open them to my mother's expectant face. She puts a finger to her lips and inclines her head, *have a look behind me*. The camera pans sideways and there's John Tannehill, an eternal sadness in his dark eyes. He tips a shy finger to his sailor's cap, as if now I know about him he should say hello. My mother squeezes his hand. How did she look at my father after she met brooding John? Were her embraces brief, the expression impatient and the arms limp? The world can take sixty years to change or happen in the blink of an eye.

Somewhere behind me the incidental music of *Father of the Bride* swells to a sentimental crescendo. My mother grimaces, no place for manipulated sentiment for her. I'd invite her back to the living room but she'd just switch off the TV and take Amber aside. *Are you sure? If you are then how do you know, how will you cope when the delusions detonate?*

When I open the door I find myself nose to nose with the Boy. He's holding a can of Stella.

'Can I have this?'

'Don't let your mum see.'

I follow him into the kitchen. He cracks the can and

166

guzzles it down, crosses to the sink and bows to his reflection in the window. Then he burps, a truly amazingly loud burp, then another, dropping into a ninja pose with each new belch. What's he thinking as he watches me watch him? When he runs out of gas he bows again. *Sometimes one's all you need*, he says.

The Boy leaves me alone in the kitchen. I look down at my silent phone. I know I can't avoid it anymore. I have to see if there's any letters in the PO Box. I have to go back to Cuba.

Before Sunset

5.30 am. Zigzags of light streamed through the slatted window. I sat up and surveyed Adelina's old bedroom, converted into tourist accommodation some years back when her parents got permission to run a *casa particular*. She was sleeping in her brother's room next door. Like her childhood, Pedro too was long since gone, working in a tobacco factory down Santiago way.

The fridge hummed, full of Bucanero beer and over-sweet Cuban cola. Apparently a fabulous dolls-house built by her father once sat in that corner. All those things that once belonged, all gone.

Sleep wouldn't return. I lay thinking of the woman on the other side of the wall. It wasn't anticipation I felt, more a see-saw mingle of attraction and unease. But no tension was apparent when I made my way onto the veranda. She was sitting on the balcony reading a book and looked up with a smile. *Good morning to you Mr Jim, what shall we do today?*

'I've never seen a horse and trap before.'
  'I used to want my own one when I was a little girl.'
  'I wanted a motorbike.'
  'I had a doll, Margarita. She was my favourite. I wanted to sit her beside me and we'd ride around the village. Every day we'd do our rounds, picking up things for my mother and father.'

'You sure you wouldn't have preferred a motorbike?'

'I still get a little bit sad now when I see the old men clipping along. It's a reminder of all those things I'll never do.'

'It's all so far away though.'

'And harder to remember as time goes by. Sometimes I have to force myself.'

'But then you start to trust it a little less.'

'We should just let them go, memories. They'll mean more if we let them come and go when they will.'

'Even if they don't come back?'

'Yes.'

'I don't believe you, I don't think you'd want to forget everything.'

'Yes I would! Well . . . sometimes. We all get older and we all get more and more sentimental. I don't want to end up like my grandmother, staring at old photographs for hours on end.

'You think that'd happen?'

'Show me a person who's not sentimental and I'll harness myself to that trap and you can ride me around the village all day.'

'I'm up for that! But what about the *neighbours*? They'd call you *el loco*.'

'Ha! You mean *la loca*. They do not need another excuse to talk about me. None of them will let me forget the past. Ever. That is why I don't like dwelling on memories.'

'Tell me about it. You know last night's dinner? If I was back home and got up in the morning and did a fart, you know, just a little quiet one, when I got to work someone would ask if I'd enjoyed my lobster and white-bean soup the night before. Guaranteed.'

169

'Jim!'

'I kid you not.'

'What I meant was – '

'I know what you mean. I stopped taking much of an interest in what people said about me a long time ago, way back in school. My reports were always saying I was "distracted", "uninterested". They were right, I *was* uninterested. In the whole fuckin lot of them.'

It should have been more difficult to talk like this. It usually was. But even the silences had no pressure to be filled. I didn't absent myself from the situation in that usual cautious way. When my wife once told me that I'd become a ghost I took it as a compliment. Being a ghost was fine, it meant never adapting to any context. Just maintain that distant presence. It was expected.

Not that I had always been a ghost. My wife and I had once talked as Adelina and I did now. The implication was obvious, but I didn't pay it much attention. The strange thing was that I had no fear in talking like this, opening up to a stranger. If I felt an occasional twinge of discomfort then what did it matter? Adelina was staying in Cuba and I would soon be going home.

All these moments? They would disappear like every other. Just leave it all to the ghost . . . Back home I would drift again through other peoples' lives, peering back at Adelina with unshared thoughts that could become anything I wanted, or chose, in the absence of ever seeing her again. So I let it go, all the little moments of that over-exposed day, all our tumbling words. I let everything drift up into blue to scroll and dart like the wings of those anonymous little birds catching the silver glinting sun.

That *sky*. A blue that stands out in a lifetime's memory more attuned to grey, a blue returned to again and again at the most incongruous of times, clearing the table, stuck in a motorway jam as the rain falls, zoning out as the TV drones. A sudden azure memory that unnerves with the depth of the possibilities it suggests. Once I was fifteen, lying on a West Coast beach and staring into a near-identical sky, suddenly so desperate to get out, into the world, wherever. I knew the insistence wouldn't last and I had to make the decision now. But I didn't. Every blue will eventually tarnish and on the edge of my gaze the clouds were already gathering.

'Why don't you come home very often?' I asked Adelina.

'I *do* come back. That's just my mother. If I visited once a day she'd want me to do it twice. I make a point of coming back, to show that I haven't run away and whatever people say doesn't matter.'

'About Floriano?'

'And Raul, my husband. He was from the village too. He was a popular man, good-looking. His father was a *guerrillero* leader in the 1950s and in Cuba that counts for a lot. No-one could believe it when one of the sons of the revolution ran off to Miami. It was scandalous, but it couldn't have anything to do with Raul, of course. It must be someone *else's* fault, *my* fault.'

'That's so unfair.'

'That was why your mother was such a friend. She never judged me about anything.'

'I have to give her that, I suppose.'

'She was right about David as well.'

'David?'

'He came from France. Toulouse. He was on a trip with *Les Amis de Cuba*. There was a social evening at the school and a friend invited me along. That was where I met him. Do you believe in destiny?

'Well I've not – '

'Good. It's nonsense. All that stuff about fate, if you think about it *anything* can be fate. But it's only the thing you're actually *looking* for that you call fate. Those other times when you find absolutely nothing? Or you find something you don't want to? We never call *that* fate.'

'Fair enough.'

'But that's not what I told myself at the time! No, meeting David was meant to be. My husband and son were gone and I wanted to disappear, I wanted this man to make me disappear.'

'Let me guess, he wanted to take you back to France?'

'I know, it's embarrassing! It was all such a beautiful charade.'

'It's nothing to be ashamed about.

'That is exactly what your mother said. She didn't try to talk me out of anything. The night before I took David to meet my parents she said it didn't matter that he was soon going home. I should just enjoy the moment for as long as possible. But she seemed so sad when she said that.'

'As if she was speaking from experience.'

'I think so.'

'It was that man in the photograph. John Tannehill. He must have been an old boyfriend. Why else keep his photo all those years?'

'Perhaps. Helen did not talk about her life before Cuba and it was not my – '

'There's always *someone*, isn't there? We have to forget them or put up with being haunted.'

'That sounds . . . *deprimente*.'

'I think my mother was haunted by John Tannehill.'

'How do you know?'

'All those years and she never managed to escape. Maybe she didn't want to.'

'If only it was so easy!'

'Is that what you want to do?'

'No . . . Of course not.'

But it was. Escape. It was the ever-present but anonymous theme in the background of everything she told me about her family, Floriano, and this love-struck Frenchman with the bald head. I saw it too in her impatient gaze as we walked the dusty street, in the overacted exchange with the old ice-cream vendor, who greeted her with loud bluster and wind-milling arms, a forced friendliness she felt compelled to match, in the sour nod from the museum attendant who suddenly disappeared, leaving us alone with echoing steps and the growing tension that comes of knowing you're not welcome here *so just go please, go now!*

Viñales. I understood the place as soon I got there. The only difference was the mind-stunning sun replacing monotonous grey. All that stuff about the multi-dimensions of global culture, all that rich tapestry of experience and attitude, it's all crap. The only difference between us is the weather. Adelina could be Inuit or Chinese and I'd still see in her the single-track roads of my youth, the smug teachers who saw the in-built limitations before I did, in the New York streets I so confidently walked in teenage movietime because I suspected that was as close as I'd ever get. Yes, I'd long-since made my peace with place. Which made her need to escape seem so naive. The thing is, in that little town, with all its beautiful strangeness that gave the world such soft-focus romanticism, I started to believe she would. It was a matter of the right *disposition*. She had it, and only lacked the confidence to know that the impossible decisions are the ones that ultimately prove the easiest to make.

We took bicycles to the San Vicente valley. We watched the clouds clear grey to wispy cirrus and spotless blue, under-coloured by full-spectrum greens, never so many shades; palms and Caribbean pine, wiry grasses, mimosa ferns palpitating at the slightest touch. No nuance but bold contrast, the white-washed wood of cottage and out-house, the iron-reds of corrugated roofs. The senses took turns, smell of dust and melting tar, humidity and sudden cool.

We talked when we stopped, glided silently through hamlets and their hidden farmers, past the little booths beside the yawning caves that took the tourists from white dazzle to ancient dark, away from peering trucks and flashing, weaving motorbikes with their unending echoes of goodbye as engines patched and re-patched bounced from limestone peak to valley leaf and finally faded, leaving bird-call, ticking heat and laboured breath. We watched each other as we cycled, glancing back or looking forward, unsure what would come next, if anything. Where the valley topped out we decided to turn back. The *caballero* we passed on the steep climb ten minutes earlier arrived with easy step and a little brown dog, an unconcerned smile. He took the offered bottle of water and touched his hat, veering into the bush, the crowding greens waving here, over *here*, but none giving him away.

I kissed her then, or Adelina me. Perhaps we reached for each other at the same time. But what does it matter. We kissed is all, in black shade by the sun-dazzled road. The salt of each other and the sweat of our hands. *I will accept no promises from you*, she said, and a little part of me began to hope. *I won't make any*, I replied, and wondered if I would.

Seven

'It's a while since you've been here, eh?'

He stares at me blankly. Has he registered the question, does he even know where he is?

'Yes, it's been a while.'

As if he's guessed: *is this the answer you're looking for?*
'I better show you round then.'

He looks down at the *Welcome* mat. He doesn't move. I'm struck again by how skinny he is. He's wearing bottle green cords and a mustard coloured tank top that hangs off him. It's a slow dematerialisation. One morning he'll be gone, a pile of clothes all that remains. His right arm hangs limp by his side. I never did ask the nurses about that. If there was a problem they should've told me, I shouldn't have to ask when they're the ones getting paid.

'Here.' His impossibly light hand slips into mine. We move along the hallway.

'Where's Nurse Davidson?'

'She's away, Dad.' The nurse had followed us back from the home to *settle him in* and helped me lug in his rise and recline chair. Soon as we set it down beside the fire she was offski.

I show him the downstairs toilet and the kitchen. He's slow going up the stairs but doesn't seem too frail. The old posters of Backstreet Boys and Westlife that I'd forgotten to take off Amber's wall briefly hold his attention, then the shelf of fluffy Eeyores. He paces around, like a cat searching for familiarity. His fingers trail along the duvet and he picks up the alarm clock from the bedside table, staring at it for a long time. 'Can you hear that tick ticking? It's like listening to your life being counted down. No, it'll have to go.'

I can't hear any ticking but say nothing. 'Cup of tea?'

'Tea?'

'Yes.'

'No.'

'C'mon downstairs.'

I've been saving the living room for last, the room where he'll spend his days. He makes straight for his hydraulic chair and picks up the remote, raising it to the tipping position. 'Technology,' he says, leaning back on the raised chair with his hands gripping the arm rests. He presses the remote and the chair whines gently back down to the sitting position, taking him with it. 'Don't you be playing with this, right?' he wags a finger, 'you'll break it.'

'Not even a wee go?'

'No.'

'C'mon, not even one little – '

'No!' he shouts.

He's not a joker, how could I forget. I think he's embarrassed then realise he's crying, staring at the unlit fire. Spatial disorientation, they call it, familiarity should be established as soon as possible, the distress triggers minimised. But I've failed already. It's mid-afternoon and last night's ashes haven't been cleaned out. This, I know from long experience, he can't abide. I have to drag him out of the ashes but all I can say is 'it's going to be strange for a while.'

His fingers drum on his knees. 'Yes. '

'You'll be ok?'

177

'I don't want to be a burden.'

'Don't say that, you – '

'Jim!' He almost spits my name. 'I want to know if you're happy for me to be here. '

'Yes,' I lie.

'I think tea would be nice.'

I get up too quickly but don't think he notices. In the kitchen I lean against the door and take a deep breath. That whining chair, rising and falling, a counterpoint to the dementia. Now composed, now anxious. Thank fuck the carer starts tomorrow. I'm glad it's her who has to watch the pendulum swing all day long. There's a lump in my throat I can't swallow.

'You don't need to sit with me,' he says when I hand him his tea.

'I thought you'd like the company.'

'I read the paper when I drink my tea.' He pats *The Times* on his lap.

I hesitate before closing the door. He's sitting stock still but his eyes are darting round the room, his cheeks wet. The newspaper's an excuse. He just doesn't want me near him as he struggles to set his new bearings. I have no way to reach him and no comfort to offer if I could. Because he's never been comfortable in my home and only some magical transference to his little old sea-side cottage would achieve that. Instead he's *here*, he's here to take his place with all the other strangers.

'Pour us one too, will you? How is he?'

'Fine.'

'You ok? You look a bit pale.'

I've managed two whiskies and a beer before my wife's got home and feel just fine. 'It's winter.'

178

'What does that mean?'

'Nothing.'

'Well here's to change, eh?'

She clinks my glass and goes through to see him. I hear the chair whine, he's obviously trying to get up, greet her like a gentleman. I have to avoid being alone with him. It'll help having the carer and the shift-work will make it easier too. Nurse Davidson said that normality is what he needs more than anything. *Simple routine Mr Drever.* Well Nurse Double D, there's nothing more routine than the awkwardness that's always underpinned our relationship.

He infuriates my wife too but she's got a better sense of duty than me. And he's always been so affectionate with her, I see it again when I go into the living room. She's sitting on the floor and he's leaning down, holding and stroking her hand. The daughter he would've preferred? C'mon, only a paranoid egomaniac would consider that. 'How about I get the dinner on?'

'Don't worry, I'll get it,' says my wife.

'No no, my turn.'

She nods. 'Uh huh.' That *you sneaky bastard* look. 'Cook away then.'

'Fish and chips, Dad. How does that grab you?'

'Yes, that would be nice.' He looks down at my wife with a secretive smile. 'In the home we had fish every Friday.'

One by one we pay our respects to the returning patriarch. It's not quite *The Godfather* but the deference is palpable. The Boy's under strict instructions and manages to be polite. Amber gives her granda a big hug and Peter doesn't have a clue what to do, eventually sticking out a hand and saying *what a privilege it is to meet you*. He keeps calling him sir for some reason. Is all this respect truly meant, or a means of maintaining our distance? Our deference is perhaps wariness, none of us knowing how his illness will be from one day to the next.

What about *simple routine*? That would mean sinking the usual two bottles with dinner. But it wouldn't be right. We limit ourselves to one glass and envious looks at the unopened Rioja.

The silences stretch. We glance at one another, all apart from my father, who picks and pushes at his fish and chips. I flash a look at my wife as if to say *should we cut it up for him*? I should've asked Nurse Davidson. These are the things, the little things that are *essential to harmonious functioning*, as my wife's gurus would have it. I don't want to offend him by asking if I can help but he's probably too proud to ask. My wife rides to the rescue, reaching across and cutting up his fish. He watches her passively. In fact, we're all watching, all trying to pretend we're not watching, listening to the knife squeak on the plate.

'Thank you,' he says.

I'm not sure he is but at least he's finally eating. His head bobs up and down as he chews. I can't help thinking about my mother's journal. The lump is suddenly back in my throat. I can't stop watching him. Bits of food dribble from his mouth onto the plate. My phone starts vibrating in my pocket. Adelina, I know. My wife's looking at me. Everyone wants something, all of them, and I've never asked anyone for anything. I can't swallow this fuckin lump.

*   *   *

Endless snow. I'm getting fevered. I don't want crump-ing boots and gritty scrapes on the salted car-park. I want to kill everyone who talks about the weather. Some find romance in endurance. Let me squat instead by the just-lit fire, staring into a distance leached of every detail.

I'm on the early shift. 5am alarm. My father's already moving about in Amber's room.

They say the elderly find it difficult to sleep. Is it a conscience thing, the remorse accumulated over a lifetime? He must be the exception that makes the rule because no more worthy a man have I ever met. Jesus himself would feel threatened. Yes, my crimes are all my own, no sins of the father rest on these shoulders. By the time I'm out of the shower he's sitting in the kitchen. I see him from the hallway and leave by the front door without a word.

I pass round by the old mash tun, onto the steps up to the stills. Stan and Ronnie stand at the top. They're leaning close, whispering away the sneaky bastards, even though no-one can hear them in the noise of the Stillhouse. They both turn and look at me at the same time.

I can't help stopping, I even look down at my scuffed boots, as if I've done something wrong. Fuckin stupid. I run up the last few steps and nod to them, nipping into the bog and glancing back. They're both still staring in my direction, not saying a word. No doubt they're discussing the strike, the fact that they scabbed. They're probably wondering about where I stand, my *position-ing*. I was at the picket but also on leave. Does that make me friend or foe?

I'm not sure myself but what does it matter. I take a new cloth from the cleaning cupboard, pour on the waxy liquid and start at number 1 wash still. Slow circles, a white smear that gradually disappears as I polish. The still gives a little burble, enjoying the massage. When I notice my face in the polished copper I see that I'm smiling. I work my way down the wash stills and back up the spirit stills on the other side. I don't need to polish them. I just do it. I like the motion, round and round so my thoughts don't have to.

'You at that again?'

I'm kneeling on the mesh walkway, finishing off number 3 spirit. Some would say it's peculiar to have a favourite still, but this is mine. No point telling Rankin that sometimes in the deepest part of the night it sings to me. I finish off the polishing and look up. Rankin's a devious bastard and has probably been standing watching for a while. In a Scorcese movie he'd be the edgy gangster watching Joe Pesci twist a ballpoint pen into the stool pigeon's eye. What he can't understand is that the stills run so much more sweetly when you look after them.

'How's it going?'

'Same as, same as.'

'Bit early for you isn't it?'

'It is that.'

Rankin's way early for his shift. 'You on secret OT? Jack won't be best pleased.'

'Got a favour to ask.'

Rankin's got this problem. Jeannie, the unrequited love of his life who manages the visitor centre. It's been going on since they were at school and they're both 35 now. Rumour goes he shagged her one lunchtime in the security guard's portacabin. Camp Gary claims he glanced at the window and Jeannie was slightly bent over, Rankin standing very intently behind her. *Both looked me straight in the fuckin eye!* Then Rankin closed the blind . . . Every day he's down the visitor centre like a love struck pup. Every day he'll offer to do a tour for her.

'S' just a wee group. I forgot I'm meeting the boss at 12.15. You don't have to do the whole tour, just the Stillhouse bit till I get back.'

'Fuck's sake.'

'You're a star.'

You're a star, when did people start saying that? I only agree to help with the tour because it means I can delay going home. It's a piece of piss really. All I have to do is stand up by the demonstration spirit safe in the exhibition area at the bottom of the Stillhouse and explain the distillation process. Crank up the accent and invoke the myths, puff my craftsman's chest.

The tour group appears at ten past twelve. I'm washing my hands and can hear Rankin belting out his spiel along by the grain hopper. Then they'll be trooping round the mash tun, peering in, Rankin burbling on about drunk cows eating the leftover draff. His hackneyed shtick in the fermentation room is to feign being stoned by the carbon dioxide and say *whoa, reminds me of Woodstock, '69.* I nip through the mash tun control room to avoid the group as it snakes back down the stairs to the Stillhouse. Rankin's not supposed to take them up there. Health and Safety. Slinky'll be there before you can say clipboard and pen.

I follow them after a couple of minutes, stopping a few steps from the bottom. They're gathered at the spirit safe with their backs to me. A dozen or so, usual outfits of Goretex and woolly hats. Rankin's on the gantry and raises a hand. He explains that the *one and only Jim Drever, our master Stillman*, the sarcastic swine, will be taking over. He even does a drum roll. The faces turn as if choreographed, a mix of non-commitment and expectation.

And I see her.

I should've clocked the duffle coat and Davy Crockett straightaway but she was lost in the crowd.

I hesitate for a moment then turn and hurry back up the steps. She's seen me, of course she has. I feel like a little boy, running away. Rankin's calling my name but when I get round to the mash tun I can't hear him anymore. Portland Bill gives me a funny look as I barge past him and down the back stairs and outside. Thank fuck for this mini Ice Age, I feel I'm burning up. I kneel down and rub snow on my face, rub until my skin is red and numb.

They're all sitting in the kitchen when I get home; my wife, father and a new presence, the top-of-the-range private nurse suggested by the manager of my father's home, salary to match. She'll do the 9-5 and we'll look after the old man at night. It's baking hot. My wife's insisted on cranking up the thermostat since my father moved in, *to make him feel comfortable.* Am I imagining the strange kind of abbreviation that hangs in the air, as if they've suddenly stopped talking about me? My father coughs and splutters but remains absent, a ghost haunting no-one but himself. He's got dried egg down his Rotary Club tie.

'We've just been talking about how everything will work,' says my wife.

'That's good.'

'This is Maggie.'

'Nice to meet you Mr Drever.'

'You too.'

'Call him Jim, for goodness sake!'

Maggie looks at me.

'If you want,' I say.

She smiles but seems unsure.

'You forgot your phone,' my wife says.

I push back the swell of panic. 'Noticed that.'

She reaches into her pocket and looks at it closely before handing it across. 'There's a number that called a few times.'

'No name?'

'No. No name.'

I take the phone. 'Cold caller I suppose.'

'Must be.'

She turns away and I stare at the phone, as if it might tell me if my wife answered or called the number back.

'You'll be late for the union meeting,' my wife says.

I didn't know there was one.

I stand by the visitor centre door, beside the display racks of postcards. An easy getaway spot. There are no cars in the car-park, no coaches. Adelina must be gone, back to wherever she's hiding. Maybe she bought a postcard to send back home, a smiling Loch Ness Monster in a Jimmy cap. This edginess, I don't know if I can handle it. The world usually leaves me pretty much alone.

Jack's persuaded Jeannie to let him use the visitor centre over lunchtime. The internal phone goes just as he stands up on a chair and scans the crowd, primed for the Big Moment. Jeannie's agreed to the meeting without checking. Slinky's informants must have tipped him off. She stammers a bit, flushes red as Rudolf's Christmas conk and hands Jack the phone.

Jack remains on the chair, delicately holding the phone between thumb and forefinger, pinkie out, the world's

185

most effete revolutionary. With the other hand he tries to quieten the hubbub. *No, your concern is unnecessary . . . There are no tours booked in and no tourists . . . Why should we hold our meetings in the Filling Store when you have a warm boardroom and all the pies and drams that an expense account can buy?* Sniggers of amusement at this, exchanged glances mixing admiration and something more complex, like embarrassment mixed with incredulity. My wife'd be creaming her best frillies if she was here.

Jack hands Jeannie the phone. 'They think they've *granted* us the use of the visitor centre. But we don't need their permission, their *blessing*. This meeting was going ahead. Regardless.'

Rankin shouts *hurrah*, his way of impressing Jeannie. He's virus-close to her, over by the pyramid of branded tumblers. Gary nudges Malky and they shake their heads. Dumb Juan they call him.

'This time last month? We were worried. That leaked memo talking about short-time working, redundancies. And what did they do? They gave us an ultimatum, stop the strike or we won't talk, like we're a bunch of children to be ordered around, threatened. But what did *we* do? We struck, we took it to *them*. And they'll talk all right, they'll talk on *our* terms!'

Fuckin right Jack. Fuckin right they will. This from a couple of the warehouse lads, Glasgow boys, not long started. There's probably about sixteen of us in here, not counting the visitor centre staff. The TV's been muted but still shows the *Story of the Spirit* on endless loop. They shot this a couple of years back, made stars of some of us; moody coopers, conscientious Stillmen. For a brief moment Jack's on both the TV screen and up on the chair.

'What now, now we've shown we won't just wring

our hands and back away? Well lo and behold another letter from the company!' He takes a sheet of paper from his pocket, slowly unfolds it.'

'They weren't expecting a strike,' shouts Camp Gary. Always takes him a while to catch up.

'They were not – '

'Couldn't believe we'd do it.'

'Absolutely, they thought – '

'They were wrong, eh?'

Jack's extended both his arms, moving them up and down like a double sieg heil, trying to get Camp Gary to shut up. This is spoiling it, he's got rhetoric to *expound*. He waves the letter in the air. *Brothers and sisters!* The hubbub's back again, a shuffle of feet as people look at each other, move their heads to get the best view. *What's it say*, shouts Rankin, managing to brush Jeannie's tit at the same time. Everyone looks a little bit more sweaty-faced. I can't take any more. I slip out as he pauses for effect, eking out the last atom of drama.

At the corner of warehouse 6 I hear a muffled cheer and glance back. The windows of the visitor centre are yellow, steamy. What's been said? For a moment I'm jealous I missed the big reveal. I cross the bridge, watching the sickly line of smoke rise from my chimney. My windows too are yellow. And more voices, ever approaching, no matter how much I try to outrun them. More voices and more questions. I'd dawdle if I could but it's too damn cold.

'Well?' says my wife.

I pull the back door shut. 'How's he doing?'

My wife rolls her eyes. 'Your dad's fine Jim. He's through in the living room with Maggie.'

187

I walk past her before she has a chance to say anything else. Maggie the carer is young, about nineteen or so. Bleached blonde hair, a few zits, and a bursting burlesque chest which probably explains why the Boy's down in the living room. He's sitting on the sofa opposite Maggie and my father, pretending to read a graphic novel. *The Sandman*. He's got no chance and knows it, just down for an eyeful, stocking up the images for a midnight wank.

'Jim.'

My wife tugs at my arm. 'Hi Dad,' I say, but he doesn't look up. Maggie turns and gives a beaming smile. *Evening, Mr Drever*. They're playing a card game and after a moment I realise its *Snap*.

It's so dispiriting I feel suddenly exhausted. My father was a man who got an Open University degree in philosophy and theology while working full-time and looking after me. Every damn night, sitting reading in that high-backed, red leather chair by the fire. He'd look at me, ever-patient, glasses slipping down his nose. I'd sit in the chair when he wasn't around and once read a few pages from the book lying there. Something about St. Augustine. I'd have been about fifteen, same age as the Boy. The only saints I knew about were football teams.

'Do I have to phone Jack to find out what happened?'

'Might be better.' My father's shaking hand lays down a card on the chair between him and Maggie. They're not even playing with a proper deck, it's one of those *Happy Family* sets. Was this Maggie's idea, does she think he's a retard, only able to deal with Mrs White, the baker's fat fuckin wife? 'Might be better. He'll be waiting, no doubt he'll be waiting.'

'Take an *interest,* man,' and she storms out of the living room.

Maggie gives a quick, uncertain glance. The Boy raises *The Sandman* to hide his smirk. The doorbell rings and my father looks up. Confusion in his eyes that slips away. For the first time he sees me.

'I'd like a new kilt too,' he says.

'A what?'

'A new kilt.'

Now I remember. The Boy and I, we're supposed to be going to town to look at wedding kilts.

Maggie looks up at me, expectant. The Boy casts a furtive glance. 'Right. If you want.' There's not much else to add. He goes back to playing cards. *That'd be nice, wouldn't it,* says Maggie, as if talking to a pet, or a child. He just takes it, even smiles as he says *yes, very nice.*

'Can I get a velvet one,' says the Boy.

'Eh?'

Maggie laughs and turns to the Boy with an exaggerated incline of the head. She's flirting and the Boy deals with it like a pro, even a little wink! 'A purple velvet kilt, I think it'd be well cool.'

And now they're both looking at me, *amused,* and I'm the one who's getting embarrassed. Only my father isn't looking at me, his hand hovering over Mr Bacon the Butcher. 'Velvet,' I say. 'Have you spoken to your mother? How much is that going to cost me and I – '

'I'm only *joking* dad.'

'About what?' my wife says, breezing back into the living room. Even if the Boy had given an answer she wouldn't have been interested, her attention now entirely focused on the person who appears behind her.

189

Jack. He's red-faced, still flushed with the admiration of his followers.

'Hi Jim. I saw you'd ducked out and thought I'd pop down and tell you the latest. I thought Katie would want to know too. It's a special feeling, knowing that solidarity still means something.'

'*Jack.*'

I haven't even sat down yet and plonk myself down beside the Boy.

'Weasel words and contradictions,' says Jack.

'Uh-huh.'

'The company was "extremely disappointed" with the strike. It's like getting told off by yer mammy! They're "taking advice" and "open to conciliation" but "reserve the right to respond accordingly".'

'Sounds like a threat.'

'Smoke and mirrors. They're playing to their own gallery. They'll be round the table in a week, mark my words.'

'Brilliant, isn't it,' says my wife.

'Is it?'

'You're right, it isn't a victory yet. The danger's still there. But I reckon they're ready to negotiate.'

'Amazing what a strike will do.'

'Damn right, Jim. The working class hasn't rolled over just yet.'

My father suddenly explodes into one of his coughing fits. Apparently they're nothing to worry about. Nurse Davidson said sometimes he forgets to swallow and then saliva builds up and goes down the wrong way. I mean, how can you forget to swallow? Maggie rubs him gently on the back and wipes his mouth with a tissue. 'Well. Am I getting a new kilt or *not*?' he blurts out. He's frustrated, angry at having drawn attention to his frailty.

'Course you are!' But I sound impatient rather than light-hearted. 'We have to get going so you better get ready.'

'Sorry,' says Jack. 'I didn't mean to hold you up.'

'Yeah, we're a bit busy Jack.'

'No hurry Jack, stay for a coffee,' says my wife.

'Well I don't know about – '

'Don't worry, we'll be a while anyway.' She raises her eyebrows towards my father. 'So you want a kilt as well, do you Dad?'

'That's kind, but I better get going,' says Jack.

'See you then,' I say.

'Peter!' My father gets to his feet, scattering the *Happy Families*. He makes his way over to Jack and sticks out a bony hand. 'What a pleasure it is to meet you. I hear you make Amber very happy.'

'I think – '

My wife touches Jack's hand, an excuse to touch, a quick smile that says *just roll with it, any explanation would only confuse him*. 'Yes,' she says, looking at Jack, 'he makes us all very happy.'

The Town. The *Town*. Land of dreams for a country boy. JC and I would come by bone shaking bus, twenty miles from the distillery. There was a cinema, a model shop that sold Gatt guns and fishing tackle, and a barman in *The Gordon Arms* who served us underage. He'd give your hand a little stroke when he handed over the change but we put up with it. It was booze! We were getting served! One day he was gone and he's probably still doing time.

The Gordon Arms didn't last much longer, like the rest of the Town, the old-skool shops that disappeared one by one, the shoe stores with the high-stacked boxes, the sticky Formica cafés and someone's granny serving, always someone you knew, the tweedy clothes shops with hostile sales assistants and an absence of customers. No much wonder the Town went nuts when the malls came. There's three hypermarkets now, we can't get enough, strategically placed on the outskirts: north, south and east, leaching the last independent life from the town centre. It's complained about, sure, but no-one really cares. If we did we wouldn't load our trolleys three feet high and keep on coming back for more, more, *more*.

The changes were insidious but I remember the winter Saturday I finally noticed. I was in a clothes store in the giant shopping mall, the Northgate. You'd hear people in the street, *you going down the Northgate . . . there's three new shops opened in the Northgate*. So there I was in the fabled Northgate, near-drooling in front of a rack of socks and all of a sudden I seemed to *come across* myself again. A few more minutes of muzak and I might have been lost forever.

That's when I opted out of any more change. Seems more authentic to be a moaning old fart, my line of retreat drawn by a slant of dusty light across those old shops, people, pubs. Strange thing is, I've become nostalgic not for something lost, but the hope I once had that the Town could be transformed into somewhere more exciting, more *persuasive*. I knew this was impossible, even back then. But the memory of unattainability is still preferable to wandering those epic stores pondering loyalty points and two for one offers.

It's hot in the car but my father likes the heat. The local radio is annoying but my wife likes the DJ. I glance in the rear-view mirror at the Boy. He's squeezed between Maggie and my father and looks anxious, probably cracked an unwanted erection. It's strange to think that his interaction with this place will be so different from my own. No doubt he'll discover his own bemusement, this era of endless choice will be his line in the memory sands.

I park in my usual place on the top floor of the multi-storey car park opposite Tesco No. 1 in the north of the Town. The Boy and his mother complain, as usual, that I haven't parked at the southern end, opposite Tesco No. 3. I know all the shops and the recently extended shopping centre are up that end but I like seeing the sagging pubs and ramshackle charity shops, the *To Let* boards that would swing in the wind if Ken Loach wanted to film an obvious metaphor.

We straggle up the High Street in a long silent line. My wife bustles ahead with me behind, Maggie pushing my father in the collapsible NHS wheelchair and the Boy bringing up the rear. He'll be checking out Maggie's arse and now I'll have to stop myself doing the same. I'm nervous, we might bump into Adelina at any moment. I feel like my teenage self, embarrassed to be walking down the street with my father, desperately hoping that I don't come across any of my friends or, horror of horrors, Samantha Christie, whom I fancy to bits.

A few years ago the Victorian arcade that houses *MacDonnell and Son, Gentlemen Outfitters* was given a makeover. Kudos to the council for trying to snag the tourists who were buzzing past the Town in ever-bigger swarms. The consultants created authenticity on steroids; hunting, shooting 'n fishing gone mental, boutiques selling tweeds, local beer and cheese, hand-crafted soaps ... And a heritage centre too, with old town ghost walks and fire-side storytelling. It's like one of those twenty-second segments between songs on the Eurovision Song Contest, an abstraction of place and identity to facilitate instant *understanding*. If I was a tourist I'd come here, darn tootin! That sets me all jumpy again, looking around for Adelina.

The kilt outfitter is one of the last survivors from my childhood. And the irony is that the shop fits right in to the pimp my heritage vibe. The more cynical visitor might think that these clustering racks of kilts, spor-rans, and dress-shirts, the ancient mustiness and the mounted stags heads, are some kind of affectation, the matronly manageress in blue apron delivered straight from central casting. But it's been like this ever since I can remember and that's the saddest thing, even the last remaining pockets of authenticity feel manufactured.

'Arms out,' she orders, tape measure round her neck.

My wife holds a hand to her lips. To stop her from laughing or crying with nostalgic delight, I can't tell.

The world is happening *to me*, again. I'm placed within it yet apart. I stand to the left of the counter, the Boy in the middle and my father to the right. We've inadvert-ently arranged ourselves in height order. If someone hit our head with a little hammer we'd make different tones, a human glockenspiel. We turn when told by the crabby old woman, saying not a word as she works her way along, taking her measurements and scribbling her notes.

194

'Tea there,' she announces, nodding towards one of those eighties teas-maids. 'Back as soon as.'

We make tea, drinking from cracked mugs and wandering among the kilts. They've got football tartans these days, and those open-necked shirts with the leather laces that got popular after *Braveheart*, like the Celtic hand-fasting ceremony. Identity rediscovered, Hollywood-style. The outfits that are handed to us fit perfectly. We don't have a family tartan and have gone with 'Ben Lawers Thistle'. It's as subdued as I could find, greys and dark blues instead of the usual lurid reds, or worse, those yellowy-greens, like last night's curry spewings.

The old matron is pleased with the results of her expertise and smiles for the first time.

We stand there in differing states of self-consciousness. My wife takes a picture on her mobile that will end up framed on the living room sideboard. The Boy says he's not wearing any pants and gives Maggie a pervy smile. She shakes her head and pretends to be shocked. My father hasn't heard, he's pulling at his bow-tie; *it doesn't feel right, Katie can you fix it?* He's shrinking in front of me, day by day becoming smaller, more hunched. But still that proud set to his jaw. He must have worked hard on that when my mother left, staring into endless midnight mirrors, wondering what this bastard John Tannehill had that he lacked.

Job done we disperse. 4.30pm, I stand at the door to the arcade, vaguely listening to the fiddle music on the tannoy. Streetlights cast a jaundiced glow on the piles of pavement slush. Rain, snow or shine, everyone hurries round here, my family no different, making their separate bee-lines to God knows where. Not that it matters,

195

we're all just happy to be released from proximity to each other until we have to rendezvous in the car-park at six.

I'm still edgy. Every corner's a sudden meeting waiting to happen. A headache is settling in for the evening. I check up and down the half-empty street before setting off. If I see Adelina I can duck back inside the arcade and make a Bond-like escape via the River Street exit.

The Post Office is just round the corner but there's a long queue. It takes an age for my turn and any moment I'm expecting my wife to walk past the window and see me standing there. The counter-girl comes back with eight letters, the first time I've collected anything from the PO Box in five years. Hardly makes all those direct debits seem value for money.

'You looked good in that kilt.'

She must have crept up the stairs like a cat. 'How long have you been standing there?'

'Can I not admire a fine figure of a man?'

'But Jack's not here.'

'Oh stop it!' A slight reddening of the neck though.

'Stop what?'

'Just stop it. I came up to give you a compliment, what's so wrong with that?'

'Thank you.'

'Eh?'

'I said thank you. For the compliment.'

She smiles, mouths a sarcastic *ok*. 'What's that you've got?'

I glance down at the pile of brochures and leaflets for alternative care homes that Nurse Davidson left behind. They've got names like Lavender Grove and Fair View

Heights, cover images of well-groomed staff and smiling residents doing flower arranging, jigsaws. 'For dad.'

'Want me to help? I can – '

'No! That's ok. It's something I want to do myself, you all made it quite clear it was my responsibility.'

'I know, but – '

'No buts!' I'm holding an arm out, as if I'm directing fuckin traffic.

She hesitates, then moves back to the door. 'As you wish.'

'How is he?'

'He's asleep. Dinner'll be a while. I'll shout you.'

How long am I going to stare at the brochures? I should throw them aside and cross to the window, look at my disembodied reflection that I want to stop mirroring my ridiculous actions and do something different, just once after all these years, do something different that might actually be useful, like gather up the brochures, walk downstairs and fling the lot on the fire. That way I wouldn't have to see Adelina's neat handwriting on those blue envelopes ever again, I wouldn't have to think about what's in those letters I smuggled upstairs among the pages of Lavender Grove and The Willows. I would just watch them burn.

The reflection lets me down. He gives an exaggerated shrug like Marcel Marceau then sits and separates the letters and the brochures. I really do have a twinge of guilt about finding another home for my father and switch on the laptop to send an enquiry email. But I don't. *Vinales2004* again. Best laid plans of mice and monkeys and all that.

I mean, what would you do?

And what of John Tannehill, the love of my life? From our first meeting onwards I saw him everywhere, I still do. The shadow cast by the lemon tree, that's him, about to step into the light with that sad, unreachable smile, the figure at the door of the midnight cantina, gone when I turn. Forgive the sentiment of an old lady, I blame the tropical sun, frazzling the synapses for the last forty years.

John returned to Edinburgh one more time. The September of 1961. He had lost weight and become more agitated. It was the morphine. He had spent time on leave in a Hindu retreat, a few weeks in Algiers with a group of French painters and writers. Haiti was 'troubled' he said, 'an uneasy place' where he'd been terrified by visions. His poems caught it all, a tumble of Basho, Snyder and Rilke.

I stayed on board for the week that John was docked. Yes, your mother chose to look after him rather than her one year-old child. He had a malarial fever but was still shooting up three times a day. I was terrified by the thought of him leaving a second time but leave he did. I stayed on the quayside for two hours after The Montana sailed.

Your poor father Edward, he should be canonised. A gentler man I have never known. The deeper I sank the kinder he became. I simply could not understand it. He would bring you to me and I would burst into tears. Yet still he would try. I spent hours alone, poring over the books that John had left me; 'Howl' by Ginsberg, Basil Bunting's 'Poems, 1950', 'Journey to the End of the Night' by Céline, searching for pieces of him that I would re-assemble in my own words, page after page that I ripped into pieces, looking for the combination that might make him whole again, bring him back.

He was such a continual presence that it seemed obvious

a letter would arrive from him. He was staying with a friend in Tottenham, north London. There was an address on the bottom of the envelope.

That was when I lost my mind. I told myself that if I left straightaway John would be there when I arrived but if I delayed even a single day he would be gone. It was the Wednesday before Easter, 1962. You were just over two years old. Your father was on an early shift and I waited until his mother had taken you out for a walk. I packed a suitcase and took the midday train from Waverley to Kings Cross. I abandoned my husband and son. Without a second thought.

Can you picture me? Do you imagine me standing like a little girl lost in the bustle of the Kings Cross commute with my one piece of luggage clasped to my chest? Do you wonder if I was wracked with guilt, ready to take the first train back north, before my disappearance was noticed? Or maybe I stood in cold pouring rain that I didn't notice, soaked but smiling as the future unfurled and all the hurrying, worrying commuters were the inverse of all the excited possibilities flowing through my mind? The truth is I was all of things, all and more. I have been all of those things ever since.

I took the Tube to Seven Sisters and spent two hours trying to find the flat John was staying at. When I finally did I spent another fifteen minutes ringing the bell before it opened a few inches and a suspicious, beady eye peered out. This was Freaky Steve.

I would come to like Steve, in time, but that first meeting I hated him. He made me stand in the freezing drizzle, firing question after question. 'I have to confirm your identity,' he said, 'anyone could have found John's letter and claim to be you.' In the end he let me in. We sat in silence in the filthy kitchen, drinking tea, Freaky Steve in an old dressing gown open to his concave stomach.

Steve rented the house with his girlfriend Sue. He'd met John a few years back and let him kip down anytime he was back in London. My heart sank when he said that John had shipped out a week ago. I was free to stay for as long as I wanted, so long as I chipped in for the rent.

John, John, I babbled on to Sue about John non-stop. How was he when you saw him? Did he mention me? I asked the same questions a thousand times, trying to ignore the pity in her eyes. 'You'll be together,' she'd repeat, ever-patient. Sue, I miss her terribly. She is still my secret diamond, cutting through everything, precious.

At the time, Sue worked in an English language school, St. David's. It was one of the first in the country, a few cramped rooms in a back street in Marylebone. She got me a start as a teaching assistant. I helped out with the conversational stuff and soon started doing some classes of my own. We sat in front of the electric fire, testing each other on tenses, grammar, pretending to be the wide-eyed children of foreign diplomats that we taught.

John sent the occasional postcard from Osaka, New York, Sydney . . . full of promises to be back in London by the spring, by Christmas . . . He had left some belongings in Steve's flat. Did I do the love-struck thing, hold one of his t-shirts to my nose and inhale his scent, close my eyes with a deep sigh? Of course! I would wrap myself in one of those shirts and read his notes, poems and books into the small hours. Rexroth, 'The Master and Margarita', Pound's 'Cantos', 'Under the Volcano', Mandelstam . . . , John was better than all of them and didn't even know it. He could have been a superstar but wouldn't have cared a jot. I adored him for that.

Sue's prediction did come true. John wrote from Alexandria, Egypt. 'Please come,' he said. 'I need you more than ever.' I will look after you forever, I thought. We would eat sweet

200

dates and drink mint tea, listen to the muezzin and make love in the softest dawn. Did I understand the implications of chasing this dream to the detriment of all else? Only vaguely, like a warning shout as you swim deeper into heavy, booming surf. I rushed headlong from London as I had Edinburgh, my motives struggling to catch up. And questions become difficult to answer in the absence of motives: was I missing you, could I even miss you?

Alexandria, how it shimmered! We had enough to rent out some rooms in a little backstreet not far from Misr train station. Even the nightmare beginning became part of the dream. The ship had been docked for two hours but there was no sign of John. I was lost in the middle of a seething quayside crowd, more and more anxious, shading my eyes and scanning every face. Then he was there, but just a glimpse. I shouted but he didn't see me and I was suddenly terrified that he would simply give up and disappear, leave me to the crowd.

Then he turned round. The happiness in his eyes has never left me. My bags tumbled as we embraced, the skinny dock boys laughing and pointing. We were the centre of the universe and I do not think I stopped smiling for the seven months we lived there. I loved the warm air and the quiet breeze, the whitewash and the dust. I loved watching John stand at the balcony in blue pastel afternoon, head down as he wrote in hot whisky night, drowsed in cool morning light. It felt so very right, the world created for us and only us. I never imagined how life could so easily flow.

You're expecting the 'but', yes? Imagine a world with no tempering of the opposite, no brake on untrammelled good, evil, sadness. Is the depth of an emotion made more sweet by its opposite, the fear it could be taken away from you at any moment? Or would it be more intense still if there was no depth it could not attain?

I wish the joy of those months in Egypt could have contin-ued forever. Even with the 'buts', the heroin John could not shake, the depression I could never reach. Today my imagina-tion is dry as the desert but back then I was convinced I could set John free if I was just able to think my way into the proper strategy. That meant emptying every last secret and fear, in the hope that myself, stripped bare, would persuade him to abandon his own self and together we would combine into something untouchable. That is why I told him what I did. I thought it would bring us together, properly and finally.

I told John he was your father.

I told him it happened during our holiday in the Highlands. I wanted to believe it myself. But the gap between wanting to believe and knowing is often unbridgeable. The hurt in John's eyes was terrible, the confusion of his dawning realisation that any reaction he decided upon was irrelevant because there was nothing he could do about it. It was too late to amend. I remember the wind rising, the way it billowed the balcony curtains. He wasn't angry, John never got angry. His voice was a whisper when he asked what your name was.

My headache has got worse. There's a shake to my hands. I lock the door to the en-suite bathroom and sit on the toilet. Mould is starting to creep along the bottom of the bath where the sealant has disintegrated. I bend down and start scraping at it, black muck building up behind my thumb-nail. Now I want it properly cleaned, I want to start from fresh.

I peel back the rubbery strip of sealant to reveal the narrow gap between the bath and the lino. The lino's grubby too, and the black tiles around the mirror, splat-tered with water marks, toothpaste. I find a scourer behind the toilet and start scrubbing, avoiding my gaze in the mirror because that reflection is useless. Adelina's letters are lying on the bed but so what? Let my wife open them, read them. I need to clean, this bathroom must be cleansed, like my mother emptied the trough of her life, the swill pooling stagnant on her balcony until it evaporated in the sun and maybe in time a hurricane blew away the last of the stench.

In the Mood for Love

Darkness and light. A consideration of explanations with no middle ground. I lay naked on top of the sheets in the dark of Adelina's old bedroom. She was there, beyond the partition wall. Red shorts and t-shirt, bolt upright in bright morning sun. The events of the day before sat just beyond me, distant enough to already be anomaly, close enough to ask a bittersweet what if?

I wasn't willing to let the day in. That meant facing each other. Across the breakfast table and Brunhilda's scanning eyes, an awkwardness impossible to disguise. I'd leave this room only when the pressure in my bladder finally forced me to just get up, go to the damn toilet.

We opened our bedroom doors at exactly the same time, startling one another. Each of us said an overly polite good morning, formalities that hung absurdly in the air. For want of filling the yawning void opening up between us, I tapped my cigarette packet. Adelina stepped back to let me pass on the narrow passageway that led to the veranda. I smoked my cigarette, trying not to think of her in the bathroom, pulling down those little red shorts.

Brunhilda bustled in the kitchen across the patio, noticing me just as I stubbed out. I waved back to her as I stepped off the veranda, in the same moment that Adelina emerged from the toilet. We may have been reaching out even before we bumped into one another.

The kiss was urgent, Adelina pulling me into her room while looking anxiously over my shoulder. But her mother was out of sight, her happy whistling drifting across the hot morning.

'You have always been a fussy girl!'
    'I get bored with fruit.'
    'Fruit is good for you Adelina.'
    '*Si, si, bueno* Jim, *bueno*.'
    Then the laugh, always the laugh. I hadn't met anyone as contented as Adelina's father José.
    'Yes, I don't know why she's so picky. I'd eat mango every day if I could get it.' Brunhilda's wizened face cracked into a smile and she gave a little wink, Adelina poking me in the ribs.
    'Don't you start!'
    Everyone laughed expect Brunhilda, whose gaze flicked from me to Adelina. She'd already picked up on the slight tension, a new shyness in her daughter when she talked to me. Her mother's gaze was burning and Adelina was over-doing the attempt to appear normal. José was oblivious for now but I foresaw an imminent briefing. He would be sat down by Brunhilda and informed, like a melodramatic Brazilian soap opera. I was glad I'd insisted on treating them to breakfast at the little café on the main street. It meant distractions.
    'Have you enjoyed Viñales, Jim?' asked Brunhilda.
    'It's a beautiful place. You're very lucky to live here.'
    'Oh, I am sure it is no more beautiful than your own home. When are you going home?'
    I looked away from the piercing glance that accompanied this question. A heat rose in my neck.
    'I have to wait until I hear from the lawyer about my

mother's financial matters. It could be a few more days.'

'Oh well that's good then. Isn't it Adelina, a few more days with your friend until he goes back home?'

Adelina's father began nodding his head. '*Si, si*. Yes, home. *Mi casa*.' He stood up and slowly lifted his coffee cup in my direction. '*Mi casa es su casa*. Me house, your house, yes?'

I smiled and raised my own coffee. 'And you would be welcome in my . . . *casa*.'

'*Gracias, gracias*.'

'If only it were possible,' said Brunhilda. 'It is very difficult to leave Cuba. You will, most probably, never see us again.'

In that moment Brunhilda definitely knew. She couldn't have missed the look that passed between myself and Adelina. The silence too was a giveaway. For a long moment no one wanted to hold anyone's gaze, all except José, beaming away as he slurped his coffee.

A shout from the roadside punctured the tension. A horse and trap had pulled up, a powerfully-built man in olive green army fatigues talking animatedly and gesticulating towards them.

The happy face of Adelina's father filled with anger, his daughter reaching for him as he began shouting at the uniformed man. Adelina covered her face in her hands and Brunhilda sat poker-straight, staring directly ahead. Across the street people gawped, listening to the furious argument so completely out of place in this sunny, peaceful place. The uniformed man was pointing at me as he shouted, Adelina's father's hands cupped like a bowl as he turned to me and back to the man in the trap, as if in supplication, explaining something indefensible. The man jumped down and stood at the bottom of the steps leading up to the café balcony. He fixed me with a stare and spat viciously on the ground.

Only when the horse's slow clip had faded away did Brunhilda return to the moment. She put a hand on her husband's arm, looking tired and drawn as she spoke to Adelina in Spanish.

'This is why I do not come home often.'

'What the hell was all that about?'

Even in the car she wouldn't tell me. The farewells had been brief. Her father was already half-way up the path by the time I turned the Audi. Brunhilda stood in the middle of the road with one hand on her hip and the other shielding her eyes, as if making sure we were gone.

The rural was always public, whatever the country. I remembered a shouting match with my father one night outside our house. I was seventeen, daft and drunk. The next day a woman I worked with in the local café leaned close to me. *Next time you take a pot shot at your dad keep the noise down eh?* It was amazing how quickly the story had transformed, transcended its mundanity in the re-telling to something more interesting. It was the first time I realised that this would happen again and again in a place where nothing ever *did*.

'I don't like bullies.'

'What's that?'

She turned back to me, tear streaks on her cheeks. 'I don't like bullies, Jim.'

'Neither do I.'

'Turn round.'

I'd just swung onto the *autopista* beyond Pinar del Rio City.

'There's something I want to tell you.'

I did as I was told and followed her directions back into the city's lazy bustle. Again that low-slung colonial architecture going to seed, sudden tapering pot-holed streets, criss-crossed by a confusion of sagging phone and electricity wires. She made me stop outside a school in a quiet neighbourhood, the dusty playground empty. Steady chanting was coming from behind the wooden classroom shutters. Times tables perhaps: I wondered if I could remember them.

'You wanted to know about your mother. Well your mother stood up to bullies. We came to this school on an exchange visit. We were helping out in a mathematics class one morning and when a student got a question wrong the teacher slapped him on the face. Your mother was shocked and asked the teacher to stop. He did it again. You want to know what your mother did? She walked up to him in front of the class and slapped *him*. He complained, yes, but the children had told their parents what happened and how they were sometimes hit by the teacher. So the parents complained and the teacher was sacked by the end of the week.'

She smiled then, leaning across and kissing me on the cheek. The diversion seemed to have helped her mood. I must have looked confused because she decided to provide me with the missing link in the morning's drama. 'The man with the horse. He is a friend of my ex-husband and the godfather to Floriano. He blames me for my husband taking Floriano away.'

'I see.'

'I doubt it. He is a stupid person and stupid people always make me feel *trapped*. I would leave this country if I could Jim, get away from all the stupid people that hate me, find Floriano and start another life somewhere else.'

'So let's do it!'

'Pardon.'

'Consider it done. Enough of the *past*. Today the future happens.'

'I don't understand.'

'We'll go somewhere else, to the mountains because it is too damn hot, we'll hide in the mountains and you'll be Mrs Drever and we'll be on holiday. You'll be looking out of someone else's eyes, just for a while.'

'But – '

'No buts! Tell me somewhere you've never been. The mountains though, *please*, it has to be the mountains, look how sweaty I am!'

* * *

Time would stand still, I reckoned, if a sense of presence could be maintained for long enough. Then the always-approaching endpoint could be indefinitely delayed. Once or twice I stood in the back garden, sure that the sounds of the distillery had ceased, that the clouds scooting across the moon had paused. What if I had caused this, breathed deeply enough at just the right moment to stop the universe? Perhaps it sometimes stopped for Adelina too, when she held that impossibly delicate purple flower on our rainforest walk, or when she suddenly stopped and stared into the deep canopy, watching the trogon bird watch her.

For me time came to a halt in other moments: in the scatter of her clothes, watching the ceiling fan while she sang in the shower, Spanish that I didn't understand but wouldn't forget.

Certainties, ever-stamped in the memory but framed by transience. From the hillside vantage of Hotel Moka the landscape around Las Terrazas village unfurled like a scroll-painting, the papaya and palms never still, walking the valley in slow-rising mist, up the hidden slopes of the Sierra del Rosario. We stayed at the hotel for two days. Each afternoon the sky erupted. Purple swelled the eastern sky and the storm darkened the green, wrapping the tree line in grey fuzz. The palms quivered even before the thunder, the rain on the leaves a frantic, multi-directed percussion. Once Adelina stepped out from the shelter of the terraced bar, twirling and laughing in the deluge, the thin cotton dress clinging to her body.

We slept together. And no awkwardness. It had been over twenty years since I'd been with another woman. Not that I felt guilty. My wife had no place here. She made sense in a cold landscape like the bones of the earth revealed, as out of place in these tropical greens as Adelina would be there. This relieved me of any responsibility to tell either of them about the other. I reached for Adelina again. My wife and children would remain *unstated*.

She lay with her head on my chest. I thought about this Frenchman, David. Maybe she made a habit out of this, I could be the latest in a line of European men bedded in luxury hotels.

'What was he like?'

'Who?'

'David.'

'Why do you mention him?'

210

'What do you think he's doing, right now?'

She sat up on her elbows, surprise on her face. 'You're not jealous, are you?'

'Course not.' But I was, a little.

'He was a romantic. And then he went home. At the moment he is probably falling in love with someone else.'

'Are we a bit old for this?'

'For what.'

'For this, I don't know how to describe it.'

'Then does it matter?'

She was right. It didn't matter. I knew that endings were written by expectations, and because I didn't have any expectation of the situation having a future I threw myself into making the most of it, letting the present unfurl as naturally as the Las Terrazas landscape. I stuck my head outside the igloo of my inhibitions and maybe she tried to convince herself that history doesn't repeat, that I wasn't another David. This didn't mean I thought of myself as a *lover*. I was too shrewd for that. Being a lover implied an end-point, a transition to another kind of relationship that was impossible. Not that this stopped me behaving as one; staying up all night, fucking for hours, uncorking the past with a drunken freedom that slightly unnerved me with its greedy need to tell Adelina all about myself, *right now*.

The hope of a different future wasn't completely absent. It revealed itself in occasional loaded silences, in the walk through the rainforest with stern Manuel, who glanced in disapproval and was peeved we didn't pay more attention, in the river where we swam with the kamikaze teenagers leaping from the high, slick rocks, in the café where we drank beer and watched swollen

211

cumulus so close we could touch, so far away we'd never get there.

'No promises?'

'What could I promise?'

'David promised.'

'I'm not David.'

Adelina, she was so open. Her words went off in my head like little fire-crackers, illuminating considerations so long forgotten I almost flinched. She talked about Floriano and I had an urge to tell her about my own children that I only just suppressed. She talked about her husband who took Floriano and I realised there were others crueller than my mother.

'Is everything broken?' I asked.

'No, everything is so complicated to put together we missed out an important bit and then it fell apart!'

'It shouldn't really *be* complicated. Isn't that the giveaway that something's not right? This. Me and you here just now. This feels right.'

'It's always right with someone, for a while, you can remember that?'

I finished my wine and motioned to the waiter for another bottle. I did remember, I remembered when it was my wife sitting across the table, a different table, snow slipping down the window. The difference was that I couldn't *imagine* it anymore. 'You're saying there'll be a time when it won't be right. Even if I stayed here, in Cuba, that time would come?'

'I don't know if it *is* right. But we're here. The only time we ever have is now, tonight, and I'm fed up with questions. Remember, no promises.'

'I think you spent too much time with my mother.'

'I think you spent too long without her.'

'That's hardly my fault!'

'I didn't say it was. I am sad. I am sad you did not know your mother.'

'I'm sad about Floriano.'

'I will find Floriano. I think.'

I was quiet then. I swirled more wine and knocked it back. I thought of my mother's collection of photographs in the wooden box and felt an overwhelming sense of futility. 'You can't give up, you know. You have to find a way to find Floriano. No matter how much time passes.'

'Your mother was going to do that, help me find him.'

'Floriano?'

'She was going to go to Miami. Then she died.'

Then she died, I thought. My selfless mother had agreed to help find someone else's lost son. And then she died. If Adelina saw the anger flare in my eyes she decided to just ignore it.

Eight

A two-day blizzard. Impassable roads. The way the world pouuuurs down. As the snow piles heavier I feel lighter, Adelina can't reach me on my island. But I know she's coming. I polish my boots to mirror black and look out my least stained boiler-suit. I'm Brando, waiting for Martin Sheen to come creeping with his machete. My wife seethes at my cheeriness, *stop whistling that tune, what the hell is it anyway*? I say I can't remember, that it's driving me crazy too. But I do, and it's not. It's *The End* by The Doors. I see tracer fire in the potter's night, the orange bloom of napalm strikes. *The horror, the horror*, I mouth as she stalks away.

She hates being cooped up but there's no chance of her getting to work. So she moans, moans about having to look after my father in Maggie's absence. They sit in the living room, hours on end, my father beside the high-banked fire and a heat that could forge steel, my wife on the sofa and the TV turned too loud. I have no place there, my father bent like a question mark, staring at me as if I'm a vital part of the present but somehow extraneous at the same time. Why doesn't it bother me more, this father who may not be my father?

He makes me think of her. My mother. I'm haunted by a throwaway sentence from her journal. *I abandoned my husband and son, without a second thought.* I watch the decision settle on her face, the slam of the door and hurried steps down Lothian Road, along Princes Street. She's anxious to get to the station but not too early, doesn't want to be sitting on the train waiting for it to depart. That would leave too much time for that second thought to arise. She times it perfectly, settling breathlessly into her seat as the guard blows his whistle.

The caricature's decaying. I worry about the layers being added by the journal. What if I can't ever shake off her complete, 3D presence? I guess I should be pleased. It's what Young Jim wanted, a solution to the Mystery of his Disappearing Mother. Old Jim aint so sure. As the details fill, the hollowness expands, my long-standing suspicion becoming dogma, I just wasn't enough to change her mind and make her stay. I was *lacking*. I hate Adelina for this confirmation but am still grateful she sent the journal, I think. That ambiguity again.

Stan's in the Stillhouse rest area, face tripping him. 'Think they mighta shut us down for a couple of days.'

'What would you do at home though?'

'I've got a life Jim, I'd fill it!'

Stan's a liar. Every time I pass his house he's slumped in front of the TV; broken, too much of a coward to admit it.

'Still, we better take the shifts while we can get them eh?'

'Why's that?'

He stares, holding back the cynical little smile trying to curl the side of his mouth. 'Strange days.'

'How so?'

'Come on Jim, *you* know.'

'Eh?'

'You weren't out either.'

215

'The fuck you talking about Stan?'

'Watch this space, s'what they say, innit?'

He's not enigmatic enough to have this performance carry the desired impact. Still, I wonder what he knows as he shuffles down the stairs. Very little, fuck all most likely, just searching for a valedictory negative from the apparent victory of the strike that he'd voted against. *Stan.* He's a whisper in your ear in the middle of the night, a saboteur of the deepest optimism.

I force him away and stare at my shiny boots. There's an undulating howl in the background. From the rest-area window the spruce silently dance, the fuuuush and ruuuuush hidden behind the moaning metal of the Stillhouse, shifting in the storm, a spaceship about to break its moorings and take me and my shiny boots up, up and away from all this.

How much, truly, do I know about Adelina? A couple of weeks of Cuban compassion does not a paragon make, as old Solomon should have said. I see her collaring my wife, bitterly spitting out the story of that time out of time, a time that shouldn't matter any more because it's past, that even when happening was almost past, a cul-de-sac off the main drag of our lives. Does she realise that in a cul-de-sac you eventually have to turn round?

My wife won't be shocked. I see a reassuring arm around Adelina's shoulder, a tired recognition of familiar disappointment and isn't it just typical of Jim to pollute another, an unsuspecting stranger who just happened to wander into his orbit. Sure, she'd do the empathy, but in a way that left Adelina in no doubt about her lesser status in their shared hierarchy of disenchantment. The two letters I'd written to Adelina, she's thrusting them in my wife's face. Then copies of her own to me, my wife's eyes wider and wider in breath-held suspense.

I haven't read those letters yet, they're hidden in an empty tin of paint in the shed, my shed, where no-one else goes, there to be read in the vice-like cold, a dram to hand and an eye on the kitchen door in case my wife appears and wonders what the hell I'm doing out there.

Not yet. The blizzard has bought me some time before Adelina re-appears. I need to steel myself before reading. Like blunt agreement the dark spruce bends in the hard wind. I bow back, hands clasped as I've seen the Boy do. If Stan's watching he'll despise me even more.

The Stillhouse ticks and clicks and creaks. So many voices tonight, too much to sift, too much in flux. Even when I put my ear to the stills I can't make anything out, the storm too insistent, and rising. Already the lights have flickered and I'm waiting for the blackout, looking forward to it, the momentary obliterating black before the generator kicks in. I can't settle, I check the temperature levels in the wash stills and immediately forget them, I'm driven back inside as soon as I open the Stillhouse door, a shove in the chest, the blizzard laughing, laughing . . . Perhaps it's *The End* right enough. I put in my iPod and scroll to the song, sing-along Jim and again the lights dim, a brief arrhythmia before settling back to steady fluorescence.

Why doesn't it bother me more? This father who may not be my father. He'll be in bed, frowning at the glow in the dark stars and moons on Amber's ceiling, or staring into the dying fire. He was always a man of the shadows, reading the lives of the saints until two, three am. Less ephemera by night, I suppose, a clearer view of the Absolute. He was interested in me too, but always

217

that distance, that suspicion that he would always be closer to God than to me. Yes, he was the original ghost, long before me. Is this why it doesn't bother me? *Father? Yes son? I want to kill you*, Jim Morrison sings, right on cue. *Mother . . . I want to . . .*

And the violence of the music drowning out the end of the line matches the storm outside, the moaning metal and the crack of the gale, the insistent whining above the Hammond organ and Morrison's shrieks and still that whining I think I recognise but can't place, that even when I glance at the control panel and see the blinking red light doesn't register as an alarm and fuuuuck, how did I let this happen, it hasn't happened for years, number three wash boiling over the neck and gushing into the spirit safe and I'm shutting down the steam, wrenching the spill pipe back to the low wines drain to stop the overflow diverting into the burn and dawn's tell-tale brown foamy scum and *The Doors* still building to that frantic crescendo and all this determinism, this certainty of followed protocols from grain to mash to distillation all counts for shit when you take your eyes from the ball and let the parameters shift, other considerations drift, and its embarrassment I feel and Stan's gloating face and why can't they all just leave me alone, my mother, Adelina, my father, my *fathers*, why won't they let me put it all back in place like the flow now slowing and the whining alarm stopping and all returning again to the Stillhouse I know and *this . . . is . . . the . . . end*.

'Hello son.'

'Morning dad.'

He's sitting in his chair, hands flat on his knees, a

218

half-lit sphinx. The fire's already roaring and it's as if he's been waiting for me to get in from the night shift, because he's got something to say.

'Still snowing.'

'It is that.'

'Still snowing.'

'Yes.'

'Never known anything like it.'

That's all he's got to say. It's laughable to think that this old man, who has dominated almost fifty years of my life, could be an imposter. I sit on the sofa opposite, still too wired to go to bed, still fretting about the fuck up in the Stillhouse. Rankin was pissed off when he came on shift, annoyed that he's got to re-distil number 3 wash. I sip my coffee, nowhere else to go since my wife handed me a mug and ordered me out of the kitchen. The blizzard's created a wedding emergency, the kitchen commandeered for Crisis Command.

I steal glances at my father's face, again. Thing is, I've never had any reason to look for any physical differences between us. Why start questioning his sharp nose, stumpy neck and big-lobed ears when my every assumption is that this man is my father? Actually, it was never an assumption because it was never a consideration. Peering at him, nothing is so obviously different in our faces to send me scurrying to Tesco's for a DNA kit. I've already dug out my birth certificate and sure enough it names 'Edward Drever' as my father. The whole thing's probably a fantasy of my screwed-up mother, some psychological excuse for running away.

A sudden racket from the kitchen has my father glancing up from the fire. He looks frightened, confused.

'Don't worry, Dad.'

'Where's Maggie? Where's Katie?'

'Don't worry, I'll have a look.'

The kitchen door is half-open. I hear Peter's and Amber's raised voices as well as my wife's. I've no intention of having a look. It's not that I don't want to help. It's that they don't want me to.

Amber's gabbling on about the wedding rehearsal that'll have to be re-arranged but she can't get hold of the registrar; Peter's complaining about mobile networks dropping like flies.

It's impressive, they must've walked the three miles from Peter's place, bent-double against the blizzard just to come here and panic. My wife's in her element. She's drawn up a spreadsheet of contingencies, conference calls on Skype, webinars, whatever it takes to make sure the wedding goes ahead. The venison farm up the glen has been contacted to set aside a hundred-weight of meat, Sammy the Keeper commissioned to get it down in the snowcat and we'll make stew, production-line style, the wedding guests all local and Malky can collect them in the Land Rover with a trailer on the back, *no bother*, and it'll be fine Amber, don't be crying darling, it'll be *different* and *exciting* and people will talk about it for years.

I sense a vague movement and glance up to see the Boy sitting half-way up the stairs. I cock my head towards the kitchen door, *can you believe this?* He says nothing and pads back up the stairs. Has he ever studied my face, fretted about whether I'm his father, which genetic legacies he's going to be landed with when he gets the miserable confirmation?

'Amber and Peter,' I tell my father when I return to the living room. 'They're a bit worried about the snow.'

'The snow?'

'For the wedding, in case it gets worse.'

'Yes. Have the kilts arrived?'

'We'll have to collect them. We might have to wear suits if the snow keeps up.'

'Snow suits?'

'Just suits. As a fall-back. If we can't get into town to pick up the kilts.'

'Yes. I see.'

'What about your wedding Dad?' A sudden welling, out before I could catch myself. But I have to ask, I have to put him right back there with my mother. For a long minute the crackling fire is the only sound. 'I mean . . . It's just that you've never told me very much about – '

'*Wind.*' He's suddenly surfaced, mid-memory. 'Always that Edinburgh wind. She had a blue dress. My shoes were scuffed, my *bloody* shoes. I polished them in the morning and scuffed them on the bus.'

'Was it a nice day?'

'I kept on seeing that *bloody* scuff, all day long. Your mother said not to worry, not to worry, she said.'

'Did lots of people come?'

'She looked beautiful that day, she truly did. I don't think she ever knew how much I loved her. I told her so many, many times but I don't think she ever properly listened, she never bloody *listened.*'

'Was John Tannehill there?'

He looks up, startled. 'How do you know that name?'

'We've talked about him before, Dad.'

He pokes out a bony finger. 'Now listen here boy, I don't want to hear that name again. He stole her.'

'My mother?'

The finger wavers in space. 'He took her away on a boat. It was a steamer, maybe. At Leith.'

'Do I look like him?'

The finger drops. A look of hurt flashes across his face. 'Why would you ask that? What does that mean?' But he doesn't hold my gaze and I know in an instant there's something here, he's never been able to lie. My mouth is bone dry, heart hammering. I feel like a little boy.

'Why would you ask that?'

His voice is breaking. He's told me everything and nothing and it does bother me, it *does* bother me.

'Why would you say that?' he repeats.

Anger hits me like a hammer, a big fuck off hammer right in the middle of the forehead. I'm up and out of the living room in a short second, down the hallway and into the kitchen. Peter, Amber and my wife look up from the laptop huddle. No one says a word as I slam the door. I step into sudden security light, harsh cold, the house lights we never remember to turn off like a ship's illuminations in mist, soft yellows with a treacherous reassurance.

I'll read her fuckin letters. Right now. I'll sit in the hard light of the shed and read all about how I miss you Jim and maybe one day I'll be able to make it across to the UK like I said at the airport when you were leaving, my aunt runs a Cuban restaurant in London and can you imagine me in a little waitress outfit and Floriano will be with me if I've managed to get to Miami and track him down and we'll get to know each other again, I'm so desperate for that, he always was such a sweet little boy, I miss him so much but I have no idea about where he is although Little Havana is still the best bet and the money you left me will get me over there soon, soon enough when I make the necessary arrangement and I hope this letter isn't intercepted, these letters that never capture exactly what I mean and wouldn't it be wonderful to sit together again at the little restaurant in Las Terrazas, the sky so blue here today, so blue, is it like that with you, Jim, it was so wonderful to read your last letter about what you have been doing and yes, I would love to climb a Scottish mountain with you and huddle beside a rock in the rain and just be close, just be close again to you and might this not be possible, one day, the world so full of possibilities so why say that you cannot write to me anymore, why after two letters must you say that, what has happened, of course the distance makes it difficult but it should also make it so much more important, so much more special and something to fight for, but I will keep on writing to you regardless and I will manage to get away from Cuba and I will see you again but I will not write anymore because there are important things that should not be said in a letter but only face to face and until then I will not be a fool any longer although I only wish you had not told me you loved me.

I love you. I repeated it in both the letters I sent her. She said the same in every letter she sent me, twice a week for five weeks before I stopped going to the post office to pick them up.

I'm surprised she kept writing for so long after that, especially without a reply. Eight more letters. I stare at the two I've just read. Six others are waiting in date order. They'll remain unread. Email, that's what matters these days, not these neat, handwritten letters. Another one's coming, another attachment. It's inevitable. It's been inevitable since I first saw Adelina.

Havana, Cuba, 21/4/1999

Havana is so soft tonight, the smell of jasmine, cooling stone. Yet I am sad. Leonardo knew, Leonardo who knows the soul. He reached across and touched my face, asked what was wrong. He holds a candle for me, as have others. But none are like Leonardo, none have ever known how to listen the way he does. I have seen the innocence of the full moon on his face so many times and felt worthless in comparison. If he says I look sad I listen, sometimes only a saint can find a way in.

Sadness and guilt are one and the same. It took me years to realise. My guilt about you has been ever-present, the sadness growing over time. They combine, now, in an emotion beyond definition.

I tell myself it is too late to amend. There is no rewind button, no re-claiming of an integrity lost a lifetime ago. This cowardice is a failing, yes, but an impassable one. Some are able to atone but I know that my ego is too strong to allow it. That is why your father loved Catholicism, he craved the wiping of the slate that comes in confession. My guilt does not give itself up so easily, my sadness cannot be consigned to oblivion by the blandishments of a priest. No, it's a primitive religion for simple souls.

Still, I sometimes wish for it, I long to blink in the clear light that will follow my long-overdue confession, I long to just be.

But I am too fearful, too fearful to let go of this diseased ego and clear the way for true atonement. As I am too fearful of you. That is why you do not have to worry about me suddenly turning up in your life like a bad melodrama, begging forgiveness. I may even have gone too far with this journal, I know. But I have to write it, if only for myself. There it is encapsulated, my terminal selfishness.

224

The last few years have been a struggle. I feel I am caught in a holding pattern, like a plane. Down I swing, round those concentric circles until it is my turn at the bottom of the stack, running on fumes. Just let death come quickly. Let that final moment be right here, up with the jumbled rooftops on my thousand-mile balcony. I am running out of patience, I cannot understand the happiness and zest for life I see around me. It nauseates me.

What a misanthrope I am!

What a facade I have built and sold all these years. My colleagues think me the life and soul of the party. They know I drink but when you couple it with eccentricity then you are not pitied for such obvious weakness but rather admired. You become a 'character'.

There was a man called in the town where I grew up in, Daft Ally. A raging alcoholic, handy with the fists on his crestfallen wife. But Ally wore a red fedora and this was enough to take the edge off, to make almost a sentimental excuse of such a horrible man. He too was a 'character'. We need their existence as a reassuring reminder of our own normality, mundanity and bland conformity.

Are you like me? Do you only allow certain very-well chosen friends to glimpse the non-public? I have two friends like that. Leonardo is one, my philosophical sounding post, a man for the strategic overview of the absurdities of this existence. The other is Adelina. She is young enough to be my daughter and please do not patronise me by seeing in her the projection of the daughter I always wanted.

While she is my necessary naivety it would be trite to say that she reminds me of myself. I do not have the temperament to exaggerate similarities. To see your self in another is like wandering across a mine-field. You are liable to blow everything out of all proportion in a desperate attempt to re-live *lost memories. Adelina, she bruises so easily. Her story would break your heart.*

I apologise for these asides. I must better hold your attention if I am to continue to indulge the delusion that you are still reading.

Tell me, how well have I tackled the subject of John Tannehill? Was the lead-in too involved, perhaps I should have broached the subject sooner? I only wanted you to have an understanding of the context, not to be excused but to offer the beginnings of an explanation. John had to be introduced, he had to grow in your imagination. To state straight-away that he may be your father would have been far too shocking. My intention was to give you the opportunity to develop a growing sense of him, certain character traits revealed, his weaknesses and his gifts. He can never be whole, I know, but who can be when edited and abstracted by words?

My enduring hope is that I have been able to present enough of John Tannehill to allow the shock of the revelation to be mitigated, for you to reflect on John as somewhat *known, slightly less of a stranger.*

You must not blame Edward. As far as he has ever been concerned you are his son. He is a good man. Why would I have risked a switch in his attitude towards you by stirring up the embers of repressed doubt? A choice revelation can corrupt even the best.

There was no certainty in any case, I had no proof. All I could offer was the fact that I wanted to believe your father was John. And while there is cruelty in most truths there is even more in a suggestion that cannot be proved. Even I am not capable of that. This is why I suspect that you will not raise the subject either. He is an old man now, why send him to his grave with such a trauma?

226

'What about my ignorance?' you shout, 'why did my sociopathic mother deign to enlighten me?' Indeed, you too could have been maintained in ignorance. But your right is so much stronger than Edward's. A better question would be why I have chosen to tell you now. I do not know, maybe it is simply death again, my closeness to it risking my disappearing without telling you. I imagine you pondering some emotional or physical trait which cannot be found in your father, something which has always triggered a vague unease. It was the slightest possibility of such moments which made up my mind.

John is long dead now. I do not suppose this surprises you. He died in a fly-blown hotel room in Guadalajara, Mexico, in 1974, his heart long weakened by heroin. I woke up beside him and cried for a year.

We had talked about you so much. He said he would wait until you turned eighteen and then make contact. Not that John would ever have done this. 'I don't want to ruin two lives', he said, meaning yours and Edward's. John is another you must not blame. I thought him so worldly but he was an innocent, too fragile for this life. I loved him. I mothered him. There is a hidden part of every woman which wants to mother her lover, don't let the feminists tell you otherwise.

We imagined a life with you, we carried you with us from Alexandria to Tangiers, New York to Guadalajara. As the years passed we wondered about the person you were becoming, the world you may change. We imagined so many futures for you and were so jealous of Edward. Not that John was bitter. He was a dreamer, a wonderful father only in his fantasies. No, I am the only person you should blame.

Does it help to know that I never allowed myself to consider what kind of mother I would have made? I abdicated that right

227

at Waverley Station, 1962. We get through them, do we not, life's traumas?

* * *

My wife mobilised Malky after the Crisis Summit in the kitchen. Any chance he could pick us up in the Land Rover tomorrow evening and take us down to 'Columba's View', the purpose-built wedding venue that opened in the village a few years back. Amber had loved it from the start and I suspect it was the irresistible appeal of Columba's View rather than the Hollywood dream-life with Peter the Chip that put the afterburners on her wedding fantasies.

The Land Rover appears out of the snowy mist like Scatman Crothers snowcat in *The Shining*. The thought of a crazed Jack Nicholson leaping out from behind a bush and planting an axe in Peter's skull is warmly cheering on such a cold night. We all cram in, me, my father, Amber, my wife, the Boy, Peter, and Vari from next door who's agreed to stand-in for the Registrar who can't make it because of the snow but who reluctantly, self-importantly, *this is a bit irregular*, agreed to email over her script so we can run through it in her absence.

'St. Columba didn't come anywhere near here,' says the Boy.

'Get stuffed,' says Amber.

'True though. He travelled everywhere by boat, and always on the west coast.'

'So what. It doesn't *matter*.'

'Matters to me. Heritage and history are a lot of shite if you just make it all up.'

I'm again startled by the Boy's insight. I haven't had

228

a conversation with him for months. Who knows what knowledge he might have soaked up? The wee weirdo might be an unknown Einstein in our midst. Is it better to have a happy idiot for a son, or a tortured genius?

'I just got another one, Mum.'

'Barry?'

'Oh God, what if he turns up!'

'Mad Bazza?' says the Boy.

'Shut UP!'

'What's this,' I say.

Peter shifts in his seat, tries not to catch anyone's eye. My wife tells me that Barry McGill, Amber's long-time ex-boyfriend, has finished his latest tour in Helmand, found out about the wedding and started bombarding her with texts. *I always loved you Amber . . . how can you betray me . . .* He was always a strange boy, scary eyes like Ray Liotta. Even as I'm reassuring Amber that it'll be fine I'm seeing Mad Bazza gliding across the snow like some special forces nutter, making his way to Columba's View, floating on the night like a Taliban compound.

Old Abe lets us in, once a cooper at the distillery and now the perma-scowled superintendent of the wedding venue. He leads us from the main building across the bridge to the little island with the conservatory-type structure where they have the ceremonies. Inside, the lights illuminate one by one in an elegant spiral from a central point in the low domed ceiling. Outside, the floodlight beams merge into the snow, no sign of the view that so appealed to the ancient Saint, the meadow that slopes down to the river, the mountains beyond. We stand in semi-circular space surrounded by our disembodied reflections in the six feet high windows, my wife moving us like chess pieces on the black and white tiled floor.

My father sits in a chair by the sleek, black granite bar, Abe next to him in mirrored pose, hands clasped on top of their walking sticks. He looks tiny in his ancient duffel coat. I remember when he filled it, chest puffed to a world faced down. Abe cracks a painful-looking smile and shares something with my father, who bends his head to catch what's being said.

He looks bemused as he straightens up, then bends down again as if waiting for Abe's repetition that doesn't come. The detachment quickly returns. Is he thinking of my mother in her blue dress? That's what we're supposed to do at these moments, isn't it? How else are we expected to find any kind of interest in the situation unless through selfish comparison with our own lives? When I catch my wife's eye I find no remembered affection, just the usual suspicion that we've each been replaced by imposters who mean as little to one another as the broken, snow-fuzzed reflections represent true images of ourselves.

Vari's no good at the registrar role, she must have a reading age of five. Amber gets upset, convinced *its going to be a disaster* and Vari's apologizing and saying *third time lucky, I promise* but we all know it won't be, *can't* be. Again I take Amber's arm in mine, my wife telling us to slow down a bit and now we're out of step and doing a strange bumpy walk across the floor and we're almost back in time when the Boy turns *Somewhere Over the Rainbow* off too soon and now Amber really is crying. Peter just stares, he looks as bemused as my father and I wonder if their personalities have quietly merged on a deep subconscious plane.

230

'We'll get through it,' says my wife, and gives Amber a hug.

'Will we?'

'Of course we will darling, we always do!'

My mother finished her latest missive with the same sentiment. *We get through them, do we not, life's traumas?* It's shocking to realise how alike my mother and my wife are. That same intense practicality and one-track mind, the bloody-minded belief that once, just *once*, they'll bend the world to their will. Ah well, 'tis said that sons end up marrying women who remind them of blah blah blah. But it's strange, the more credulous would say profound, to think that even though I've never known my mother my wife can be so similar. They'd have got on like a house on fire. I can just see her sitting beside my dozing father, another figure in this sagging tableau, where everyone holds their stage-managed position, their breath, the only movement the floodlit flurrying snow. I know for sure that she'll haunt me, the ghost of someone I only came to know after death. I have no idea which has more repercussions, this imagined haunting or the bona fide one awaiting me when the snow stops.

The next day the blizzard does, of course, stop. There's no need for the contingencies that have been readied anyway, Malky bribed with a bottle in case the Land Rover's needed again, a lake of venison stew made and frozen, spare suits checked and passed for wearability.

I wait for Adelina. I try not to think of her letters. I'm edgier with every passing car, every arrival that might be her. My wife and Amber escape for the Hen Day. I watch them from the bedroom window and I'm still standing there an hour later. Two days until the wedding. One more shift and I'm on leave, my wife and I heading to the Costa Blanca after the happy nuptials for a week's holiday neither of us want. *A second honeymoon*, she said. I had to admire her willingness, although it sounded more like a question she wasn't sure about asking.

I've been given a list of things to do, including cleaning the house. When I questioned why I was told *just do it, people might come round*. But why would they when we'll be seeing and feeding the buggers at the wedding? At least I don't have the chore of looking after the old man. Maggie's made it through the snow and I won't have to cancel my shift.

It passes too quickly. Many find it unbelievable I take so much enjoyment in working the stills after all this time. *It's the contrast between the ever-shifting soundscapes and the never-changed process.* Imagine I told Rankin that, held a hand in front of my face and rubbed my fingers, like a flouncy art-critic looking for the right words? I wouldn't be trusted again, how could a man who likes his job, who finds *pleasure* in it, ever be trusted? But there's always something. Today it was the dappled stains on the wall running the length of the Stillhouse. Eight hours I wandered back and fore, conjuring shapes from the grubby marks, wondering when they happened, what they meant, if they'd emerged over time like liver spots.

She's there when I come off shift.

I pause beside the Dark Grains Plant on the other side of the bridge from my house. Seeing her opens the floodgates, the content of the letters I've spent the last few days holding back now rushing over me, an amorphous whole, without detail, the collective crushing weight of emotional failure, failure now demanding anger, anger to overwhelm everything else.

She's standing by the garden gate. Behind her the living room window glows in the failing light, maybe a shape moving behind the net curtains. It could be Maggie, wondering who's standing out there in the cold, too uncertain of her authority to go out and ask what she wants. Des is walking a bit ahead of me and gives Adelina a stare as he passes and looks back at me. She's moving from foot to foot, thumping her arms against her sides. When she sees me coming she suddenly stops and takes off her Davy Crockett. She smiles, but only briefly.

I can't bring myself to cross the bridge. I stare at the walls of the Dark Grains Plant. More stains, that alcoholicy mould again. The Angel's Share Fungus, I finally looked it up, can't remember the botanical name, black and creeping and if I stand here long enough I'll see it move, fingering out and writing my name, some message, wisdom on these disconsolate walls.

The amorphous jumble of distillery noises becomes distinct, louder, the thrum of the Stillhouse and the machine room whine. The fizz from the pipe taking the draff from Mashroom to the Dark Grains Plant swells to a white rush. She's still there on the edge of sound, unmoved. I look to the sky, as if the blizzard might suddenly return and again delay the unavoidable.

Everything in every life is ever-approaching, some situations as inevitable as the Reaper's rap on the midnight door. To mention death isn't overly dramatic. After all, Cuba has irrevocably passed. Adelina and I are dead. She knows it too, I've seen it in her dark eyes. My unwillingness to come to terms with the loss could be the very reason I've avoided her. Those memories, I was once so careful with them. I told myself when I came back that I didn't want over-familiarity to give way to corruption. In truth I don't mind embellishment, selective forgetting, all the unconscious stratagems that bring our lives a little bit more drama.

So how will I remember this moment? Adelina, I'm angry with her for making absolutes of those memories when I thought they'd be ever-living, as untrustworthy as any other story.

Eternal Sunshine of the Spotless Mind

Adelina stood naked in the little bathroom. Through the doorway I lay on my mother's bed. She looked at her reflection in the mirror, turning her head from one side to the other, comparing the profiles, leaning forward and tracing the lines on her forehead. She let her hands wander across her body, lightly pinching the skin here and there, testing the elasticity.

Did she always do this when drunk? She smiled at me, her gaze moving to the jewellery box on the bedside table. A questioning raise of the eyebrows, a swirl of the drink in her hand.

My mother had some lovely pieces, delicate threaded bead necklaces, painted wood, silver and pewter bracelets, two endless-knot Buddhist pendants in turquoise and coral that she must have picked up when she taught in Kathmandu. Adelina placed the turquoise pendant round her neck, stepping back for a better view in the mirror. It suited her, hanging between her smallish breasts, still quite pert, not bad for a thirty-five year old. She trailed her fingers slowly across her chest, lingering on the nipples with little circles until they swelled, moving on to the pendant, maybe brass, copper, tracing the knot round and round.

Adelina sat down beside me and cradled my head. I moved round and placed my mouth over her nipple, my tongue tracing little light circles, as her fingers had.

I began sucking her, greedily, like a child. She tried to push me away but I kept my mouth where it was, my hand moving roughly between her thighs. But her gaze was empty when I pushed her back on the bed. She understood the significance and would still let me do this. I didn't take my eyes off my mother's pendant as I fucked her, trying to ignore the part of me that wanted to hurt her.

Afterwards we lay sweating. The floor fan thrummed, moved slightly from side to side on its wobbly legs. Beyond the balcony the unseen moon lightened Havana's night to cemetery grey.

'What happens now?'

'We sleep.'

'And then?'

'Then it will be day.'

'You know what I mean Adelina.'

She pulled her legs up to her chest and seemed to have no intention of answering.

'My flight's at 2 o'clock the day after tomorrow.'

'I am on holiday. I'll come with you.'

'Come with me?'

'To the airport. Don't worry, I don't mean I'm taking the flight!'

'I didn't mean it like that.'

'I know.'

She didn't turn round when I placed a hand on her shoulder. I pushed back a treasonous swell of sadness, rising from the place that wanted her to pour out every futile word.

'You can keep it, if you like, the pendant. You can have all her jewellery, I don't know what to do with it.'

'Is there nothing you want?'

'Why?' I rolled away and reached for the bottle, pouring myself a large, straight *ron*. 'I had no memories of her to begin with, nothing except one photograph. Why would I want that to change?'

'Will you take the photos?'

'No. Nothing. You know what? I'm not frightened of her any more. I think it's because I can imagine her now.'

She didn't believe me. She couldn't miss my anxiety every time my mother was mentioned. This wasn't something I could ever lay to rest. Did she feel sad for me, for Helen, who had caused this pain long before Adelina knew her, that person she wouldn't have recognised?

I got up and padded across to the balcony, still warm underfoot. Down below, the streetside café was still open. A few old men played dominoes in the dirty yellow light, lazy cackles mingling with the clatter of the occasional scooter. Sure enough the old waiter soon appeared, staring up at me. What did the old guy want? I imagined my mother standing here, drunk as I was, looking to the building across the street where the ancient woman with the enormous pendulous breasts sat in insomniac night, staring back at her from the hidden shadows, wondering again what had brought the white-haired gringo woman to Havana.

There was no way of knowing. Adelina was only able to pass on the story of my mother's last few years. It seemed enough, to know something about her final manifestation and only the odd echo of a past now forever closed. Her abandonment of me was a lost story, so too John Tannehill. My overriding feeling was relief that Adelina had been unable to shine any light on potential explanations. I'd blamed myself for years but wasn't enough of a masochist to torture myself with a truth that would only solidify the guilt.

I listened to Havana. As she once listened on this very spot. I didn't know enough to forget about her.

* * *

Rodriguez went on and on about it. How his wife had said *if it was flu you wouldn't have got out of bed!* But the child was screaming again and he couldn't stand it. Better just to agree it was a heavy cold and get to the office where he could get some peace. He then spent an hour in a bus queue and when it finally turned up it broke down after a few hundred yards. A not uncommon occurrence but most unwelcome today. Yes, Havana was a shitty place to have a cold.

'I hope you get better soon,' I said.

The lawyer's mood probably wasn't helped by Basilio. It obviously wasn't the first time his assistant had screwed up, going to the Inglaterra to collect us when he'd been told to head downtown to my mother's apartment on Brasil. Rodriguez's watery eyes kept roving back to Adelina, his gaze lingering awhile, amusement flickering. All those years in the profession, all those divorce cases, he'd probably developed a pretty keen nose for the whiff of sex.

'My apologies for keeping you waiting for so long on this matter Mr Drever.'

'That's ok. I've had a chance to tidy away my mother's things and do a bit of sightseeing.'

Rodriguez glanced again at Adelina. 'I am glad. Life does go on. I hope the . . . sightseeing helped your grief.'

I shrugged.

'The papers have come through. I have the sad but necessary duty of releasing your mother's estate.' Rodriguez shuffled in his seat and drew his shoulders back, looking from me to Adelina and then settling his gaze on me. He clearly loved this bit, his enjoyment almost sexual.

'12,000,' he said, quietly.

I leaned forward. 'Come again?'

'The value of your late mother's estate. 12,000.'

'Pounds?'

'Convertible pesos Mr Drever. As I say, a not insubstantial amount, about –'

'6,000 pounds,' I said.

'Yes. *Un poco menos, probablemente.*'

'A little less,' Adelina translated.

'Less?'

'*Poco.* And we have deducted tax, of course.'

'Of course.'

Rodriguez wiped his forehead with a handkerchief and reached for a plastic bottle full of cloudy yellow liquid. 'A guaranteed cure for the cold my mother-in-law tells me. I have to take a glass every three hours. It looks like the old *bruja's* piss and tastes like it too. Tell me Mr Drever, what is it like to live in a country where so much money is so meaningless?'

'What are you laughing at?'

'My mother.'

'What about her? Her money?'

'This was never about her money. Think about it, why would she want me to come half-way round the world for so little money?'

'It goes a long way here, Jim.'

'I've spent a few thousand coming here! That isn't it. I don't think she ever let go of the idea of getting back in touch. But she was too much of a coward to do it when she was alive – '

'So she arranged it when she was *dead*?'

'Exactly.'

'Come on, you can't really – '

'Think about it. What's the best way of getting the attention of the son you've never met? You offer *cash*, a little carrot that makes him think "yeah, fuck you, I *will* take your money, it's the least you owe me". I mean, if she was just dead, and not dead and potentially loaded, would I have bothered? So I wing my way over and get to find out all about her. See where she lived, meet her friends. This is her way of finally making contact, when she's dead! Even dead she's still running away. And the best thing? There's hardly any money!'

'Do you really believe all that?'

'You have to admire the *beauty* of it.'

'I think it's taking things a bit far.'

'I don't think so. Now I know all about her when she knew absolutely nothing about me. She never wanted to.'

'I hope that my son, Floriano, never thinks that of me.'

I thought about her ex-husband. Every day he might be sitting little Floriano down, telling the boy anything he wanted about his mother, constructing a myth that would lock her out forever. She had to find him before he became like me, steeped in revulsion for the mother who abandoned him. The rest of the walk back to my mother's apartment passed in silence.

The truck was waiting for us, a decrepit Soviet flat-bed

truck owned by one of Adelina's friends. The school would take charge of my mother's belongings, find homes for her books, her clothes. *I am sure this is what she would have wanted*, said Adelina. It took an hour to carry the boxes down from her roof-top rooms, supervised by a mournful Luis who followed us from floor to street, street to floor, like a confused child who'd lost his way. He shook my hand and said something in Spanish. I looked at Adelina but this time she didn't translate.

Across at the café the old waiter had been standing watching, hands held delicately in front of his spotless apron. I felt his gaze again, the old man who stared at me as he passed, who always seemed to be looking up when I leaned over my mother's balcony. I watched the waiter walk towards me with slow, deliberate steps. Then a strong handshake and more awkwardness as I accepted the condolences I didn't want because they meant so little.

Adelina translated in staccato bursts. *I am Leonardo, a friend of Helen's. We stayed up many nights . . . We believed in time, we helped each other's clouds pass . . . She is eternal now, only blue skies . . .* As the truck spluttered off I watched Leonardo in the side-mirror, disappearing into dust and diesel. Another enigmatic stranger with something to tell, if I allowed myself to be interested. The old bitch had guessed right. She knew if she got me to Havana I'd want to find out more about her, my *mother*, the woman who left only sadness behind.

The sadness lingered into the evening, made heavier by the humidity, the silences ever more difficult to fill.

Adelina cooked for me in her echoing flat. Black market lobster and *arroz con frijoles*. We ate in the cavernous living room under the crumbling cornicing.

241

I was uncomfortably hot, the balcony door open but no breeze at all to ruffle the curtains. The roses she'd bought earlier seemed to droop lower with each passing minute, even the street noise subdued. Havana waited impatiently for rain and we ate, our cutlery scraping into the silence.

Our last night together. I didn't know if it was the wrong or right time to retreat to a critical distance. On one level I wanted to be disappointed, waiting for an off-hand comment to puncture the romance and offer a short-cut back to normality, something unpleasant that would allow a line to be drawn under this impossible situation. On another I waited for Adelina to say something transcendent, a redefinition of what was possible, regardless of normality and screw the consequences. Instead, I saw my own fear reflected. Neither of us wanted to be the first to follow the concentric rings downwards, deeper into the other, adding different, more consequential memories to the stack that was already difficult to ignore. So it was inevitable that nothing very much was said at all. The setting of our final meal would instead define the memory, the rickety table with its white tablecloth and wilting roses, the echo of voices in the stairwell, my sweaty brow and the green bow in Adelina's hair.

I thought about David. An easy role to play, if I wanted. I understood why the Frenchman had laid on all those romantic clichés and impossible promises that Adelina told me about. Anything was possible if you drew a distinction between yourself as existed in this strange situation and your *real* self, who saw this episode as a deviation from reality. The same justification explained sex-tourism, those fat Europeans fucking the local teenagers. It all centred on the ability to delude yourself that it wasn't really you doing it. Problem was, David had fallen in love at the same time and couldn't handle the tension between those two selves. The poor fool wanted to be a continued presence in Adelina's life, not a memory. He couldn't handle being forgotten, his love nothing but ego-driven narcissism.

At the same time, it was kind of appealing to step outside myself like that. For a while anyway. It was another reason to keep quiet. I didn't trust myself enough in the pressing heat, with a head full of Cuba Libres and half a dozen beers, not to blurt out something stupid, impossible to reel back in. The silence was just as bad, dripping with expectation, begging to be filled with whatever hokum tip-toed into my traitorous gob. I was glad of the sudden, insistent hammering at the door, Adelina hurrying to find out who it was.

The old woman who bustled in to the living room behind Adelina's near shouts was about four feet tall, near-bald, and improbably round. She bowled around the room, bug-eyes darting here and there, babbling and gesticulating as I stared and Adelina shouted. Eventually she spied the vase of roses on the table and swiped it up triumphantly, quickly trundling to the door where she suddenly stopped and turned. *Quien te crees que eres?* she hissed, looking from me to Adelina with utter disgust. Then she was gone, the door slamming and Adelina returning, bemusement on her face and a bunch of dripping roses in her hand.

'What the hell was all that about?'

'That was Esme. My grandmother borrowed her vase. The day after my grandmother's funeral she was round here demanding it.'

'Bloody hell! Imagine what she'd have been like if you'd slept with her husband.'

Adelina's face crinkled up. 'What a horrible thought.'

'I dunno. She's got a certain . . . *something*.'

It was crazy Esme, I realised, looking back, who turned the evening inside out. The old crone freed us from the oppressiveness of my last night. There wouldn't now be a premature goodbye, Adelina wouldn't have to drink the second bottle alone. Instead we laughed for fifteen minutes then made love on the dark balcony, quietly and intense, the city's silhouettes crowding close, all Havana echoing with our unacknowledged expectations.

Afterwards we listened to JC's music. Guitars and accordions. Sorrowful and so apt. And then to the ocean, down along the Malecón, an iPod earphone each. Where the seawall stretched away below us a floodlight blinked, briefly illuminating white froth, broken concrete and a little Cuban flag painted by the waterline. Looking closer I realised the flag was actually a jigsaw, stuck onto the wall. One side was incomplete, the missing pieces stuck loose beside the finished section, as if waiting for someone to come along and complete it.

'Quite a metaphor,' Adelina said.

I said nothing.

'Cuba is crumbling for me. Piece by piece. I don't have any reason to stay.'

'Everyone's got a reason to stay.'

'My reason is in Miami, growing up without me.'

Still she stared at the little flag.

'It isn't easy but other people manage to leave here all the time. My stupid husband managed it.'

'Would you really do it? Leave the country.'

She turned then, eyes flashing in the floodlight's blink. 'If I could? Of course.'

'I can help you with that.'

Only at the airport the next day did Adelina accept the money. My mother's money that is. 6,000 pounds could get her out of Cuba. A little left over to set her up in Miami. *People come and go from our lives*, I said. *Don't let your son be another*. She held me for a long time at the departure gate. She told me she'd return to that spot beside the painted flag to stare at the sea and listen to JC's sad guitar. That was when I said it. I don't know why. Cuba had become such a parade of impossibility that maybe I even believed it. 30,000 feet and 4,000 miles later I was more willing to consider the alternative, that I was emotionally illiterate, unable to read situations properly. So what was the truth? It didn't really matter. I was going home.

'I've fallen in love with you.'

Nine

At least, that's how I remember Cuba. I think. Maybe that's just how the story should've unfolded.

The detachment I look back with suggests a certain lack of authenticity. My life has been mainly imagined, after all, hyper-edited for dramatic effect like a shitty reality TV show, my characters pre-assigned to roles that each cut simply reinforces. Adelina might think I'm real when she pulls back on me as I drag her round the side of the house but in truth I'm my own derivative concept. My persona's as hollow-shelled as a production lot at Paramount.

She wants to know why I'm being so rough. Des has stopped again a few houses down the road and is looking back at us, Maggie staring out of the living room window bold as you like, the net curtain slung back. I want Adelina out of sight, back in the recesses where she's been for six years. *Let go of me*, she's saying, but I don't until I get her into the shed.

I push her towards the back wall and down onto the old wooden chair. When she stands up I push her back down and realise she's scared. Our breath rasps as we struggle, fogging the cold sawdust air. I smell her, a hint of a perfume I think I remember. I don't want to get aroused but can't help the swelling hard-on and feel immediately disgusted at myself.

'Please Jim,' she pleads, a near whisper.

I let her wrists go. She immediately barges past me and throws open the door. I sit in the chair, head in my hands. I'm shivering, can't get it under control. The distillery pulses in the background, a cosmological constant. She's probably fled to the front gate and gone, run into the house in the hope of denouncing me to my wife. But when I look up she's still at the door.

'I missed you,' I say.

She stares at me for a long, long moment. 'No you didn't.'

Is she right? She could say anything and I'd believe her. 'What are you doing here, Adelina?'

'You never told me you had a wife, a family. Why did you never tell me?'

'Is that why you're here? To break it up?'

She looks as if she's about to burst into tears. 'I would have walked away. If you had told me.'

I feel that familiar lump rising in my throat.

'I made it out of Cuba. I couldn't have done it without our money. I wanted to thank you.'

'I'm happy for you.'

'It wasn't easy, I – '

'Why are you sending me my mother's journal?'

She shuffles on the snow. 'I found her notebooks after you had gone home. They were in a drawer in her teaching room at the school. I decided to make them into computer files, to make them easier to send to you. If you wanted. Then you stopped writing to me. You just stopped.'

'What's that got to do with anything? Why didn't you send it?'

Her fists suddenly clench. 'Because I hated you. For a long time. Almost as much as I hated myself.'

247

'Course you did.' This coldness, again I feel I'm forcing it, creating anger to smother the guilt.

'You didn't deserve it. Do you understand that?'

'Why do I deserve it now? All of a sudden. Why the endless drama for fuck's sake, sending it one piece at a time?'

She seems to sag then. She stares at the ground, foot scuffing the snow, round and round in little circles. 'You said you wouldn't read any more of my letters. You told me the situation was impossible. But I got out of Cuba. In October I finally made it to London, to my aunt. I cannot begin to tell you how difficult it was. Over five years. Those journeys made anything seem possible. We were in the same country now. We might be able to see each other again.'

'After five years!'

'Why not?'

'And the journal?'

'Because I knew you would read it, you would not be able to ignore it. You were so eager to find out about Helen, but so fearful. I thought she might be a way back. Each time you read her words you would think of me, you would wonder why I was sending these emails, what I wanted. I wanted to be in the back of your mind. I wanted you to think of me again.'

'You think I don't think of you?'

'No, I don't.'

'I do.'

'I don't believe you. I think you decided to lock me out, like you locked your mother out. You're right, it is a drama, the emails, me being here. But life *is* a drama. Your money got me *out* Jim, to Miami. It would have been impossible without you. I will forever be grateful.'

248

I want to go to her, hold her so tight, but I'm terrified of the implications. 'Why just turn up like this? Why didn't you write anything in the emails, give me some kind of warning?'

'You ignored my letters. You would have ignored my emails. But what if you had replied? What if you told me not to come? I might have changed my mind. I did not want to be persuaded *not* to come. I was so sad when you ignored me after your friend's concert, I did not know what to do.'

'No. Me neither. You can't make this shit up.'

'I am not trying to steal you away.'

'Thanks for the heads-up!'

'Why are you being so hostile?'

'You brought me my mother's past, all that stuff I didn't need to know about, that fucking *journal*.'

'I don't want you to have the regrets that your mother had.'

'What regrets?'

'About losing someone.'

'Look, just go back to London. That person in Cuba, he doesn't exist.' I sound angry even though I'm not. I just feel exhausted, defeated, as if I've felt the first breeze of old age.

'You have to talk to me!'

She's still talking as I cross the garden to the back door. The night's stumbled in, bunker-like. Those first evenings back after Cuba, mid-September, warm as it gets up here on the moor. But all I remember is a chill emptiness and a lack of colour. A flatness, a lack of her.

Apparently email was a swine to access in Cuba so snail-mail it was. I set up the PO Box, as agreed. I wrote her a letter. I said I missed her, *loved* her, my dodgy poetics scavenged from JC's songs and fuck the embarrassment. Then I wrote one more. She's right, I told her the situation was impossible and just *stopped*. I think I'd been back for a couple of months.

There was no great revelation behind the decision. The present had quietly re-imposed, simple as that. The rhythms of this place are carefully programmed to avoid alternatives, at least none that might be deemed serious. Fantasy's fine, we might be trying to live someone else's life but that doesn't mean we'll choose it. I turned into David the Frenchman after all, the same ridiculous promises and disappearing act. Why didn't I close the PO Box down? Maybe I was leaving the door open to possibility. Maybe I just couldn't be arsed.

It's Adelina's turn to grab and pull at me as I open the kitchen door. There's a whiney edge to her voice, a high-pitched noise like the condensers make when we drain the pipes. As I lock the door behind me I remember her son Floriano. Did she find him, did she manage to bring him to London? She's hammering at the door, her figure vague behind the frosted glass, dematerialising in front of me. I switch off the kitchen light and she disappears into black.

My father leans forward on his chair. He wants to know what I'm burning. Maggie the carer looks fit to burst, desperate to ask who that woman was but too much of a stranger to know how I'll react.

Unread or read, Adelina's letters burn all the same. I can make out sentences, blue lettering darkening to purple as the pages brown and curl, still legible until the sudden flame. I throw on more pages, angling my body so there's no chance of the words being read over my shoulder. *Thinking of long mornings . . . do you remember the cycle . . . if only life did not create such sad. . . .* I read and I remember, for as long as it takes the paper to become ash.

Some people look back on their past and don't recognise themselves, as if we're different people at different times. I've never bought into that idea. Seems like an abdication of responsibility, a way to absolve your conscience by blaming failure on a less-evolved self.

Me? As I was then, so am I now. That may be the problem, what if I'm unable to evolve, locked by self-built parameters into flawed mediocrity? Still, I'm glad I'm not sitting here fretting about another self, a *man in my position*. It all comes down to what gimpy face you're happy to see in the mirror, the latest model of smiling confidence who'll one day be cast out in embarrassment, or the same old mug worn like a shapeless jumper you can't bring yourself to get rid of. That's not to say I haven't changed. No siree, I'm on the move all the time, if you walk in circles you'll find yourself back the start. There's a song in there, I should tell JC.

'What are you burning?' says my father.

I turn round.

The old man points at the fire, the last of the letters lying like black feathers across a smouldering log. 'What have you been *burning*? I know you, what have you been up to, eh?'

The same questions as I'm helping him into bed. *What was it, what were you burning?* A more coaxing tone of voice. He knows I'm preoccupied, the old bugger's always been a psychic barometer. Not that this is necessarily borne of concern, more his lifelong quest for full-spectrum control. He used to find things out sur-reptitiously. Now he wheedles like a child.

It must be unnerving, the dementia leaving ever-larger blank spaces where every piece of flotsam is grabbed at. I can't think of anything reassuring to say and leave him wide-eyed in the pyramid glare of the bedside lamp. In my own bed I realise I'm mirroring how I left him lying in the next room, the duvet pulled right up to my neck, fingers of both hands gripping the fabric. If he's not my father how come I've got the full-face frown and chickeny jowls? How does that work? Either proximity triggers biological convergence or my mother was a deluded fantasist. The one thing we've never had in common is temperament. Unlike him my own old-age caricature will be totalitarian indifference, my wife too awed by its impenetrable defences to com-plain any more about my lack of interest in her life.

It's just after 3am when I hear her getting in, back from the Hen Day. She takes an incredibly long time on the stairs, which means she's pissed, trying to be quiet. When she opens the bedroom door she's got a pair of high heels in her hand and her orange and white mini-dress has ridden up her thighs. She smiles, lascivious, and puts a finger to her lips, blowing a *shhh*.

'I was hoping you'd be awake.'

The crappy strip-tease takes a while, the dress gets stuck on her head and she can't undo the bra, fingers clawing as she giggles on the end of the bed. I'm sur-prised by my reaction. Both of us are. She wants me faster, *harder Jim*, and I'm trying to stay in *this* moment, trying not to think about Adelina, standing by the fence, hammering on the door, looking up at the window through lilting snow to catch sight of me. And sudden as you like I'm not thinking at all. The world takes on a fish-eye perspective and I feel a spreading lightness, as if I'm underwater, effortlessly moving, knowing I can go on all night if I want to, if she wants me to.

* * *

Tuesday, 2pm. A convoy of Audis sweeps up the distillery road. Malky tipped me off. At lunchtime he leaned over the fence to say he'd been told to snowplough the road. *Slinky's orders, big-wigs must be comin.* He was near bursting to speculate, but Malky would cheat at Chinese Whispers to see what shite the final person comes out with. He lures you into these rapid, staccato conversations. *Probably nothing*, said I. *Shit storm*, said he. *You reckon?* said I. *Telling you*, said he. *Wonder if the crows will come back with them*, said I. *Eh?* says he.

There's only one crow sitting on the telephone wires strung across the road as the six Audis pass underneath. A bit different from the vast flock that had followed the same cars out of the distillery a few weeks back. The crow looks bored, as uninterested as the gossip will be fevered when word spreads that the suits are back. Jack's said nothing. Sure as shit he would've told us if he knew a board meeting had been called. He's bound to be pissed off. I make myself a cuppa, thinking I'll have a custard cream too. Accusations of complacency could be levelled against me, sure. But I'm with the crow. The world happens, regardless.

And it happens around me. For the next three days I seem to stand in the middle of the kitchen drinking the same cup of tea as the world around me accelerates, a blur of doors opening, people coming, going, the table set for breakfast, cleared, dinner, cleared, my wife gesticulating and my daughter anxious, happy, my father leaning on his stick by the door, by the sink, the Boy making Maggie laugh, the Boy getting shouted at, three days happening in the ten minutes it takes to sip my tea and eat my biscuit, the last three days of wedding build-up.

My wife tells me to stay out of things. My solitary task is to pick up the hire kilts and the champagne that'll have me on OT for months because *it just has to be champagne not bloody cava, ok?* Not that I escape as lightly as that. Twenty-four hours to go and she corners me in the Den. *Pete, deal with him.* There's no other information, just a wild-eyed stare.

I find Pete on the living room couch, opposite my father. He looks crestfallen. Maggie glances from me to Pete and scarpers. The Boy's in the window seat, headphones in.

It's not that I don't love her, Peter says. It's a wonder it took so long but that doesn't make the inevitability any less depressing. I mean, he's called *Sneaky Pete*, it was fated that he'd revert to the unreliability and cowardice witnessed across the years. Not for the first time I realise how much I distrust him. He's a man rehearsed, impossible to read. I can't help thinking that this is a deliberate attempt to impress me, to seek my wisdom, to *allow* me to change his mind, some kind of bonding moment that he wants us to look back on and laugh about.

'Pete?'

We both glance round at the Boy. 'Aye?'

'If you don't marry my sister I'm going to batter fuck out of you.'

Pete squirms in his seat. 'There's no need for – '

The Boy gets up and stands in front of him. 'I mean it. I'll take you outside and batter *fuck* out of you, you *cunt*.'

'Jim?'

I put my latest mug of tea down on the floor. I must've drunk more tea in the last three days than I have in three years. My father's lost in the flames. He didn't even twitch when the Boy swore. Thirty years ago I'd have felt the old man's hand before I got beyond the 'f' of the first fuck. *Jim*? Peter repeats. Daylight is quickly slipping into the black and white of dusk. There's no more sound, just the crackle of the fire. No-one moves. We're waiting for a shout of *cut* that doesn't come, the silent sequence stretching on and on. In a moment John Tannehill enters the frame and sits beside me, John Tannehill as he was in that photo I found in my mother's wooden box in Havana, heavy sailor's jumper and a smell of tobacco. He seems intrigued by how I intend to deal with this situation and I'm going to impress him with a high-falutin' monologue that'll shine a powerful, universal light on the hackneyed theme of a groom with cold feet. But when I clear my throat to begin he's gone. Just the old man in profile, staring into the fire. I want to shake him, make him tell me what he sees.

'You sorted it then?'

I pull the kitchen door closed behind me and lean back against it. 'Just a minor bump in the road.'

'A minor bump . . . I've had Amber sitting in tears for the last hour. You know Pete's hardly spoken to her for days?'

'I know where he's coming from though.'

'How's that?'

'Before our wedding. I had second thoughts too.'

'So he *was* having second thoughts.'

'No, I mean – '

'You breathe one word of this to Amber and I'll kill you, right?'

'Why would I even – '

'I mean it Jim, I've even given her a Prozac to take the edge off.'

'Prozac?'

'Yes. One of mine.'

'Eh, since when have you been on Prozac?'

'Oh for God's sake.' Her voice is rising and she takes a breath, reigns it in. 'Look, it doesn't matter, we can talk about this later.'

'When were you going to tell me?

'Why do I have to tell you? Do you think that'd help?'

'It'd help me.'

'How's that, how can it help you? What's it even got to do with you Jim?'

'I'm your husband.'

'And?'

'We should share things like that.'

She looks at me as if I'm insane. 'Yes Jim, we should share things like that. Because you're such a tremendous support.'

She knocks back the rest of her glass of red wine and shoves past me. The bathroom door slams a moment later. There's still a puffiness to her eyes when I get into bed a few hours later. She's in that pose, sat up with the pillow behind her, staring into space. Once upon a less compromised time I'd easily have found the right words to deflate the treacly atmosphere and leave her giggling like a little girl. Now I can't be bothered and neither can she.

'What did you mean by having second thoughts about our wedding?'

I stand there with my slippers in my hand. When did I start wearing tartan slippers? 'I've told you that before.'

'No you haven't.' Still that flatness to her tone.

'Well it wasn't a major panic or anything. I just wondered if we were doing the right thing.'

'And were we?'

'Course we were.' But I'm too quick to say it and sound too sure. The words hang in the air, synthetic.

'I think so too.'

Her words ring even less true than mine. This isn't a subject to broach, not now, perhaps never. It'd be too easy to read our own thoughts in the other's eyes. I stare down at my stomach that droops further towards the crotch every day. 'How's he getting on with that ice sculpture?'

'That's all he's been doing apparently, holed up in his shed with that bloody swan.'

'I thought you liked the idea?'

'Not now Jim, I'm not going to fight with you the night before the wedding. Let's make sure it's a good day.'

Like ours? Luckily I hold back from saying it. That would be the tin lid, far too ambiguous given the context, a high-tech suggestion-bomb scattering shrapnel in all directions.

I know we're both lying here thinking about our wedding day. That's the thing about weddings, they're a bugger for making you think. My father'll be doing the same; my mother's blue dress and his scuffed shoes, he's obsessed with shoes. 7am the next day he orders me to polish his brogues again. Afterwards he inspects them, close enough to blacken his nose. He wets a thumb and

257

starts rubbing away at an invisible mark. The Boy and I stand in matching kilt and dicky-bow, watching him, listening to the squeaky sound made by his thumb.

'Think he'll turn up then?' asks the Boy.

'Pete?'

'Pete's a pussy. I mean Mad Bazza.'

I'd forgotten about Barry. 'I doubt it.'

'He's been sending Pete texts as well. Wouldn't put it past him.' The Boy sounds almost gleeful about the prospect of Amber's ex-boyfriend putting in an appearance. 'I can handle Pete, not Bazza.'

It's my fault. I bought him that Bruce Lee box-set for his birthday and now his bedroom's a shrine to Kung Fu. He's even started lifting weights. Factor in the ninja moves he's always doing and on some level the Boy believes he *is* Bruce Lee. He stares at his squeaky thumbed grandfather who may not be his grandfather, a second generation of obsessive alienation in the same room and me to make three. A Trinity! All those years the old man rammed God down our throats and we end up haunted by the Unholy Ghosts of each other. When Jack calls my mobile for the fourth time this morning I'm almost eager finally to answer him.

'I take it you've got the letter?'

'What do you mean? I haven't checked the post. It's a bit busy here, Jack.'

'I know. I'm sorry. I'm just calling round everyone because this is important, they've – '

'Look, Jack. Not now ok? I'll see you at the reception.'

'It'll just take a minute Jim, have – '

'Columba's View' does funerals too. Next time I'm here it might be my father's turn, the old man on the terminal

258

trolley, angled towards the windows for the final view. Now and again I've thought of his eulogy, what I might say. Is this morbid, does it cross the mind of every son?

The mourners, they'll be expecting mumbled, bumbled and brief. I want to see the looks on their faces when I deliver words of such perfectly measured poignancy that they splutter their free drams all over each other. You've got to give the punters something to remember, it's *the* lesson to be taken from the sheer banality of most funerals. But banal is the one thing death isn't. Death's waaay out there, such an *exaggeration* that a bit of artistic licence is obligatory. I'm not talking *Four Weddings and a Funeral*-type bollocks, but something a little bit rehearsed but not obviously so. A few choice lines for people to chew on, something they won't expect from me. Something they'll know is truly meant.

What would you call it, this entrance with Amber? It can't be walking up the aisle because we're not in a church. And to call it 'crossing the sticky floor' hardly fits the ambience. *Aye, she looked right bonny crossing the sticky floor.* How about *approaching the window* or *seeking the bureaucrat*? I swear the registrar just checked her watch. That smile must have been grafted on by a surgeon with the DTs. Then I clock the old man in the front row and start thinking about his funeral again. I can't help it, there must be something wrong with me.

What would all the guests think if they could peer inside my head? Would they be more embarrassed by my creepy thought processes or the fact that it is indeed *Somewhere Over the Rainbow* on the PA? The old man doesn't seem to hear anything, he's almost completely absent, staring out the big semi-circular conservatory into the snow. There's no reason for me to hate him,

I know. He's bound to have considered the Tannehill Factor. When did he let it go? How long did it take for him to accept that in the absence of John Tannehill and my mother there was no way of ever finding out, no way of proving it one way or the other?

I hand my daughter to the polyester registrar and sit down beside my wife. She's crying already, dabbing at her eyes. She pats me on my hand as if I'm a child who's done a good job. My father blinks, blinks, but sees nothing. Peter sweats through his simplified vows. Amber's eyes are wide. She looks terrified; the implications of a life with Peter the Chip have finally detonated. But there's no freak out and flee. It's almost disappointing. I glance across the rows of smiling guests as we stand to clap and cheer after the declaration of husband and wife.

It's nerve-wracking. I'm expecting the throng to part any second and reveal Adelina at the back of the room. I'm no good with contrasts. To see her sitting in one of these pink-cushioned chairs is as improbable as me standing at a balcony watching a storm sweep towards that hill-top hotel in Las Terrazas. It's all about belonging to your own space. I'm Jim Drever, Stillman. I'm known for certain patterns of behaviour. And indulged, most likely, for the same reasons. I've spent my whole life soaking up the lessons of the master, my father. He sits here beside me and how could it be otherwise? He makes sense *only here*, nowhere else. It took a few months after I got back from Cuba to remember that I am exactly the same.

Problem is that improbability always leaves the door open to the possible. Adelina's nowhere to be seen as we file out to Bryan Adams, *Everything I do, I Do It For You*. But that doesn't mean she's gone. My wife grips my arm tightly, still beaming and dabbing. Botox couldn't make my smile less believable and I'm paranoid about how my kilt is loosening with every step. Behind us the Boy helps the old man and we all slow to a crawl so they don't get left behind. Amber and Peter's steps have synchronised, they could be about to lay a wreath on a war memorial. The weather too is more in keeping with solemnity, the hard-flurrying snow, the grim half-light filled with grinning ghosts. Here come my mother and John Tannehill.

They look nervous, unsure whether they should have come. But this is a *family* occasion, they belong here too. John's a big, physical guy, I could see him working the barrels. Have to keep the writing quiet though, wouldn't want a confrontation with Malky in some warehouse corner; *yer not one of those . . .* poets, *are you?* No way his attraction to my mother could be kept hidden. There'd be knowing looks, *nudges of arms*. He's a man of stillness is John, a man I could like. What does it matter if he's my father or not? I know almost as little about the old man, even after all this time. One big dysfunctional family, that's us.

'I need to talk to you,' whispers Jack as we pass. He's on factory setting, intense. His lingering glance at my wife drifts breastwards, *hungry* it could be called. Her arm stiffens in mine.

'Later, Jack.'

But later means ten minutes later when he spots a gap in the line of guests shuffling along to congratulate us. After the obligatory kiss on my wife's cheek, *both* cheeks, he puts a hand on my arm.

'Did you get the letter from the boss this morning? You're the only one I haven't spoken to.'

'That what you were phoning about?'

'Did you get it?'

'Might have. Other things on my mind, strangely enough.'

'What's happened?' my wife asks.

'They're shutting us down.'

'*What*?'

Even I'm interested. 'The fuck you talking about?'

'They're shutting the distillery down. And they're saying I assaulted Ronnie on the picket line.'

'You? It was *me*,' says my wife. 'And I'd do it again!'

'I'm sorry about this. Today of all days. They really are cold-hearted bastards.'

'It's a bluff,' I say. 'They're upping the ante so they can back down.'

'What, and that's better is it, short-time and layoffs? Who do you think'll be the first to go?'

'Well I – '

'Everyone who went on strike! Doesn't affect you, though.'

'Not my fault. I was on leave.'

'Yes. Yes you were.'

'I saw the Audis coming in the other night. I knew something was up.'

Jack eyes me closely. 'Course you did. You always know when something's up, Jim.'

'What's that supposed to mean?'

'You work with Stan?'

'And?'

'Just saying. Just saying.' He turns to my wife. 'I'll take the rap for Ronnie, Kate, don't worry. I didn't know it'd come to this.'

'No way. I'll tell them. Bloody right I will!' She gives him a long hug. I might as well not be here.

'What's the plan then?' She says it softly, affectionate.

'We occupy.'

'The distillery?'

'Monday morning. Run the place ourselves. Build a media campaign. We know it's profitable, we've got the documents from central office that prove it. And we've got access to the order book.'

'You're serious?' I ask.

'Yeah. I'm serious,' says Jack. 'You should try it one day. Just try it for one fuckin day.'

I leave them to it, glad-hand my way to the black granite bar and pour three drams into one. Peter's at my shoulder before the first sip. *Thanks Jim, I really mean that.* Then gone.

The evening will come and go in the same way, a swell of reddening faces, compliments and an odd mingle of BO and vanilla. I take a breath and plunge under, surfacing for the procession across the bridge in the snowstorm to the main reception venue. It's like that scene from *The Seventh Seal*, I wait for the guests to break into that strange dance on the horizon line. Back under the choppy waters I go, rising to strained laughs as I plod through my after-dinner speech. Funny how I can stand outside myself like this. One moment I'm at the back of the reception room, eavesdropping on the flirting bar staff as I watch myself at the top table, the next I'm floating above the tables, peering down, listening to my well-rehearsed lines. Back under the waves I go. I swim with strong, smooth strokes.

There's no drama.

Another disappointment. We've had the big build-up, the farce with the run-through and all the contingency plans, even a daft groom with cold feet. The story's supposed to peak in an unforgettable dramatic episode, yes, *yes*? But the wedding's slipping away without incident. Even the aspiring bourgeois among the guests, of whom there are a few, may reluctantly declare it a *triumph*. The cherry on the baker's best bun is, incredibly, Peter's ice-sculpture. It's wheeled in for the first dance, a six feet swan beating its wings. The whole room's applauding, not out of sniggering disdain but at the sheer unexpected elegance. Amber's in tears as they waltz round the sculpture, mirror-ball flickers catching the ice.

No Mad Bazza? JC asks as the band set up. He sounds almost hopeful. *Nope. All's quiet.* Too many Hollywood movies and airport thrillers, that's the problem, too many telegraphed three-act dramatic arcs. There's nothing here but the usual corner cliques, drunken casualties being carted to the toilet, and glittery-eyed cola kids. This is my life, our lives, unfurling as they always have. That's why Jack doesn't need to worry. He's going from colleague to colleague whispering in their ears about occupations, blockades, and Malky's pissed, shouting *burn the fucking office down*, each word punctuated with a jab at Jack's chest and Jack calming him with arms on both shoulders. *Channel the anger, be angry but be focussed.*

'I love you, Daddy,'

'I love you too.'

So speed the reels and batter the drams, let the faces flush and let us all dance, the snow blow to a furious peak and no matter if we're marooned, stuck here, because it can't be otherwise. Jack's never got it, the essence of this place, never realised that because it exists *by itself* it will always exist, almost out of time. Change can only happen within the parameters of that truth. And that's why there will be no closure, no mothballing. To exist is to endure. Melancholy, yes, but that's the price of determinism's comfort. It's why there's no laughter when everyone notices my father alone on the dance-floor between songs, arms holding an invisible partner and tears on his face. It's because we all know what it means.

'Don't we?'

'You're pissed!'

'Course I am. It's my daughter's wedding! So are you.'

'Fuckin hope so,' says JC.

We're standing outside in one of the smoking shelters. To our left vague shapes move behind the bright fogged windows of the reception room. Wedding hits leach our way, Abba and Queen. The Monkees. *Cheer up sleepy Jean* . . . I take a drag on my roll-up and lean on the railing, looking across the pristine car-park, the cars disappearing under snow.

'You know what I mean though?'

'I never managed to figure it out.'

'You went away, you came back. Tells a story, JC.'

'And I might have to do the same again?'

'How's that?'

'Ruth's needing a change. We always said we'd do a few years up here, a few years down south. We're going to move to Sheffield. No reason we can't run the label from someplace else.'

There it is. That odd mix of scorn mixed with envy I always feel when someone moves away. 'Traitor.'

'Yokel.'

'Turn-coat.'

'Yi darn shit kicker, don't be tripping over those dungarees your whole life!'

'You'll be back.'

'I hope you're still here when I do.'

'What's that supposed to mean?'

'The distillery. It's looking pretty serious. You need to sit down and talk to Jack.'

'Don't get me started about Jack.'

'Fuck's sake, Jim. Don't be so complacent.'

The music swells as he opens the door, ready for the second set. I roll myself another smoke.

Complacency, does that also explain this sudden surge of affection I feel towards JC, this night, the snow that'll never stop? Fuck it, I'm still breathing and that's the name of the game.

My mother and John Tannehill, they'll be sitting at their table realising what they've been missing all these years. I'll have a word with Old Abe the caretaker when the last guests have gone, slip him a twenty so they can stay behind and take the empty floor, holding close, dancing through the years to that first moment in Milne's Bar, my mother reading again his first poem, those weeks in Alexandria. I can't hate them, not on a night like this.

* * *

I've always disliked Sundays. The day of rest never seemed like much of a rest to me. As a kid my father had me up even earlier than on school days. We had prayers *before* going to chapel. Then into the best clothes and shoes and off to Mass, the never-ending mundanity of Mass. Why did it all have to be so stern? If spirituality is such a chore then why bother? The churches were as dull as the priests, as if they'd been designed by a local authority planning officer.

I felt cheated when I first saw pictures of cathedrals like Chartres and Salisbury, almost outraged by those high-flying buttresses, baroque pulpits and soaring chancels. If I had to suffer the Word then I wanted the setting in all its crazed glory; doors that were called portals, heavy incense and echoes, the broken reliquaries and deep shadows of pressing time. I needed something to hold my attention as I sat there bursting for a piss and trying to catch the eye of the girls in their own Sunday fineries with their own boredoms and hormones.

Yes, Sundays are long-ruined, I've been conditioned by guilt to get up at the crack of a sparrow's fart. Even today, despite not getting back from the wedding until after two. My wife's asleep beside me, almost too quiet, arms coffin-crossed on her chest. I stare at her until I'm convinced she's still breathing. There's a fusty, eggy smell in the air. I might still be a bit pissed. Is my father awake yet? I hope he's lucky, that the memory of last night's sad, solitary dance isn't one that plays on endless loop. Soon enough he'll be struggling out of bed and down onto his bony knees to say the prayers that haven't been answered for all these years.

The house is freezing. I get quickly changed. I start in the living room and wander round the house from room to room, downstairs to upstairs in the usual way. What would they say if they could see me, my wife and father, the Boy? The way I carefully lift and place my slippered feet, avoiding the floorboard creaks long memorised. I'm just pacing, I'd say, but it wouldn't be enough, because it's peculiar, maybe even deviant, to wander

267

around the house in the half-light of dawn. Bugger it all, I have no explanation other than the silence. I like the silence. And the steam. I like the way the steam from my coffee disappears into the gloom.

I stand listening outside each of their bedrooms. It's not that I'm making sure everything's all right because I know they'll be fine, regardless of me. They don't need me and I know that. I don't think they ever have. Maybe I'm listening in the hope that they've finally disappeared and I don't have to suffer these permanent reminders of my superfluousness.

My phone's blinking on the kitchen table, insistent. That's the word for these times. All these TV channels, the 24 hour news cycle, super-fast techno-change, it's like being constantly tapped on the shoulder. Once upon a time a phone rang once and if you missed it so what. Now it still rings but even if you don't answer it still blinks at you, *lookatmelookatmelookatme*. I don't, I switch it off and go into the living room to clean out the fire.

Here, *here* is my Sunday rest. Sitting feeling the heat grow, watching the swelling daylight leach round the edges of the heavy curtains. I may even fall asleep, and who cares if I've decided to sit in my father's hydraulic chair. No, nothing to be done, we can't avoid what we must become. Of course he's my father, why else would I sit here, using the remote control to tip me back into a reclining position and yes, *yes*, I see why he likes it, the perfect angle to comfortably rest my head and watch the flames leap and settle and lull me to sleep.

Although only briefly asleep I still dream. It's unnerving how quickly they rush in, just waiting for the slightest close of the eyes. Other times they leave me alone for

268

months. I let the images go; my mother, John Tannehill and something about a boat, a sinking boat. The fire's already faltering and no logs in the basket. That means facing the wood pile and the butcher's cold, the Cuban-like azure skies already giving up the pretence and reverting to grey, the snow skulking in from the north as if embarrassed about yet another appearance. I feel the first flakes at the same time as I hear vague music coming from the front of the house.

How long has Adelina been there?

She's standing with her arms folded in front of a blue Renault Megane. The music is drifting from the driver's opened door. I think it might be one of JC's albums. She watches me walk along the path, the expression on her face both empty and overflowing. I know if I ignore her she'll wait all day, all week, wait with the patience of a ghost for me to appear again.

'Jim, I – '

'Why am I not surprised?'

I hesitate for a moment then walk down to the gate. I feel absurd in my wife's pink dressing gown, my green Hunter wellies over my pyjamas. Hardly the costume for a confrontation.

'*Jim.*' She holds a hand up. 'You don't need to worry. I'm leaving.'

She says it so abruptly I have no reply. 'Keep it down,' is all I can manage, looking up to the bedroom window but nothing stirring behind the curtains as nothing has stirred for years.

£quote'You didn't give me a chance before, to talk to you.'

I can't argue with that. I can't decide if she's looking at me with pity or defeat.

'But I have to, I can't – '

'Adelina, this is my – '

'I *know* it's your home.'

'We can't be together, you must know that?' It's bizarre, listening to myself say it.

'I've known that for a long time. Since the letter you sent.'

'Why are you here then? Did you just want to hear me say it? Is it as simple as that?'

'Nothing's as simple as that. Tell me, how do you think the pieces of a life fit together?'

'What?'

'The pieces of a life. Your life. How do they fit together?'

'I don't have time for this.'

'You don't have time for anything but yourself.'

'You told me not to make any promises!'

'I'm not asking you to make a promise, I just want you to listen.'

'I'm listening.'

'No you're not. Maybe one day you will. I didn't want to be disappointed but I am used to that, I've spent a long time being disappointed.' She walks over to the car and opens the back door.

The little boy who holds her hand is wrapped up in a one-piece ski suit and a woolly hat. He scuffs his feet in the snow and looks from me to Adelina. She's managed to find Floriano after all. As soon as the thought occurs to me I realise the boy's too young to be Floriano. Floriano should be about ten by now. And I suddenly understand. I know what she's going to tell me, much as I know that I'm going to ask her to repeat what I've already grasped.

'This is your son. Alejandro.'

The hollowness in my stomach is sudden. My wavering voice lets me down as well. 'What?'

'Your *son*. I want you to have the opportunity. Ask yourself, do you want him to read your story after you're gone?'

'My son?'

'I asked you how the pieces of a life fit together. How do you *want* them to fit together?'

I take a half-step forward. JC's *Martini Red* is playing on the car stereo. Solo acoustic, his high plaintive voice. The snow makes that squeaky crunch that sets my teeth on edge. Alejandro's staring at me. What colour hair does he have? It's the first question that pops into my mind but I don't ask. I think my first full memory was around his age. I'm sitting in front of a 3-bar electric fire watching TV. It's *Doctor Who* and I'm eating a chocolate bar, a Mars Bar, although these details may have been made up later. All of it could've been made up later. Five years old. It could be me standing there. I don't want this to be his first memory. Association is everything and it's so cold out here, cold and strange. Or is it me? Is it simply me I don't want him to remember? The presence of this little boy is incredible, literally incredible, not Camp Gary saying something like *I literally died laughing*. Alejandro, he's called. He was always a possibility, I suppose, from the moment I first saw Adelina, an unlikely one but a possibility nonetheless. Can a possibility be literally incredible if it comes to pass? I need some advice. I glimpse movement behind the living room window from the corner of my eye. My father most likely. That life I don't understand ticking on and on. Behind me. Behind glass. And me looking

271

in. From the cold. A little boy called Alejandro and the muffle of snow. He's got snot dripping from the end of his nose and I have a tissue in my pocket. I could wipe it off, a direction to step in if I want to.

I need some advice. I could turn to my father and get him to open the window, ask him what to do. *Can you see*, he says, *can you see him in you as you see yourself in me?* Alejandro looks up at his mother and might be thinking the same, wondering why his eyes are so big and so dark and my own so blue and how can it be so when the saying goes that it's all in the eyes, these connections between us, it's all in the damn *eyes*? There's a flicker of amusement in those dark eyes, the kid's a watcher, like me, only he's watching me, patiently wondering what I'm going to do next, why he's been brought here and how long does he have to stand in the cold watching this strange man with the pink dressing gown and green welly boots who at least is amusing him, making him forget the cold but who is he mama, who is he? I smile too, sharing his amusement and all of a sudden he looks anxious, looking up at his mother again. Adelina says something. Now they both seem unsure, perhaps wondering what I'll do next, if I'll walk away. Not back to the house but away from them, from the car, the music the distillery, onto the moor, into the distance and never looking back. I have an almost overwhelming desire to hold out a hand. I imagine him recoiling violently at my touch, as if he's been burned, his mittened fingers tightening around Adelina's. No, it wouldn't be right, it might suggest something I can't ever live up to. He's at that age, I can't risk the first touch of his father's hand being his first memory, a touch that was both a hello and a goodbye.

I look at my hands. *Love* and *hate*, Preacher Powell's tattooed knuckles. What would Robert Mitchum do? I begin to hum. *Leeeaning, leeeaning, leaning on the ever-lasting arms*. Alejandro meets my gaze again. His eyes, so big and so dark and my own so blue. Adelina says something else I can't be sure of because I'm singing. *Leeeaning, leeeaning, leaning on the everlasting arms*. They stare at me, Alejandro and Adelina, another intervention I still have time for. How about a silent long shot from their perspective? Jim Drever walks slowly into a grey, greyer distance, his figure becoming vague, vaguer as the snow thickens. Hold the shot for two, three minutes until he finally disappears. Or something schmaltzy, big on the strings. Drever's indecision, a close up on his face, ambiguous wetness on the cheeks that could be tears or just melted snow. Which would be more believable? Because that's the thing about a story, it has to be *believable*, doesn't it?

* * *

Havana, Cuba, 22/4/1999

If I read of this situation in a magazine I would find it heart-less. A mother writes a journal for her son, yet leaves instruc-tions for it to be sent after her death. He would have questions, surely, questions that her death had rendered mute. Is there lesser cruelty in silence?

I am unsure.

Can I bear to forever remain a stranger to my only child? Would I not rather be the approximation here glimpsed and misunderstood, now one thing, now another, than a stranger? I find it difficult to settle on your perspective, imagining you

273

both burning these pages, unread, and greedily devouring every one. I do not know if your life deserves an infusion of either or whether I should stay hidden.

The night he died John asked me, 'how do the pieces of a life fit together?' We were drinking beer in a midnight cantina in Guadalajara. He was wearing an open necked white shirt and seemed melancholy, as if he somehow knew that the poem he'd just finished would be his last. I remember a group of men at the next table burst out laughing and maybe their laughter inadvertently revealed the answer. Why worry, it doesn't matter. A life fits together as it will, as the story demands, as valid in its own humdrum way as any other.

No, that little anecdote should not be read as justification for leaving you. I do not want to make the suggestion that I did not care. My words are only meant to relate, to reveal, what my story demanded.

All these ill-considered details, spilling as I write, once in the open they run free with a life of their own. That is not to say you should disregard what I have written to this point, only that as the journal continues you may wish to re-assess what has gone before. Such is the way of every true story, the reassuring lack of absolutes.

However, I fear I am too self-indulgent, too erratic, to be an engaging storyteller. My intention is to help you project, I want you to step towards me with empathy. Empathy rather than judgment, after all, is what we truly crave from one another. Perhaps you will grant me the relief of the former if I suggest that John's early death was the price I paid for abandoning you, the equal and opposite reaction that could never be avoided, your pain balanced by my own.

What an intense few weeks, once I start writing I am up until dawn. There is so much more to come, much I have forgotten which is spilling back into the light. I have seen more stars in the last month than the last ten years. Aha, I hear you say, a shamed conscience preventing sleep, fevered regrets pouring down like silver starlight, one after the other? You would be wrong. To admit regrets is to suggest there may have been an alternative narrative. This is not to say I have not missed you, never reached out and imagined your life. But regrets? I cannot allow myself to consider such thoughts as regrets. That path leads only to madness.

Shall I let you read any of this?

To be forgotten is everyone's greatest fear. There would be a measure of justice in my accepting that, drifting unknown to you into the ether.

One day you may come to Cuba. You might see the palm trees on Varadero beach silhouetted against the darkening sky, the individual fronds becoming an anonymous mass, shifting in the rising wind into whatever shape you wish it to be in that moment. If my wish is simply to be whatever you want me to be then I have so much more to tell you. The decision will come. In the meantime I will keep on writing. You may read these words, you may read those to come. You may know that I am here, was here, with the pieces of a life to fit together.

Mexico blues

it's a mystery to me
three attempts at a landing
three times the mist and the mountains
I reach for you

my lips as dry as my body's tired
I can't take the crowds
I'll breathe a cityful of dirty diesel
if it helps me sleep

Guadalajara's broken
the child lies in the street chest heaving
I look in every mirror
but what can really be trusted?

every stranger's a
mockery of ever presuming to know
each smile a knife
I never realised I knew how to use

I touch your troubled face
your little hands
I try not to admit
these are acts of remembrance

I imagine your own forgetting
a naked dance
in our empty room
the music only you can hear

JT, Guadalajara, Mexico, 1974

276